POPULAR PUBLICATIONS · FACSIMILE EDITIONS

Dime Detective Magazine #9 (July 1932)

Dime Detective magazine was the flagship detective pulp in the Popular Publications stable, running for almost 300 issues over twenty years. The July 1932 issue contains stories by J. Paul Suter, T.T. Flynn, Erle Stanley Gardner, James A. Goldthwaite, and Maxwell Hawkins, and includes installments in the Horatio Humberton and Dick Bentley series.

Authors:

J. Paul Suter, T.T. Flynn, Erle Stanley Gardner, James A. Goldthwaite, Maxwell Hawkins

Illustrators:

William Reusswig, John Fleming Gould

10 DIME DETECTIVE MAGAZINE

EVERY STORY COMPLETE   EVERY STORY NEW

Vol. 3   CONTENTS for JULY, 1932   No. 1

FOUR COMPLETE MYSTERY-ACTION NOVELETTES

SMASHING SHORT STORY OF A MURDER-MASTER AND THE LAW

Watch for the August Issue   On the Newsstands July 20th

Published every month by Popular Publications, Inc., 2256 Grove Street, Chicago, Illinois. Editorial and executive offices 205 East Forty-second Street, New York City. Harry Steeger, President and Secretary, Harold S. Goldsmith, Vice President and Treasurer. Entered as second class matter Feb. 26, 1932, at the Post Office at Chicago, Ill., under the Act of March 3, 1879. Title registration pending at U. S. Patent Office. Copyrighted 1932 by Popular Publications, Inc. Single copy price 10c. Yearly subscriptions in U. S. A. $1.00. For advertising rates address H. D. Cushing, 67 West 44th Street, New York, N. Y. When submitting manuscripts, kindly enclose sufficient postage for their return if found unavailable. The publishers cannot accept responsibility for return of unsolicited manuscripts, although all care will be exercised in handling them.

OPPORTUNITIES
are many
for the Radio Trained Man

Don't spend your life slaving away in some dull, hopeless job! Don't be satisfied to work for a mere $20 or $30 a week. Let me show you how to get your start in Radio —the fastest-growing, biggest money-making game on earth.

JOBS LEADING to SALARIES of $50 a Week and Up

Prepare for jobs as Designer, Inspector and Tester—as Radio Salesman and in Service and Installation Work—as Operator or Manager of a Broadcasting Station—as Wireless Operator on a Ship or Airplane, or in Talking Picture or Sound Work—HUNDREDS of OPPORTUNITIES for a real future in Radio!

TEN WEEKS of SHOP TRAINING
Pay Your Tuition After Graduation

We don't teach by book study. We train you on a great outlay of Radio, Television and Sound equipment—on scores of modern Radio Receivers, huge Broadcasting equipment, the very latest and newest Television apparatus, Talking Picture and Sound Reproduction equipment, Code Practice equipment, etc. You don't need advanced education or previous experience. We give you—RIGHT HERE IN THE COYNE SHOPS—the actual practice and experience you'll need for your start in this great field. And because we cut out all useless theory and only give that which is necessary you get a practical training in 10 weeks.

TELEVISION *and* TALKING PICTURES

And Television is already here! Soon there'll be a demand for THOUSANDS of TELEVISION EXPERTS! The man who learns Television now can have a great future in this great new field. Get in on the ground-floor of this amazing new Radio development! Come to COYNE and learn Television on the very latest, newest Television equipment. Talking Picture and Public Address Systems offer opportunities to the Trained Radio Man. Here is a great new Radio field just beginning to grow! Prepare NOW for these wonderful opportunities! Learn Radio Sound Work at COYNE on actual Talking Picture and Sound Reproduction equipment.

PAY for YOUR TRAINING
After You Graduate

I am making an offer that no other school has dared to do. I'll take you here in my shops and give you this training and you pay your tuition after you have graduated. Two months after you complete my course you make your first payment and then you have ten months to complete your payments. There are no strings to this offer. I know a lot of honest fellows haven't got a lot of money these days, but still want to prepare themselves for a real job so they won't have to worry about hard times or lay offs.

I've got enough confidence in these fellows and in my training to give them the training they need and pay me back after they have their training. If you who read this advertisement are really interested in your future here is the chance of a lifetime. Mail the coupon today and I'll give you all the facts.

ALL PRACTICAL WORK
At COYNE in *Chicago*

ALL ACTUAL, PRACTICAL WORK. You build radio sets, install and service them. You actually operate great Broadcasting equipment. You construct Television Receiving Sets and actually transmit your own Television programs over our modern Television equipment. You work on real Talking Picture machines and Sound equipment. You learn Wireless Operating on actual Code Practice apparatus. We don't waste time on useless theory. We give you the practical training you'll need—in 10 short, pleasant weeks.

MANY EARN WHILE LEARNING

You get Free Employment Service for Life. And don't let lack of money stop you. Many of our students make all or a good part of their living expenses while going to school and if you should need this help just write to me. Coyne is 33 years old! Coyne Training is tested—proven beyond all doubt. You can find out everything absolutely free. Just mail coupon for my big free book!

H. C. Lewis, Pres. RADIO DIVISION Founded 1899
COYNE ELECTRICAL SCHOOL
500 S. Paulina Street, Dept. 82-5E, Chicago, Ill.

Mail Coupon Today for All the Facts

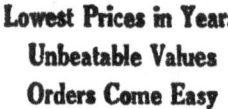
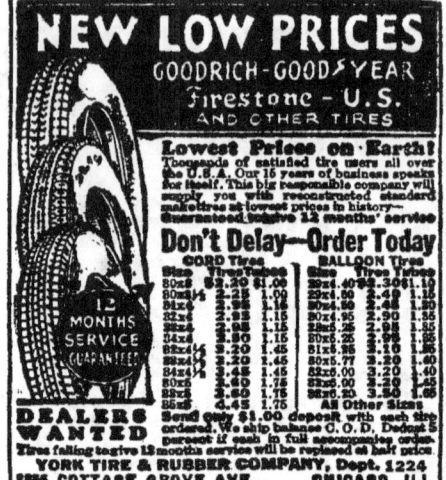

AGENTS! SHARE THE PROFITS
WITH ME ON THIS *NEWLY IMPROVED* TOM THUMB ELECTRIC WATER HEATER *WHICH IS*

Listed and Approved by Underwriters Laboratories

FREE Heater To AGENTS

Deposit $3.75 with us for sample outfit. After you send in 24 paid up orders, the $3.75 deposit is refunded and the heater is yours F R E E.

Get Instant Running Hot Water from Cold Water Faucet

Show housewives, factories, etc. how they get instant running hot water from cold water faucet and make up to $40.00 a day.

KITCHEN

SHAVING

LIGHT WASHING

DOCTOR | FACTORY

Again Tom Thumb leads! The first and only portable electric water heater approved and listed by Underwriters Laboratories to be absolutely safe and non-hazardous for 110 volts, a.c. on medium branch circuits. Tell this story. Show how it is possible to get instantaneous, continuous running hot water from any cold water faucet. When your customers see this and know they can enjoy this great convenience for only $3.75, they will buy on sight demonstration. Price includes everything. Nothing else to buy—

No installation expense—just stick it on the faucet, ready for use.

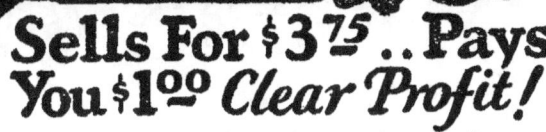

Sells For $3.75 .. Pays You $1.00 *Clear Profit!*

Tom Thumb electric water heater has many uses and an unlimited market for sales. Sells for $3.75. You collect $1.00 deposit on every sale, which is your cash commission.

No Installation — Stick On Faucet and Sale Is Made

Tom Thumb doesn't have to be removed when hot water is not wanted. Easily detached and carried to any part of house where cold water is running and hot water is wanted. Made entirely of aluminum. Cannot rust—no moving parts. Unbreakable—nothing to get out of order. Do not be fooled by porcelain heaters which are easily breakable. Do not sell an unsafe heater which is not listed and approved by Underwriters Laboratories. Sell TOM THUMB. Fire authorities, insurance companies and even the police forbid the sale of an electric water heater unless it is listed and approved by Underwriters Laboratories. Stick a Tom Thumb on the faucet and tell the wonderful story about convenience, safety and low price and your sale is made.

Rush Coupon If $40.00 A Day Sounds Good To You

This new scientific safe invention offers tremendous sales possibilities. At low price of $3.75 you should be able to sell at least 40 a day. Sign your name and address to coupon for additional facts, or, better still, get started selling and earning at once by attaching money order for $3.75 to coupon and rush to me. I send complete selling outfit containing one Tom Thumb Electric water heater, 110 volts, order blanks, selling particulars and everything necessary to get you started earning at once.

Terminal Products Co., Inc.,
Dept. 508 , 200 Hudson St., New York.

I have checked below the proposition I am interested in.

[ ] Enclosed find money order for $3.75. Please send me 1 Tom Thumb, 110 volts, order blanks and selling information. It is understood upon receipt of this sample outfit I will be permitted to take orders and collect $1.00 cash deposit on every Tom Thumb I sell. I will send orders to you and you will ship direct to customers C.O.D. for balance, plus postage. We refund the full price ($3.75) paid for sample after you have sold 24 paid up heaters.

[ ] I would like to have additional information before acting as one of your agents. Please send this by return mail free of obligation.

Name ....

Street ....

City .... State ....

Canadians send cash with order at same price (U. S. A. money). Other foreign countries $1.00 extra cash with order.

The
ANGEL
of the
DAMNED

by

J. Paul Suter

It hovered there—batlike, horrid—glowing with poisonous, twisting fire. And before it, groveling in ecstasy, the thing which once had been a man. What did it mean? What awful message flamed from that hell-pit angel's eyes—The Angel of the Damned!

CHAPTER ONE

Moonlight—and a Dead Man

HORATIO HUMBERTON rose from his chair in the book-cluttered study at the rear of the Humberton Funeral Parlors, and shook an admonishing finger under the prominent nose of Dr. Sigmund Bensen, Curator of the Tate Archaeological Museum.

"You are playing with fire, Bensen," he declared. "This thing, into which you are going so scoffingly, may be real. So far,

"Do you mean this thing came to life—grew up, and throttled them?"

you have not been hurt. Be thankful, and let it alone."

A moment before, Dr. Bensen's straggly gray beard had been a silky and docile adornment to his intellectual face. At Humberton's words it seemed to bristle. He had been sitting upon a nicely balanced pile of books—the study's usual hospitality to visitors, since there was seldom more than one vacant chair to be found at a time. The pile sprawled into a heap, as he too stood up.

"Real?" he roared, in deep bass. "Such rot real? I tell you, Humberton, the whole history of Spiritualism has been one long tissue of lies. Frauds and dupes—that's what they are. And as for the 'spirits'—when you lay a man in his coffin, he has just one more engagement this side of oblivion—an engagement with the worms! *Spirits!*" He laughed, sardonically, and rearranged the books. "My sole object in joining Weekoff at his seances has been to expose the whole business. I mean to show him the truth."

As he sat down again, Humberton smiled—a slow smile, which barely lifted the corners of his large mouth. He helped himself to a long, black cigar from the box before him on his work table, and blinked rapidly a few times behind his thick glasses as the potent smoke began to curl upward. But he did not speak.

"How many people have you buried?" the curator demanded in a moment.

"A few," his host replied, modestly.

"You've had dead bodies here—a good many of them lying around, at one time or another, eh?"

Humberton nodded. "Two in the morgue now," he volunteered.

"Very good. Then this ought to be a ghostly place, if there ever was one. Ever see a ghost here? Ever see one anywhere else?

The tall necrologist smiled again, and looked at his watch. "Half an hour before midnight," he announced, cheerfully.

"How far is Weekoff's house from here?"

"How far?" Bensen's heavy brows lifted. "Why—twenty minutes walk, perhaps. But I haven't asked you to go there."

"You are going to ask me. Why didn't you remain at Weekoff's this evening?"

"How could I remain? No one was there."

"Yet you had been invited to a seance?"

"I had. He has them every Wednesday evening—my assistant, mind you—my right hand at the museum—a man who preserves the scientific attitude in all other directions—yet he believes this rot. I have been going with the idea of awaiting the favorable moment, then exposing the thing completely—so that he can't fail to see through it. But I feared to act prematurely. I—"

"Precisely. You went into the house and found no one there?"

"I couldn't go in. The door was locked—everything dark."

"Now we are progressing. Really, Bensen, you are insufferably hard to pump. This is a cool night—yet when you came in a few minutes ago you were sweating. You've been glancing behind you at the hall door. If I ever saw terror in a man's eyes it was in yours when I answered your ring. What happened to you at Weekoff's?"

The curator shook his head, with a touch of defiance. "Nothing!" he snapped.

"Tell me about it."

"There's nothing to tell!"

FOR a moment, the eyes of the two men met; Bensen's a trifle bloodshot, Humberton's gently humorous behind his thick lenses. Then the pile of books was scattered again. The curator had rolled sidewise.

Humberton's reaction was calm and almost automatic. He knelt beside the unconscious man, pushed him over upon his back, and unbuttoned the rather tight collar. He was fumbling behind the row of books on a lower shelf for a bottle of ammonia when the front door of the undertaking establishment slammed. Footsteps approached down the long hall. Presently, the bluff voice of Detective Clyde, of Central Police Station, addressed him from the study doorway.

"I'm on late trick tonight, Ho. Remembered I had a key to this place, and that you're always late, too. What's this? Murder—or just one of your regular patients?"

Humberton looked up into the round red face of his official friend who was filling his pipe and staring down with interest at the man on the floor.

"This is Curator Sigmund Bensen of the Tate Archaeological Museum," the necrologist informed him, crisply.

"The hell you say! What happened to him. He's alive all right."

"I rather think he has seen a ghost."

"No!" Clyde built himself a pile of books, with the deftness born of frequent visits to his friend's study, and sat down, puffing at the pipe. "Don't hold the ammonia too close, Ho. Illegal to suffocate him, even if he is crazy. Does he say he saw one?"

"On the contrary, he denies it." Bensen's eyelids were fluttering. Humberton set down the bottle, and regarded him closely. "But his protestations are just a trifle too emphatic. There, Bensen! Don't try to get up yet. Lie on the floor with this book under your head. You'll be perfectly fit in five minutes."

The detective was grinning. "Pick out a soft book, Ho! Any objection to my horning in on this? It's been a quiet day. A little excitement would make me sleep better."

Bensen sat up abruptly. His head moved slowly from side to side. As his dull eyes rested on the detective, they lighted up with immediate recognition.

"Detective Clyde!" he exclaimed feebly.

"Sure! Hardly thought you'd remember me, professor. Didn't know you, at first. I helped out a few years ago, Ho, when they had some junk stolen from the museum. Ho tells me you've been seeing things, sir."

Helped by Humberton on one side and Clyde on the other, the curator rose to his feet, and sank with a sigh into his host's arm chair. He smiled, apologetically.

"I fear I've made rather an exhibition of myself. I have had a severe shock—so severe that I've been tempted to fence with words instead of telling my story. I started out tonight to attend a spiritualistic seance, Mr. Clyde—a thing in which I take no stock, whatever."

"All the spirits they ever have at those places come in bottles," the detective agreed.

"Exactly. My friend, Weekoff, who conducts the seances, has been experimenting with 'elementals', so-called—a supposed lower order of spirit, of evil tendencies, which never has been incarnate in flesh."

The detective's red face was an absolute blank; perceiving which, Humberton inserted an enlightening word. "Imps, Clyde," he prompted.

"Oh—imps! Sure! I've heard of them. Go on, professor."

"Of course, such things are figments of the imagination. Yet the imagination can be decidedly terrifying—as I have had reason to learn tonight. I was delayed in starting for Weekoff's, so it must have been all of eleven when I reached there. The place was dark. Nothing extraordinary in that—they darken it for the seances. But I hadn't expected the front door to be locked."

"So you went around to the back?" Clyde suggested.

"I did. You must understand, gentlemen, that Weekoff lives in a small cottage. From the window of the back door one can see through to the front."

THE detective seemed to sense that something important was coming. "Is there a window in the front door?" he demanded.

"There is not. I looked in from the rear, gentlemen—I looked in—"

Humberton was standing at the archaeologist's left. He leaned forward expectantly. "What did you see, Bensen?" he prompted.

"Something—something—looked out at me. Merely—looked out." The curator wiped his high forehead. "It was imagination—of course. Don't ask me to describe it. Certain things are beyond words. I am not easily upset Humberton, but this had such an effect upon me that I could think of nothing but to come here. You'll pardon me? I will go now."

"Just a minute, Bensen," Humberton put in. "Did you realize at the time that it was imagination?"

The curator shook his head. "I was too much overwhelmed."

"Clyde—" the necrologist turned to his friend of the official force— "I have known Dr. Bensen quite well for some years. He is a scientist; also a materialist. I have never credited him with much imagination. Are you too tired to stroll out to Weekoff's house with me?"

"You mean he really saw an imp?" The big detective was trying not to grin.

"Mean that some imps do not come directly from hell. Weekoff's house may be worth looking into."

The curator rose. "I am quite in command of myself again, gentlemen. No doubt conditions weren't right at Weekoff's; they went to some other house to complete the seance. There were three of them—Johnson, another assistant at the museum, and Tyler, who works in a bank.

A very small circle, but Weekoff preferred it so. We need hardly go out there at this time of night."

But the detective had caught Humberton's eye. He was pushing the study door open.

"It's a fine night for a walk," he observed. "Nice and cool and crisp. I've been spending the last eight hours tailing a bird who never stirred out of the same speakeasy he went into for lunch. Give me a chance to uncramp my legs."

"I tell you what I saw was imagination! There are no such things as 'imps' —as you call them."

But the necrologist had shrugged himself into a long overcoat ,and perched a high-crowned soft hat on his head. He helped Bensen on with his overcoat.

"You feel equal to the walk?" he inquired, solicitously.

"Certainly. The air will do me good. But I tell you—"

Humberton snapped out the light in the study. "Take Dr. Bensen out, Clyde," he requested. "I'll join you after making sure the morgue and the embalming room are locked up for the night."

A FILM of snow lay on the sidewalk outside. The curator walked carefully, meanwhile enlightening Detective Clyde as to his views on the unreality of spirits—a position with which the detective heartily agreed. Clyde was not deterred, however, from seizing the first opportunity—when Bensen was lecturing them learnedly on the reasons behind 'Poltergeist' phenomena—to put a rather paradoxical question to his friend.

"What did you mean about imps not coming from hell, Ho?" he inquired, guardedly. "Where in hell would they come from?"

He received small satisfaction.

"I merely wish to find out what he saw," the necrologist replied.

"Well, any man that imagines he sees

something fierce enough to make him faint must have a bad mind," was Clyde's reflection.

Paced by the long strides of Horatio Humberton, the walk to Weekoff's street was brief. The necrologist himself made it mainly in silence; though when Bensen pointed out the little cottage where the seances had been held, he glanced up at the moonlit sky and put an abrupt question: "Was the moon out when you were here before, Bensen?"

The archaeologist hesitated. "I believe so," he concluded.·

"Then it must have shone on the rear door of this cottage?"

"No doubt. I was too much perturbed to observe."

"Front and side window blinds down," Clyde remarked, with professional briskness. "Is that usual, professor?"

"Always, when there is a seance. The so-called 'spirits' perform best in the dark."

"They would," the detective growled. Now that they were at the scene of action, he was taking charge. "Might as well go round to that back door where you saw—whatever it was you saw."

"It was nothing—merely imagination."

"Sure! Then we'll see whether my imagination is working good, too."

As they walked down the narrow brick path to the rear of the small house, Humberton brought up the rear, peering, with the painstaking care of a near-sighted man, at the dwelling itself, the picket fence to the left, and even at the trailing vine along the fence. He was thus the last to arrive at the tiny, square back porch. Clyde already was looking through the window in the door.

The detective stared fixedly for several long seconds. His hand slid into the side pocket of his coat. He brought forth a flashlight, and, without taking his gaze from something within, levelled its beam into the interior of the kitchen.

At last he turned to the necrologist.

"Come up here and have a look, Ho," he said, coolly. "Imagination didn't get into this so big, after all. Moonlight did —moonlight and a dead man."

CHAPTER TWO

Digits of Doom

WHATEVER could have been said about his imagination, pro or con, Detective Clyde was proficient in the more material details of his profession; for instance, in breaking down a door. His substantial shoulders struck the rear door of the cottage, and it trembled. Twice more he hurled his weight against the panels, and a sharp snap resulted.

"Both of you keep back!" he growled. "This part is my job. Come in when I tell you."

Flashlight in hand, he stepped into the little house. The door swung idly behind him. Without hesitancy, the tall necrologist, coolly disregarded his instructions, and entered almost at his heels. He was in time to see the first revelation of Clyde's flash, as the circle of light embraced a sprawling body, just beyond the kitchen sink at the left.

The detective glanced over his shoulder at his friend. "Couldn't wait, could you, Ho? Suppose there had been a bozo in here with a gun!"

"In that case, I might have been in time to provide you Christian burial," Humberton retorted, calmly. "Shall I call Bensen in? Bensen, can you identify the dead man?"

"Just a minute—there ought to be electricity in this place." Clyde swept his flash along the wall. "Here's the button. Now, professor."

The curator had remained on the lowest step, in meticulous observance of Clyde's instructions. He resopnded slowly. When at last he forced himself to look at the body on the floor, his breath came sharply, and he quivered with emotion. But he did not speak.

"Well?" demanded the detective, with a touch of impatience.

"It is Weekoff."

"That's this spiritualist guy—the one that worked for you?"

The archaeologist nodded, silently.

"Well, let's see if we can figure out what killed him. We won't change the position of the body. I'd rather wait till the coroner comes for that. But maybe we can tell something just by giving him the up-and-down."

"If you don't mind, I will not touch him. I have a deep-seated fear of the dead. Even mummies, which I occasionally am called upon to handle in the course of my work, fill me with horror."

Yeah?" The detective had paused to light his pipe. "To tell the truth, I don't like to chum round with 'em, myself. Humberton here would sooner take a dead one for his little playmate than he would you or me. But I didn't have you in mind, professor, when I talked about examining this fellow. You can just stand back and watch. Ho and I—where the devil is Ho?"

The necrologist was not in the kitchen. Clyde, who had knelt beside the body, stood and looked about him. His eyes rested on the lighted doorway to the next room.

"He's lighting up the other parts of the house. Not a bad idea, at that." He raised his voice. "Everything all right, Ho?"

Humberton appeared in the doorway. His somber, rather heavy face, betrayed more emotion than was usual with him.

"Possibly we had better call the coroner at once, Clyde," he suggested, soberly. "And I think we should request Dr. Bensen to step into this room. The seance appears to have been held in it. Two of the participants are still present."

The big detective started, as if stung. "Do you mean they're dead, too?" he demanded.

"They are."

"Come on, professor." Perhaps a certain ill-timed flippancy had been perceptible in some of Clyde's remarks. That was one of his failings. If so, it was gone. His mouth clamped shut in a grim line. His blue eyes reflected the horror in those of the curator. As he stepped into the room where Humberton stood, he grasped Bensen by the arm and half forced him along.

"I want you to identify these bodies, too—if you can," he said.

IT was not a large room. Part of it was taken up by the cabinet—evidently a home-made job, built of wall board—which stood in a corner. The side of this cabinet farthest from them, and facing a small bedroom at the left, stood open. Clyde's rapid glance swept the place. He moved toward the cabinet.

"One minute." Humberton turned to the curator. "Before you look, I should like to ask a question. Is it usual Dr. Bensen, for more than one person to occupy a cabinet at a spiritualist seance?"

Bensen shook his head. "Certainly not," he emphasized. "The medium occupies the cabinet. The theory is—"

"I know." Humberton nodded and led the curator around the corner of the little enclosure. "First—even before you identify them, Dr. Bensen—notice the position of the bodies. Is there anything in your knowledge of spiritism to explain that?"

Clyde pushed the open section of the cabinet a little farther. Light streamed in, from the chandelier in the middle of the room. It revealed the bodies of two men. They sat back to back in two straight-backed chairs—and they were bound tightly to each other and the chairs, with ropes around necks, waists, and ankles.

The curator recoiled, with a cry of horror. "That's Johnson!" he cried. "He was married only a month ago. How can we ever tell his wife about this? She wouldn't have a thing to do with these seances. She warned him against them—I happen to know that because he told me. My God! And the other one—" He leaned far over, visibly fighting his repugnance. "Yes—it's Tyler. He worked in the Commercial Bank."

"You have not answered my question," the necrologist reminded.

"No." Bensen shook his head, weakly. All the violence he had shown an hour before, in his visit to Humberton's study, had vanished. "I know nothing of this. Sometimes they tie the medium—but never, so far as I have heard, to anyone else. But of course, I am not a spiritualist. My knowledge—"

"Possibly my information is more extensive than yours," the necrologist interrupted. "I have studied the subject. Under exceptional circumstances—for instance, where experiments with two mediums have been tried—the two might have been bound together. Were both of these men mediums?"

The curator turned slowly from contemplating the bodies. He met the near-sighted yet intense scrutiny of Horatio Humberton, and shook his head again. "They never had the slightest claim to mediumistic power—if there is any such power. I have heard Weekoff talk of that. They felt rather keenly about it."

"Was Weekoff himself a successful medium?"

'I am told so." Horror still trembled in the curator's deep voice. "You understand that I don't believe in the thing, at all. But they say Weekoff was unusually effective in raising 'elementals'."

"Imps," supplemented Clyde, half to himself.

"Precisely. And in physical phenomena, too. Perhaps you noticed some broken dishes on the kitchen floor. They might have been broken in some such way."

"They had been swept to the floor from the end of the sink nearest the body," Humberton commented. "I see a telephone in the front room. Suppose you call the coroner now, Clyde."

The tall necrologist busied himself in a rapid survey of the contents of the room. Bensen dropped into a chair—one from which the bodies were hidden by the cabinet—and buried his face in his hands. Presently, the detective's heavy voice became audible from the next room, as he telephoned.

EXCEPT for the cabinet and half a dozen chairs, the room in which the seance had been held was nearly bare of furniture. Evidently Weekoff—a bachelor, living alone—had taken his meals in the kitchen, for there was no dining table. A tambourine lay on the floor, just at the entrance to the cabinet. In one corner, a stand supported a cheap vase, empty of flowers. Three of the chairs were in the middle of the room—one of them overturned. Three others had been ranged in a line against the wall. Bensen sat on the chair nearest the front room, in this line, and as he rocked backward and forward, with hidden face, an occasional dry sob shook his broad shoulders. Humberton glanced at him once, but said nothing.

In his methodical examination the necrologist paused at length at the stand and the vase. "Haven't the 'elementals' a habit of breaking things of this sort?" he inquired.

The curator looked up. "Weekoff mentioned that vase to me only today," he returned. "We had an argument—rather a warm one, I fear. I was trying to dissuade him from this seance—as I always have tried to do. One of the minor points

I brought up was the damage done his furnishings by this senseless phenomena —or charlatanism, or whatever it is. Less than a month ago, quite an expensive vase of his—an antique—was smashed to bits. He told me this afternoon that he had replaced it with a cheap vase, so that the 'elementals' could indulge their destructive propensities at less expense to him."

Humberton nodded thoughtfully. He was unobtrusively studying the depressed face of the museum's learned chief.

"Suppose we assume that these 'elementals' really exist," he said, slowly. "We can do that for the sake of the discussion. You have never had any experience with them, yourself?"

"Positively not!" The reply came with something of the curator's former vehemence.

"But no doubt Weekoff has told you a good deal. Would you say he regarded them as dangerous?"

"At times. According to his belief they were mischievous, to say the least. Some of them I think, are classed as distinctly evil spirits."

"Would they do a thing like this if they could?"

"They are the devils of old-time legends. No doubt they would."

Clyde reappeared at the doorway to the front room. "Got a nice break, Ho. That's the beauty of having a real, honest-to-Jake doctor for coroner instead of a politician. Dr. Sollerby had just blown in from a case. Hadn't taken his shoes off yet. I told him about things out here, and he said he'd be with us in ten minutes. No waiting till morning for him! Now, you take the coroner we used to have— that lazy loafer—"

The detective stopped abruptly. Humberton's long, thin hand had slipped into the vase, and when it came into sight again, with the swiftness of a juggling trick, something small and red and very curious appeared between the necrolo-

gist's forefinger and thumb. This in itself might not have halted Clyde's characterization of the former coroner. But the behavior of the little curator was curious, too. He rose slowly to his feet. His breath came in gasps.

"The Angel of the Damned!" he whispered.

"What's that?" Clyde took a step into the room. "Look's like a funny angel to me—the kind I'd not care to meet in a dark alley! Maybe that's a real clue! Let's see it, Ho."

But Humberton had placed the little figure gingerly on the stand.

"I think we shall do better not to handle it, Clyde," he suggested. "My own fingerprints will appear at the very top and nowhere else."

"That's right. Sure! And I'm supposed to be a detective! We'll stuff some paper into the vase and take it that way for our finger print department to play with. But that angel stuff—did you say 'angel', Dr. Bensen?"

THE curator sank back into his chair. Perspiration appeared on his forehead. He seemed unable to turn his eyes away from the queer little image—the figure of a flying creature, about three inches high, with spread wings and outstretched arms, made entirely of cut, red stones, bound together by minute settings of gold.

"You haven't heard of it?" he asked.

Humberton, too, had been staring at the image. He was kneeling by the stand, to examine it from all sides. At Bensen's question he nodded. "I have read about it a number of times," he returned. "Very valuable and very old. As I recall, it is owned by the wealthy collector, Wallis Reddington."

"It was," the curator corrected. "For some time it has been the property of the museum."

"A gift?"

Bensen nodded. His self-control—apparently shaken by the discovery of the tiny image—was beginning to return.

"A gift in anticipation of death, I think. Mr. Reddington is a very sick man, and has been for some time. A year ago, I was called to his bedside, and he gave me that jeweled statue—called 'The Angel of the Damned'—together with the necessary papers conveying its ownership to the museum. I have kept it in one of our strongest cases until I could persuade the Museum Board to put through an appropriation."

"For a special case?" the necrologist prompted.

"Also a special watchman." The curator sighed. "There are drawbacks even to gifts. That little object is enormously valuable. You could group together half the exhibits in the museum, picked at random, and it would outvalue them all. Unless Mr. Reddington takes account of the fact, and leaves us a sufficient annuity in his will, his gift is likely to burden us. It must be guarded. It—"

Abruptly, his voice trailed off.

"Good Lord, what am I doing?" His hand swept over his forehead like that of a man awaking from sleep. "I'm taking it for granted, Humberton—taking its presence for granted. How in the name of sanity did it get here? Is it at the bottom of all this? Did someone try to steal it? It could easily be resolved into its component stones. They could be sold for an enormous sum. But why didn't he steal it? Why is it here?"

Humberton was still on his knees at the stand. He had picked up Clyde's flashlight, and by the help of a pocket microscope of his own was examining the curiously built-up image with painstaking care—remarkable care, considering the fact that his long hands never once touched it.

"Possibly, when we can answer your question, we shall know who killed these men," he returned soberly. "I feel the need of more data—facts concerning this Angel of the Damned, as you call it. Tell me about it, while we are waiting for the coroner. Why is it called that?"

"Have you looked at its face?" the curator fenced.

Humberton nodded. "Devilish!" was his appraisal. "The hands, too, are like claws. I notice that while the remainder of the image is built up of separate stones, these parts are exquisitely carved. The Lord would never own this sort of angel."

A faint smile relieved the pallor of Bensen's countenance. Isn't there a Lord of Hell?" he suggested. "Both name and image come down to us from medieval times. The thing was used for purposes of witchcraft. No doubt of that, at all. It is supposed to have the power of calling up familiar spirits."

"Then it might have its place in a seance?"

The curator started. "Yes!"

"Could Weekoff have borrowed it for that purpose?"

"He had the keys."

Humberton rose slowly to his feet, dusted off the knees of his trousers, and, with hands in pockets, gazed down reflectively at the little image.

"Are the gold mountings, which connect the stones, of medieval workmanship?" he inquired, presently.

"The whole thing is medieval."

"Meaning that it is how old?"

"Perhaps seven hundred years."

"I seem to recall, Bensen, that you are an expert, yourself, in this sort of work—the mounting of precious stones and the like."

The curator smiled again. As long as he kept his eyes averted from the cabinet, and from one still, sinister foot which it did not quite hide, he appeared master of his nerves.

"As a lad in Sweden I served apprenticeship to the jeweler's trade," he said, with a touch of pride. "It is still a hobby with me. I have mounted many precious and semi-precious stones in the museum, where the old mountings were falling to pieces."

"Take this little image." Humberton nodded toward the figure on the table. "I see you can speak as an expert. Would you say that the mounting is as old as the cut stones?"

"Not quite. Of course, I examined the Angel pretty carefully when it came to me. I estimate the mounting to date back not more than two centuries. One can tell by the style."

THE front door opened and closed. Clyde, who had been listening in silence to the conversation, turned expectantly.

"Hello, doctor! Glad you didn't wait to knock—I unbolted the door for you. Step right this way."

Dr. Sollerby, the coroner, was fat. That would have been anyone's first impression of him. With the unobservant, it might have been the only impression— a huge, flabby mountain of a man, slow in movement, ponderous of voice, wheezing like a locomotive. The unobservant might have missed his remarkably steady gray eyes; also the straight, alert line of his mouth. The eyes now appraised the room while he took in the company with a comprehensive nod.

"Glad to see you, Humberton. Suppose you take the bodies to your morgue when we get through here. Three of them, you say, Clyde? Nice of you to wait for me. I shan't be long." He was on his knees at once behind the cabinet, working silently.

Clyde nudged his friend and whispered: "That's one of the things I like

about him, Ho. The other bozo used to talk all the while he was giving a stiff the once-over. When he got through what he really thought was nobody's business till after the inquest. Sollerby shuts up till he's done. Then he spills it."

Soon, the big coroner rose, and trudged heavily into the kitchen. In a few minutes, he was back.

"Got any ideas, Humberton?" he inquired, cheerfully. "I notice you generally hit the cause of death pretty close. It seems fairly obvious in these cases."

"A blow on the head for the man in the kitchen; strangulation for the other two," the necrologist suggested.

Dr. Sollerby nodded. "That's about it, I guess. You carry a microscope sometimes. Got one with you now? I want a better look at the marks on the necks of these two in here."

With the little instrument—and Clyde's flashlight, which the detective proffered —he knelt again beside the bodies.

"Come over here, Humberton. Take a glance at these marks. Anything funny about them?"

The necrologist did as requested. In a moment he looked up. His eyes met the keen gray ones of the coroner, fixed on him questioningly. Sollerby smiled.

"Damned funny, don't you think so? If it was a pair of hands that strangled those fellows, then the hands had six fingers, besides the thumb—steel fingers, judging by the abrasions. Not only that, but as far as I can tell without measuring, the finger marks are spaced exactly the same on both necks. That's not natural."

Humberton did not reply at once. Instead, he rose, and walked over to the stand on which The Angel of the Damned still stood. He knelt beside the little figure, and examined it again through the microscope.

"Look at these hands, Sollerby," he said. "And you, too, Clyde."

Sollerby took the glass, and knelt by the figure. Before he could speak, however, the curator seemed to come out of a lethargy.

"Seven fingers to each hand," he volunteered. "That is characteristic of certain medieval images used in the black arts. It dates back to ancient Egypt."

The fat coroner straightened, suddenly. "You haven't any kind of measuring device handy, Humberton?"

Horatio Humberton shook his head, with a smile. "Your eyes are good, doctor," he returned. "I thought no one but myself would see that point. It is odd, isn't it? The marks on these dead throats seem to be spaced exactly the same as the claws of the little image!"

Detective Clyde started. "Do you mean this rummy thing came to life, then grew up and throttled them?" he demanded.

The necrologist shrugged his shoulders. "I wonder!" he said.

CHAPTER THREE

Cult of the Demon

THE group which gathered the following evening in Horatio Humberton's study, beneath the swinging electric bulb, was rather odd in its make-up. It included the coroner and Humberton, also the necrologist's hearse-driver and general right-hand man, Ted Spang, whose sleekly smoothed, glossy black hair and sharp, alert features contrasted strongly with the obese Dr. Sollerby, who sat beside him. The other member of the party was small, dark, and unmistakably Jewish. His curly brown beard constituted the only adornment of that character among the four of them. The outstanding fact concerning the group, however, was that though its members had come together to dicuss an atrocious crime, no police officer appeared. The absence of Detective Clyde fairly cried for explanation.

Sollerby seemed to feel this. When Humberton had shut the door into the corridor and had carefully bolted it, the coroner put his thought into words.

"Clyde coming?" he asked.

The tall necrologist smiled. His fingers toyed with the tiny Angel of the Damned, which stood before him on his work table.

"I requested Clyde not to come," was his reply; then, before any exception could be taken to his remark: "Sollerby, to what extent are you bound to keep within the letter of the law?"

The fat coroner looked perplexed. "Why—to the same extent as you or any other good citiezn."

"To the same extent as Clyde?"

"Hardly." Sollerby's keen eyes flashed the ghost of a smile. "I'm not a policeman. I might stretch a point, now and then, in the interest of justice."

"I wish you to stretch it tonight. Before the evening is over, we may plot a violation of the law. Clyde, being a city detective, would be bound to report that impending event. How about you? You still have time to leave."

Coroner Sollerby was a man of deliberation. He slowly fished a cigarette from his pocket, passed the package to Ted Spang, and lit up while thinking the thing over. At last he came to a conclusion.

"Go ahead," he said. "I'm not the coroner, tonight—I'm just a doctor. If you kill a man and ask me to sit on the remains, I'll turn back into the coroner."

The necrologist nodded his satisfaction. He leaned back in his swivel chair, with the jeweled figure in his hand.

"Pretty little thing!" He held it up to the light. "See the red gleam in the heart of those stones! Red for blood! By the way, Sollerby, I am not sure that you and Mr. Isaacs have met. Have you ever pawned your watch?"

The stout coroner shook his head.

"Then you have not met. Mr. Isaacs is the squarest private banker of my acquaintance. He is also an expert in precious stones—an expert unhonored and unsung in the seats of the mighty—whose judgment I rate a trifle higher than that of any jeweler in the city. He knows the history of stones—their psychology. Am I correct in saying that this figure, Mr. Isaacs, has no psychology?"

"None," the little Jew replied, quietly and very decisively.

"Neither has it any fingerprints of value. Clyde reported to me, when he was kind enough to lend me The Angel of the Damned, that headquarters could make nothing of it. Too many prints have been imposed, one upon the other. We must use the figure in a different way."

The coroner nodded, absently. "While I think of it—" he interrupted— "I mustn't forget to tell you this. I dropped into the morgue this afternoon and went over the bodies carefully—while you were out. Odd feature about the two in the cabinet. I checked it in a number of ways—there's really very little doubt. Both of them had received terrific blows on the head before they were strangled. Understand—they were still alive when the strangling took place. But I don't think they were conscious."

"What killed them?" Humberton inquired.

"Both causes, probably. Either by itself might have been enough. The combination made a sure job of it."

"Were they tied together before death?"

"Oh, yes."

THE necrologist rose lazily and stood in apparent contemplation before the well-filled book shelves at his right. His eyes traveled upward and came to rest at a row of corpulent volumes on the topmost shelf. He pulled the swivel chair over, mounted it with painstaking care, removed the pair of books at the left of this top shelf, and from the space behind them produced a ponderous tome, which he dusted with his sleeve as he resumed his place at the table.

"Here, gentlemen—" he gazed at his auditors with the peering benevolence of a pastor about to address his flock "—you see one of the gems of my library. It is a first printed edition, written in medieval Latin, of Julius Servetus' *magnum opus* on the Cacodaemons, or Evil Spirits. Some of the most curious treatises on the care of the dead are couched in that tongue, so I have made myself familiar with it. You've never taken it up, Sollerby, by any chance—as a hobby, perhaps?"

The fat coroner shook his head.

"You might do worse. Just now, for instance, you'd be interested in a certain chapter of this book—the one dealing with the fallen angel, Beltonus, known as The Angel of the Damned!"

The three others reacted variously to this startling item. Sollerby's eyes opened rather widely, and he sat very straight in his chair. The little Jew turned his gaze sharply to the tiny, bejeweled figure, now set upon Humberton's table, as if that might explain the reference from Servetus. Ted Spang blew a smoke ring. Emotion seldom found a toehold in Ted's mind.

"The worship of Beltonus was one of the many obscure cults of the middle ages," the necrologist went on, didactically. "Not much is known about it. For instance, not even Servetus can explain the symbolism of the bound worshippers, trussed together two by two and back to back, which characterized the secret rites. The demon had seven fingers counting the thumb as one. He took possession of his sacrifices (can't you guess this, Sollerby?) by throttling the victims. Servetus hints at the exact manner of this death, but the language there is obscure—something about fingers of steel—I can't quite make it out. The point seems to be that Beltonus himself, materialized by certain infernal rites, appeared and claimed his own. Sometimes, he merely came. On other occasions, he killed. His worshippers seem to have taken their chances on that. He was always dangerous."

"Where did they meet?" the coroner inquired.

"Deep in the darkest and most lonely recesses of the woods. And of course at night."

"Well—" the coroner grinned "—it's a darn good thing I'm not superstitious. I don't recall whether you saw me do it, Humberton, but I fished a blotter out of my pocket last night before we left that house, and used it to take an impression of the claws of your ugly little image. No—I didn't gum up the fingerprints; I held it with my handkerchief. This afternoon was harder. If you ever tried to take an exact impression, to scale, of fingerprints on the neck of a corpse, you know. But I got them. Not only that, but I used what I got as the basis for some interesting figuring. Mathematics always was my dish."

HE WAS slipping a fat finger into each pocket of his vest, in turn, then into his coat pocket. At length, he stood up ponderously and tried the pockets of his trousers. Sitting down, he grinned again.

"Left the figures at home! I'm always doing some fool stunt like that. But I can tell you what they showed. In the first place, suppose I choked both Mr. Spang here and Mr. Isaacs to death—"

Ted Spang merely turned his head, with languid interest, toward the speaker. The little Jew started, perceptibly.

"—I should undoubtedly leave some marks on their necks. Would the marks coincide? That's the point. Would the

distance from the mark made by the forefinger to that made by the middle finger on one neck be exactly the same as on the other? And so on? I ask you!"

Horatio Humberton silently shook his head.

"Certainly not! One never picks up two things in succession with quite the same spacing of all the fingers. Try it some time. A precision instrument, with a micrometer gauge, such as I used this afternoon, would show a difference somewhere."

In the heat of his remarks, the stout coroner had let his cigarette burn down too far. The glow reached his finger. He dropped the butt, ground it beneath his heel on the floor, lit another cigarette, and when it was puffing to his satisfaction, resumed.

"Point Number One! Allowing as well as I could for the difference in size of the two necks of these murdered men, the distance between finger prints seems to have been exactly the same. In other words, they seem to have been strangled by a pair of seven-fingered hands which had no lateral movement between the fingers, as human hands have. Can you explain that, Humberton?"

"Not yet."

"I did some pretty delicate work with the prints on my blotter. Used a pantograph, and extended them out until they reached the same scale as the neck prints. When I did that, they corresponded exactly. That is Point Number Two!"

"Which brings us to Clyde's suggestion that the image came to life and grew up."

"Darned if it don't!" the coroner agreed, cheerfully.

"Perhaps—" Humberton glanced at the black-letter book on his table "—we might profitably give a little thought to the supernatural angle. I am no more superstitious than you. The fact remains, however, that these men had met with the deliberate intention of trying to communicate with certain intelligences not yet recognized by science. They were particularly interested in 'elementals.' Now, 'elementals'—granting their existence for the moment—are evil and mischievous spirits of sub-human intelligence. They are not spirits of the dead. They have never been clothed in flesh, at all. If there is a vestige of truth in the thousands of stories of demons and hobgoblins that have descended to us from an earlier day, it seems likely that these things were 'elementals.' To come down to cases, Beltonus would have been one."

Sollerby's eyes twinkled. "Go on," he said. "This is getting good!"

"What does the presence of the Angel of the Damned indicate? We don't have to go over to the supernatural to theorize about that, do we?"

"This fellow Weekoff stole it from the museum, to see whether he could put on a Beltonus meeting," the coroner suggested.

"I think so. Perhaps 'borrowed' would be as accurate as 'stole.' He seems to have been trying to duplicate the conditions of those dark orgies of the middle ages. He may have known the very incantations they used. According to Bensen, Weekoff was quite a learned man in these matters. He and his friends sought to raise Beltonus, let us say. Or they were experimenting, to learn whether such a thing—if it ever had been done, at all—were still possible. And Beltonus came!"

"That's not your solution of this case, is it?" the coroner demanded.

"Perhaps not." Humberton smiled. "I am not a materialist. I believe in ghosts —to a certain extent. It might be the solution—but for one very disquieting fact. That fact changes the whole complexion of our inquiry. It is the reason why I brought Mr. Isaacs here. It explains the question I asked you at the outset, too, Sollerby—whether you object to viola-tions of the law. When we have settled this point, with all that it implies, I fear we shall no longer be respectable citizens. Isaacs, let me hand you the image."

THE little Hebrew rose and received the proffered figure. He stood thoughtfully a moment gazing at it in his hand, then sat down again. A quizzical smile played about the corners of his mouth.

"Isaacs, is that image a good example of medieval workmanship?"

"Very good workmanship." The private banker nodded emphatically to reinforce his appraisal. "The man who executed it is a master. Very good, indeed. I should say—but not medieval."

"Go on," Humberton requested. "I want both Dr. Sollerby and Ted to know as much about it as we do. We are all in this together."

"Someone with the original figure for constant reference has made a copy," the Jew went on. "An excellent copy! Binding the stones together with the gold bands was simple, but this face! These hands! The work is marvelously done. Marvelously—but for all his skill, the artist who did it missed the precise medieval twist in the gold. You see, gentlemen—" his mild brown eyes lighted with the enthusiasm of the expert "—every age has its own peculiarities. The zeitgeist—the time spirit! No other age can quite duplicate it. Always there is a difference somewhere. I see that difference here. I can't explain it to you. Yet it is present."

"And the stones?" the necrologist prompted.

"Good, commercial imitations. I saw the originals a number of times in Reddington's collection. I know how good these imitations are. These stones are not rubies, at all."

"I don't get this!" the coroner exclaimed. "How closely did you have to examine that figure to know it was a fake, Mr. Isaacs?"

"Not very closely. Does a poultryman have to sniff more than once at a bad egg? I am a poultryman. This is my egg."

"All right—isn't Dr. Bensen a poultryman, too?" Sollerby pursued, accepting the metaphor.

"Oh, yes, indeed!" Isaacs smiled, ingenuously. "I am quite a vain man, Dr. Sollerby. I hold that only one person in this city is more expert in precious stones and jewelry than I. Dr. Benson is that person."

The coroner's keen eyes swung swiftly to Humberton's face. What he saw there enlightened him. He grinned.

"Gets better, doesn't it?" he commented, dryly. "Excuse me if I seem a trifle dumb. I've got it now. You're trying to tell me that Bensen knew all along this figure was a fake, but for some reason he wasn't saying anything. What was that reason?"

Horatio Humberton's long hand slipped into the pocket of his coat and brought out a huge bunch of keys.

"The keys of the Tate Museum," he explained. "They were on Weekoff. Clyde was kind enough to lend them to me without asking questions. Mr. Isaacs here, also Ted Spang and I, intend to break into the museum tonight. These keys will be a great help. I am not asking you to go with us, but I do request that you keep our little expedition secret. There is a chance—just a chance—that my theory might be wrong."

"Your theory? You think—"

The tall necrologist nodded, solemnly. "In my mind, it has almost gone beyond surmise. Everything points to one conclusion. Dr. Bensen is the murderer!"

"But why should he do a thing like that?" Sollerby flung the words almost defiantly.

"Because those he killed knew too much."

"What did they know?"

"I am going to the museum to find out," Humberton answered.

CHAPTER FOUR

The Museum Murder

WHAT the Humberton Funeral Parlors gained from their proprietor's repute for learning they perhaps lost in other ways. For one thing, he might, with decided worldly advantage to himself, have devoted more time to building up business for the parlors. Business was bad. It never had been very good. In consequence, the limousine, skillfully driven by Ted Spang, in which the necrologist himself, with Sollerby and Mr. Isaacs, sped toward the Tate Museum, undoubtedly ranked with the shabbier funeral equipages of the city.

It being night, the party could not observe the car's moth-eaten upholstery. But every roughness in the pavement emphasized that the springs were not what they once had been; and some annoying mechanical trouble, lightly characterized by Ted Spang as "a bit of piston slap," made conversation difficult.

These minor discomforts troubled Humberton not at all. He devoted the trip to the museum, which lay well toward the outskirts, to an exposition of his reasons for suspecting Dr. Bensen. His voice was strong and clear. Dr. Sollerby, who had insisted on being one of the party, was not anemic, either. So most of the dialogue was theirs. Mr. Isaacs' speaking tones tended toward the quiet and refined. He listened.

"If he did it," Sollerby objected, in stentorian accents, "why did he come to you? Why did he court investigation?"

"What better way of disarming suspicion?" the necrologist retorted. "There was every chance that one of his three victims might have mentioned to someone else that Bensen was going to be there. He couldn't hope for an alibi."

"But I understand he actually fainted in your place."

Humberton laughed. "Oh, I mentioned that, did I? After all, what else could you expect of a high-strung man, after he had committed a triple murder? Bensen is a man of the highest intellectuality, you know. I could make out a very good case for a genuine faint on his part. By the way, his was not genuine!"

"The devil you say!"

"Of course, he knew me to be merely a necrologist—not a physician. But even with me, he should not have come out of it so completely all at once. Then, too, when he had called with the fixed determination to get me out there—that was very obvious—he should not have pretended to change his mind, as if the matter were of no consequence. His acting there was very poor. In fact, he alternately over-acted and under-acted. And you heard about the face he said he saw in the window?"

"Clyde told me."

"That was to account for his excited mental state. But people don't see faces at windows and then faint half an hour afterward—even in imitation faints."

"No." The coroner shook his head ponderously, and a street light they were passing revealed the movement. "You're entirely right there. Men of his type either faint at the time or not at all." He reflected a moment. "Why the bound bodies?"

"Another point against him. Almost as damning as the fact that he did not at once brand the fake image for what it was. How many people in this city, do you think, know of the Beltonus rite? Very, very few. Weekoff did. Perhaps he engineered the ceremony. But Bensen did know of it. And another thing—did

you invite him to examine the bodies?"

"I hardly think so," the coroner replied, slowly.

"Clyde did. He refused, on the ground that the examination of dead bodies— even of mummies—completely unnerved him. That was a defect of memory. He forgot that I was with him on one occasion when he unwrapped a mummy— showing no more emotion in the process than if it had been a side of beef. Don't you see?" Humberton wrapped his knuckles, for emphasis, against the back of the front seat. "Touch him where you will, he rings false—false!"

"All right, sir!" Ted Spang's strident rather high-pitched voice hailed his master from the driver's seat. "Another block and we'll be there. Going to drive up to the front door and ring the bell?"

EVIDENTLY Ted surmised Humberton's answer, for he was drawing to the curb. The necrologist released the door catch and stepped out.

"Quite right, Ted," he returned. "We will walk the rest of the way. Perhaps I had better explain our tactics before we go closer."

"What I want to know is, why are we going at all?" Sollerby cut in. "As far as I'm concerned, this is a blind lead. I'm in on it because it looks like an adventure. But why am I in? Why are any of us in? Do you realize that as soon as we set foot in that museum we shall all be burglars in the eye of the law?"

"Not quite so bad as that, Sollerby. Not quite! I know the night watchman. I telephoned him this afternoon. It took some persuading, but he is willing to stretch a point in my favor and let us in. A reputation for honesty has some value."

"Front door?" the coroner inquired, quizzically; but Humberton, in the act of igniting a cigar, shook his head.

"Perhaps 'let us in' is not entirely accurate," he explained. "As a matter of fact, there is a small basement door at the rear, used chiefly by the fireman. That door will happen to be unlocked. If it came to a burglary charge—which it won't —the watchman would clear us."

The museum loomed ahead, two stories of stone, white in the darkness. The investigating party stopped talking. Only their footsteps sounded faintly on the cement pavement. Sollerby, the heaviest man among them, trod most lightly, while the diminutive private banker walked with a shuffle noisier than the tread of any two of the others. Even Isaacs, however, became comparatively quiet when they had rounded the corner of the museum and were following Humberton down an inclined runway to the basement level.

The necrologist seemed to know his way. He led them around a second corner, where the sub-grade path became level again, and so halfway across the rear of the building to a small door. The handle yielded readily. Humberton laid his half-smoked cigar carefully on the sill of a little window to the right of the door, and stepped inside.

"Furnace room," he whispered, out of the darkness. "One of Bensen's peculiarities is that he does not favor lights after closing hours. He says they are an aid to burglars—just the opposite of the usual view. His watchman carries an electric lantern, but keeps it off most of the time."

"Then we're likely to run into the watchman before we know it," Sollerby objected, also in a whisper.

"Hardly. Ted is remarkably good at seeing in the dark."

"What are we here for, anyway?" the coroner persisted.

"No time to tell you now. Come!"

He gave the others no opportunity for further whispering. Their attention was concentrated on following his lead, as he swiftly skirted the warm furnace and took a diagonal across the cement floor. In a

few moments, his feet found the first step of a narrow stairway. He stopped.

"Ted!" he whispered, cautiously.

"Here, sir!"

"Keep beside me. I want the benefit of your eyes. You still wish to come, Sollerby?"

"I'm in this thing to a finish," the coroner declared.

WITHOUT further comment, Humberton climbed the stairs, accompanied by the useful Spang. Sollerby and the pawnbroker followed closely. A door at the top admitted to an even darker place than the basement. Humberton released the flash of an electric lantern. It revealed a large room, cluttered with boxes and packing cases.

"The receiving room—where they unpack the exhibits. Don't fall over the boxes."

He used the light again, for the benefit of the others. They threaded a zigzag path among the boxes to a door on the farther side. Humberton snapped off the lantern once more and pushed this door open.

"The great hall. It runs from front to rear, the length of the building. Careful, now. We are almost there."

They crossed the hall and stood in an enormous room—one of the exhibit rooms. Dim windows at the left let in enough light from the drab night sky to show in vague outline the rows of cases in which the exhibits reposed. Humberton placed his lips close to the coroner's ear to whisper again.

"Bensen is an expert in mental work. He could pull off the most intricate jobs without a jeweler's help."

"What of it? What's that got to do with this business?"

"Don't you see?"

"I'll be hanged if I do!"

Petulance raised the fat coroner's voice somewhat above a whisper. Humberton placed a cautioning hand on his arm.

"Never mind. These keys I have are numbered to correspond with the cases. Isaacs!"

"I am ready," the little Jew responded, coolly.

"Take the flashlight. When you find a case you wish to examine, let me know its number."

"The little circle of light, guided by Isaacs' hand, darted into the nearest case. A moment's pause, a shuffle of feet, and it was in the next one. Humberton followed closely. Sollerby, grumbling under his breath, turned suddenly upon the imperturbable Ted Spang.

"Do you know why we are doing this, Spang?" he demanded, in a penetrating whisper.

"No more than the man in the moon, sir."

"Humberton!"

The necrologist looked around; but at that moment Isaacs spoke. "Seventy-two," he said. "The number is on a metal disk on the side of the case."

"No time now, Sollerby." Humberton fumbled among the keys. "Watch Isaacs. Here is the key to seventy-two."

The side of the case swung open under the private banker's left hand. He reached in, withdrew a bit of delicate jewelry, and scrutinized it in the light of the electric lantern.

Apparently, a few minutes were enough. He laughed, quietly and rather grimly. "Imitation medieval, very skilfully done. Would you like to examine it, Mr. Humberton?"

"No. Put it back. Now do you see, Sollerby?"

The coroner's reply came in an exasperated growl. "Confound it, man, you don't have to speak in riddles! I see there's something wrong, if that's what you mean. How did you know he would find imitation jewelry in this museum?"

"I did not. I merely suspected. If an imitation angel, why not other imitations —things lower than the angels? Yes, Isaacs?"

The little Jew held a second small object in his hand. "Another!" he declared.

"Very well. Put it back. I think we will go to the upper floor. The most valuable exhibits are there."

"Is there only one night watchman?" Sollerby inquired; at which the necrologist laughed, softly.

"Good, conservative citizens serve on these museum boards," he returned. "They believe in economy. Perhaps they are right. Museum pieces are easy to identify and hard to sell."

THE coroner followed quietly for a few minutes, as, under Humberton's direction but with Ted Spang's keen-eyed guidance, they skirted the somber cases toward a back stairway. Presently he put another question: "Did Bensen make the substitutions?"

"I think so."

"Could he sell the originals without causing suspicion?"

"Hardly. Not in any such quantities as seem to be involved here."

"Then why—"

The necrologist laughed again—rather too loudly for safety. "You're a doctor, Sollerby. Put two and two together. What kind of man plans profoundly, then makes the most ridiculous and elementary mistakes? What kind—"

"Begging pardon, sir," interrupted Ted Spang, in low-pitched but penetrating tones. "You're broadcasting kind of loud."

"Very true, Ted. I must be more careful. Ah, here we are at the top of the stairs. I see a light!"

They stood at the rear door of a large exhibition room—the Egyptian section. It was dark. Through its farther entrance, beyond the mummy cases and the stiff rows of votive offerings, flowed a narrow stream of yellow light from an unseen source.

"It comes from the left," the necrologist diagnosed. "No doubt from Bensen's private office. Ted, suppose you go on as quietly as possible, and see whether anyone is there."

"Right, sir."

The agile hearse-driver went very quietly, indeed; so much so that in a moment, though they could see his alert figure against the background of the lighted doorway, they could not hear his footsteps, at all. He paused, and peered cautiously around the door jamb. What he saw must have reassured him, for he vanished. Almost at once, he was back at the door. He beckoned.

The keen-visioned coroner started. "That fellow has seen something! Don't you catch his expression? Come on!"

He took the lead. Ted remained motionless at the door until they had joined him.

"What is it, Ted?" the necrologist demanded.

"Step this way and see for yourself, sir," the hearse-driver answered, coolly. "You won't wake no one!"

Humberton knew his assistant too well to waste words. The source of the light was plainly visible. It came from a little room just around the corner at the end of the upper hall. Through the half-opened door of that room, a roll-top desk, with its top pushed up, and the green glass shade of a lighted desk lamp upon it were to be seen. Sollerby was first in the room, with the tall necrologist just behind him. They saw the body of a man sprawled on his back between the desk and the wall.

Humberton ran forward. "Lyons!" he exclaimed. "The watchman!"

"The man who let us in?" Sollerby inquired. He was already kneeling beside the body.

The necrologist nodded, silently.

"Well! Not a bad idea to have the coroner along on this job, at that! Don't we need the police, too?"

Humberton nodded to the hearse-driver. "There's a telephone here on the desk, Ted. Call up Clyde, and be ready to let him in at the front door. Tell him it's another murder!"

"It's all of that," the coroner agreed. "Men don't shoot themselves through the forehead after tying their hands behind their backs. Feet tied together, too!" He looked up gravely at the necrologist from his position on hands and knees beside the body. "Do you know, Humberton, this thing is getting interesting?"

Horatio Humberton also dropped to his knees, carefully avoiding a sinister pool of blood on the rug. His long fingers deftly untied the cord about Lyons' ankles.

"Clyde won't mind my doing this," he exclaimed. "I rather think we need to work fast. How long has he been dead, Sollerby—an hour?"

"Not any longer. I'll have to see whether I can tell about these cords, off-hand. The others were tied before death. I wonder if these were."

Humberton glanced at him with a smile —the smile of the specialist with whom the horror of tragedy counts for nothing as compared with the niceties of his calling.

"I can answer that question," he declared. "This man was shot before his feet were tied. The cord evidently fell into that pool of blood." He held up the dangling evidence. "There is blood inside the knot as well as outside!"

But the coroner's interest had become diverted from the cord. He leaned over the pathetic figure on the floor until his eyes were within a foot of the upturned neck. His breath came rapidly.

"Humberton!" he whispered. He looked up, to find the necrologist's eyes, through their thick glasses, focused on the marks he was examining. "I can't measure these marks right now. But they were made after death. I'm certain of that. And, I'd be willing to hold up my right hand and swear they are identical with the fingerprints on the other bodies. That damned angel has been getting into this, too!"

CHAPTER FIVE

Through the Passage

DETECTIVE CLYDE stood in the doorway of the curator's little office, his face flushed somewhat more than usual from the exertion of stair climbing, and his eyes narrowed into an expression of considerable severity. Behind him, Ted Spang calmly lighted a cigarette.

"I get it!" the big detective declared, bitterly. "I get it sweet and pretty, Ho, just from looking in here. You've been law breaking again. Burglary this time. And you want me to square it because it's a short cut to justice. Well—I can square most of your stuff. Maybe I can even square burglary. But if this is murder, too, I can't square that!"

Humberton had seated himself in the open roll-top desk, the height of which from the floor suited his long legs nicely. He indicated the curator's chair to Clyde. Sollerby stood beside the body, still studying it gravely.

"Sit down, Clyde. I wonder whether you saw anyone else, out in the hall?"

"There was a bozo sitting on the top stair. I don't get—"

"You wouldn't. He is Mr. Solomon Isaacs, profoundly learned in precious stones and in all the intricacies of the jeweler's art, but not in the least bloodthirsty. He is sitting out there from choice. Mr. Isaacs, Clyde, has been very interesting, tonight. He has demonstrated that a number of the finest pieces in the Tate Museum are not so fine as the public imagine. Bluntly, they are fakes. The genuine pieces have been removed, and others substituted."

"The devil—"

Humberton cut short his friend's vigorous rejoinder. "I don't wish to seem hasty. But really, we have no time to lose. What I must know is—are you willing to come with me at once and take the responsibility of breaking into a private residence?"

"Without a search warrant?"

"We shall not be searching. We are going to arrest a murderer."

Clyde stood up, briskly. The prospect of immediate action had cleared his face as if by magic.

"I'm taking that kind of responsibility right along. Where do we go from here?"

"Just a minute." Humberton spoke rapidly, with a curiously grim intensity. "I can't let you come without a full understanding of the danger. You don't believe in the supernatural?"

The detective shook his head, with a half-grin.

"The little figure of the angel—The Angel of the Damned—was thought by its worshippers in the middle ages to have terrific powers. It could kill. It killed by throttling. And the marks it left on the necks of its victims were in exact scale to its own tiny fingers."

Sollerby interrupted—though not with words. He leaned over the body on the floor and silent exposed the throat to Clyde's gaze.

"Hell!" was the detective's earnest comment.

"The man we are going after is expert in this particular mystery. He knows how the angel kills. And he is bright enough to anticipate our visit and arrange a reception for us." The necrologist slid to his feet. "That's all. I wanted you to appreciate our problem. Shall we start?"

"Right now!" The detective rubbed his hands together like a ballplayer waiting for the throw. "Just you and me, Ho?"

"I'm in on it," the stout coroner put in.

Humberton nodded. "You may as well

come, Sollerby. Any of us may need the services of a coroner before the night is over. As for you, Ted—"

"Here, sir!" the hearse-driver interjected, quietly.

"You will take Mr. Isaacs home. Unless I am mistaken, that is what he desires more than anything else. Then come back and park in front of Dr. Bensen's house."

Spang nodded understanding. "Got you, sir. His house is right beside the museum, ain't it? I'll be back so quick you'll think I knocked the little chap on the head and dumped him somewheres."

"I'm not so good at seeing in the dark, Clyde. Suppose you take the lead. Head for the back door. I think we are justified in forcing it."

"Not unless you're pretty sure he's the man, Ho."

"I am sure."

THEY were descending the broad front stairs of the museum. Ted Spang and the little private banker had gone ahead. Their footsteps were audible on the tiles of the lower floor. Quite in his element now that physical danger threatened, the big detective put a cheerful question: "How do you think he'll try to get us, Ho? With a gun?"

"Very likely."

"Be waiting behind the door, maybe. Or shooting through it. That's the kind of thing that makes this job interesting!"

The night had changed. As they let themselves out of the front entrance to the museum, a fine drizzle met their faces, driven by enough wind to give it penetration. Clyde descended the broad stone steps so rapidly that he slipped and came near finishing the descent head first. The tall necrologist took it more slowly. On his way down, he stopped several times to peer upward into the thick night.

"Expect something out of the sky?" Sollerby asked, walking beside him.

"In a way, yes. I was thinking of the moon. If it were out now, that might make a difference."

The coroner, about to put a puzzled question, suddenly started and nodded his understanding.

"I think I get you. Certainly I do! You mean a difference in what we may find— the supposed influence of the moon on insanity?"

"Exactly."

Clyde was waiting rather impatiently, at the foot of the steps. "Got a gun, Ho?" he inquired.

"No," was the necrologist's curt response.

"I never carry one," Sollerby volunteered.

"Then mine is the only rod in the party. You fellows lean pretty hard on your guardian angels, don't you? Better keep close to me."

A fence of old-fashioned iron pickets separated the two-story brick house next the museum from the property of the institution itself. Clyde asked no questions concerning the house. He led the way in silence through the street gate in the fence, and so around to the rear. The fact that the eccentric and learned curator had lived alone in this pretentious dwelling since the death of his wife, ten years before, was fairly well known. He took his meals out, and kept no servants. The public knew that, too. Newspapers had carried stories upon it. How successful he had been as his own maid-of-all-work was harder to determine. Inquisitive reporters had never penetrated farther than the small square reception hall.

The raiding party stopped when they had reached the rear. Clyde looked about him with professional acumen.

"Two doors," he ruminated aloud. "Steps leading up from the yard. Door at the top of the steps opening into the kitchen. Furnace-room door under the steps. In my house we always lock the upstairs cellar door at night. If Bensen does that, we'd have two locks to force. So what do you say to the kitchen, Ho?"

"Much the best," the necrologist agreed.

"You boys stay back in the yard. Or wait—doctor, are you handy with a gun?"

"I haven't shot a revolver for twenty years," the coroner replied.

"That's that! And I don't think Ho knows which end to point. I was going to ask you to cover me while I broke the lock, but we'll forget it. Stay here. If I don't come back, use your own judgment."

He climbed the flight of wooden steps, leading to the door. Entirely disregarding his instructions, Humberton followed. The coroner hesitated a moment, then, with a suppressed laugh, brought up the rear.

Thus it was that both of them were just behind him when Detective Clyde, as a preliminary to more forceful methods —and no doubt to learn where the bolt was placed—cautiously turned the knob.

The door was not locked.

SLOWLY, the detective pushed it open. Protecting as much of his body as possible by the door jamb, he peered into the darkness. Then, with a sudden swift movement, he snapped on his flashlight, swept the luminous circle once around the kitchen, and turned it off again.

He turned to whisper to his companions, waiting until his face was close to theirs, and pitching his heavy voice so low that their ears were strained to catch the words.

"No one in there—no one that I can see. Ho, I'm asking you. I'm asking it as a favor. *Will* you stay out here while I go in?"

"No," the necrologist answered, curtly.

"Oh, all right." The big detective's voice was moody. "I didn't think you would. You wait here, Dr. Sollerby.

We've got to have somebody to take charge of our bodies."

"Nothing doing," was the coroner's rejoinder.

"Come on, then, you darned fools!"

He stepped into the kitchen. They followed. Clyde had seen enough with the fleeting help of his flashlight, to know the directions. Though the darkness was nearly complete, he led the way confidently.

It was a broad, old-fashioned kitchen. They were about in the middle of it, dimly perceiving each other's figures in the blackness, when abruptly they found themselves looking into one another's faces. The lights had come on.

Clyde's mouth opened as if for speech. But he said nothing. His eyes were fixed on the outer door, which they had left ajar. He leapt for it—a little late. It swung shut sharply. He wrenched at the knob. He hesitated a moment, then retreated a few steps with the obvious intention of charging the door and forcing it.

"I wouldn't do that, Clyde," Humberton suggested, quietly. "Put in your time on this door to the left—the one that leads into the house."

"That's right." Clyde pivoted, crossed to the inner door, and glanced at it. "This ought to be easy. Wait till I see if it's locked."

His hand was almost on the knob— not quite on it—when the door opened. It was a thick, oaken door. Humberton looked up at its top, which his height enabled him to see better than the others, and nodded comprehension.

"Simple, but effective," he observed. "There is a lever at the top, which fits flush when the door is closed. Controlled by an electric button from the interior of the house. It strikes me, Clyde, that we are expected."

Clyde's reply was to produce a heavy revolver from his pocket.

"Come on!" he said.

The door had opened, not on another room, but on an extremely narrow dark hall. The light from the kitchen penetrated only a few yards. Beyond that point the passage evidently changed direction.

With something resembling a growl, the big detective plunged in. Humberton caught his arm.

"Easy, Clyde!" he cautioned. "You don't know where this leads. It's a trap."

"I don't care if it leads to hell, I'm going in," the detective retorted. "If you're afraid, stay in the kitchen."

Humberton released his arm, and followed. Just behind him, he could sense the coroner. They rounded the first twist in the passage. Then he could hear the stout medical officer's grunts and muffled imprecations, for the corridor had grown still narrower.

The necrologist whispered over his shoulder in the blackness. "Go back, Sollerby. You may get stuck."

"Go back, nothing!" The coroner was quietly laughing, with grim enjoyment of the situation. "You didn't see what I saw. You were around the corner by that time. Before I rounded it, the door behind us swung shut—I heard the lock click. We're in this, old boy, for better or worse, till death do us part. I only hope I shan't get stuck before the fireworks begin!"

THE passage twisted again, and began to slope gradually upward.

Suddenly, the detective chuckled. "Why don't I use my flash? Can you beat that for dumbness? Get it out of my right-hand coat pocket, will you, Ho? If I try, I'm liable to scrape my elbow against this damned wall."

Humberton, the only thin member of the party, still had plenty of room. He patted the detective's pockets—first the right, then the left.

"You laid it on a chair, when the lights came on and you charged the door," he said, mildly. "Did you pick it up again?"

"Would I pick it up?" the detective demanded, bitterly. "Did you ever know me to have brains? How about your flashlight, Ho? You generally carry one."

"No doubt Issacs handed it to Ted," the necrologist returned. "He forgot to pass it back to me."

"Cheerio!" Clyde quickened his pace, slightly. "We can sit around and laugh at this, boys—after we're killed and talking it over in heaven. Come on! Ouch! Damn!"

Humberton found himself jammed abruptly against his friend's broad back. The next moment, Sollerby had run into him.

"All right—back up. I just skinned my knee against the wall. Either this darned place twists again, or else—" The detective was silent a moment, while the others backed away and left him more room. "Yep, that's the answer. Blind alley! We're at the end. We can't go any way but back—and we can't go back."

"One minute." The necrologist's voice was low-pitched and calm. "Suppose you stand perfectly still, Clyde. Try not to breathe so hard, Sollerby. I should like to sound the walls."

He took the right-hand wall first. His long fingers traveled slowly upward, tapping every few inches.

"Find a thin place, and I'll bust through it so quick—"

"Be quiet!"

Humberton's hand crept rapidly up the left wall. Suddenly, it plunged, about shoulder-high, into space.

"What is it, Ho?" the detective whispered, excitedly.

"A side passage, up in the wall."

"Wide enough to walk through?"

"I can't tell. To crawl through, perhaps. It doesn't seem to be very high."

"Let me at it! Remember, I'm leading this party. Give me a boost."

The necrologist complied. Clyde was big, but athletic. He required little help. With the fat coroner, it was different.

"I'll go second," he suggested.

Humberton, tall and exceedingly thin, possessed a reserve fund of wiry strength. He assisted Sollerby's climb to the passage. The stout coroner stuck a moment, but a vigorous shove started him forward. Humberton himself, as soon as the others had progressed far enough to leave him room, easily wriggled in behind them.

The new passage sloped gradually upward. In the narrow hall they had just left, they had been unable to see one another. The darkness had been absolute. Here too, it pressed upon them, a palpable presence. Soon, however, there was a change in the air—a fragrant, freshening change.

Clyde's hoarse whisper floated back: "Darned if I don't smell pine woods! What's doing it?" Before either of his companions could reply, he spoke again. "Here's the end, Ho. No blind alley this time. Just a jumping-off place. That you behind me Sollerby? Let me grab your wrists. It's wider here—I can turn around. Ho, you hang on to Sollerby. I'm going to let myself down."

HUMBERTON'S long fingers closed on the coroner's ankles. In a moment, he heard a shuffle ahead in the thick darkness, and felt Sollerby's muscles tighten. The big detective was descending. His voice came to them in a cheery whisper: "O. K.! I've touched bottom. Must be a room of some kind. You fellows wait there."

But the coroner was obstinate. As Humberton released his ankles, his feet were drawn swiftly away. There was another shuffle, then a crash.

"All right!" he said, cheerfully. "No damage done. I landed hard, that was all!"

"You darned fool—"

Clyde's reproaches stopped, abruptly. The darkness about them was not quite the same. Some subtle change was taking place. An instant before, it had been impenetrable. Now, as Humberton lightly dropped to the floor beside the others, he could see them faintly. The odor of the pine woods was strong, but it was a hot and heavy fragrance, like the woods on a summer night, when there is no breeze and the clouds hang low.

"Ho!" The detective's deep voice quivered slightly. "What's that? What the devil is it?"

Humberton strained his near-sighted eyes. He was conscious of a faint rosy glow in the darkness. A suppressed exclamation from Sollerby told that he saw something more than that.

"It seems a little lighter, Clyde," the necrologist observed, calmly.

"A little lighter—hell!" The detective had drawn his revolver. "Can't you see it?"

The glow deepened. Behind them and just above was a grind of cogs, with a scraping sound. Humberton glanced up, over his shoulder. The light had become strong enough for him to see, gaping blackly in a wall of delicate iridescence, the opening of the passage through which they had come. As his gaze reached it, the diameter slowly narrowed. Unseen mechanism was forcing some sort of sliding panel across the passage from left to right. As the panel completed its journey, the entire wall reflected the shimmering radiance. There no longer was an opening.

CHAPTER SIX

The Angel of the Damned

HUMBERTON had watched the movement of the entrapping panel with a kind of fascination. A muffled exclamation from Clyde recalled him. He calmly turned about again. Then calmness forsook him for an instant.

"The angel!" His voice sounded strangely in his own ears. "The Angel of the Damned!"

A gigantic figure confronted them. It was the source of the ruddy light. It *was* the light. From its flaming eyes to the tips of its batlike, outstretched wings, so broad that they extended from wall to wall, it glowed with flickering, twisting fire. A heap of snakes from the Pit, burning unquenchably, molding their poisonous lengths together to form the figure of an angel, might have shone with some such glow. The eyes of a fallen spirit, damned forever, yet once built on a greater pattern than man, could have blazed thus hopelessly.

The necrologist took a step forward— an unwilling, involuntary step, drawn by the evil wonder of the angel's eyes. For that moment, his companions were forgotten. He thought himself alone with the figure. The majestic head of the angel inclined toward him, and he took another step. The focus of the light had changed—had come nearer. It dazzled him. He lowered his gaze instinctively —and saw the contorted face of Dr. Sigmund Bensen, with glaring eyeballs and protruding tongue, beneath the angel's feet. At that moment, too, he realized that the room was a death trap. The gigantic figure, with its spread wings, seemed to leave them no room to pass around it. Toppling forward, it would crush them to the floor like ants beneath a heedless foot.

The spell was broken. Humberton leapt lightly backward. The red light picked out with unnatural clearness every detail of the room—a room glowing with jewels, set into niches in the walls and even in the ceiling, and decking the shining angel. It showed him his two companions, backed against the wall. The coroner's shoulders were squared and his face rigid, with the expression of a man waiting for death. Clyde stood, one foot advanced, revolver in hand.

"Clyde! Sollerby! We must stop it! Bensen is committing suicide. The image is crushing the life out of him!"

"It's alive!" Clyde's voice was almost unrecognizable.

"No more alive than any other statue, man! It is falling forward. Help me push it back before it crushes us, too!"

The descending angel, now at half of a right angle, seemed to hesitate. Bensen's face was not to be seen. The necrologist flung himself against the glowing body. It was hard, smooth like glass, but only slightly warm. A second later, Clyde and the coroner joined him.

THE figure had only appeared to stop, for that instant. In reality, it had been slowly, inexorably, moving downward.

"Hold it, Ho! For God's sake, hold it!" The detective's voice was normal again—the voice of a man struggling to the limit of his strength.

Sollerby's breath came in sobs.

There was another instant when they seemed to be holding. Then the heels of all three slipped backward along the polished floor.

Humberton suddenly flung himself clear. His eyes, desperate yet cool, took in the whole of the room still remaining visible: the glowing back wall, a small portion of the walls at the side, the majestic menacing head of the Angel, now almost directly above, between the outstretched wings. Suddenly, he perceived a vital, incredible fact.

"Throw yourselves on your faces!"

Clyde, catching at the note of hope in his voice, also leapt backward and asked, eagerly: "Where, Ho?"

"Here in the middle, with our faces to the wall. I think we have a chance."

"Let me try to crash the wall, first."

"By all means, try."

Three times, in rapid succession, the big detective hurled himself. He was gathering his forces for a fourth attempt, when the descending Angel grazed his head. With something like a sob, he reeled to the floor beside the others.

"All right, Ho," he gasped. "I guess we're done."

Humberton did not reply. He was on his back, where he could look up at the descending death. His eyes scanned it in every detail as it came closer. The others had flung themselves on their faces.

The burning orbs of the Angel were very near—so near that his myopic vision could detect the electric lighting behind them. They came nearer. They were a blur. There was a jar, a moan from the coroner, and they stopped.

"Got you pinned, Sollerby?" the necrologist asked, cheerfully. "I still have plenty of room. Try to bear it till I can wriggle under and find the controlling switch."

"Ain't we going to be killed, Ho?" Clyde demanded, incredulously.

"Not this time, Clyde." Humberton's laugh, a little high-pitched for him, was otherwise not noticeably nervous. "I fear Bensen overlooked a point. The wings of his angel project forward a trifle—just far enough, in fact, to make all the difference for us! I, at least, have room enough to crawl around it!"

IT WAS in the room back of the ruddy angel—a wide, barnlike apartment, in part a workshop, in part the studio of an artist or a sculptor—a shop or studio cluttered beyond reason. Horatio Humberton had propped himself upon a convenient sawhorse. His long legs reached the floor with ease. Part of a marble statue, which lay upon its side in a corner, served Detective Clyde for a seat. There was a sofa. Upon it the coroner sprawled, his face white and strained, the breath not yet coming easily in his stout body. He seemed more interested in a long bronze instrument he held in his right hand than in this physical discomfort. The instrument was a kind of tongs, with six powerful metallic fingers and a thumb.

Sollerby suddenly flung the bronze tongs from him. They bounded on the floor and came to rest not far from something covered by a sheet, which lay in the middle of the room.

"The confounded things frighten me!" the coroner said, explosively. "How many people have they killed? Three, to my present knowledge."

Humberton nodded. "To your *personal* knowledge," he corrected. "To reach the full total you should have a view extending over perhaps seven centuries. This is a real antique, Sollerby. None of the stage properties which affected our nerves a while ago have any danger in themselves. These have."

He stooped and picked up the tongs.

"You don't mean they are dangerous without him?" the detective put in. He glanced toward the sheeted object on the floor.

The necrologist shook his head.

"No." He agreed. "Without him they are quite harmless; at least, unless someone else turns up to use them. Down through the centuries they have been the instruments of poor, distorted minds like his. Perhaps no other such mind will ever direct them. We can hope so, Clyde. After all, they are out of place in the twentieth century, when men no longer worship Beltonus in the forest."

The detective lit his pipe. "What I want to know—" he began; then stopped and puffed twice, with an air of bewildered determination. "Well, I'll be darned if I can tell you what I do want to know, Ho. But I'm all mixed up on this thing. I see why you suspected Bensen, all right. You explained that before we came here. And I can savvy why you hit on this house for his hideout. When a fellow has lived alone for years, in a big joint like the one we're sitting in, and nobody is ever allowed inside, that's naturally the first place to look for any funny business. But why all the hoop-lah stuff? Why the dark passage, and the phony doors, and this damned angel that had me scared out of a month's growth? And why the murders? Was the man crazy?"

"Do you doubt it?" the coroner demanded, languidly.

The big detective scratched his head, meditatively. "Well, maybe not," he admitted. "No, I guess he was bughouse, all right. Think he was always that way, doc?"

The coroner emitted a long yawn, which ended in a groan. "My ribs won't feel natural for a month," he complained. "I'm a doctor, not a clairvoyant, Clyde. I don't know whether Bensen was always crazy. Perhaps he suffered a head injury at birth."

CLYDE shot a suspicious glance at the reclining Sollerby; but the latter went on, languidly: "Natal brain lesions are curious things. They've been known to change the characters of men who have lived blameless lives for years. Perhaps that was Bensen's trouble. I don't know." He yawned again, long and profoundly. "He started by being interested in the Beltonus cult, I suppose. Studied it intensively. At last it got him. Eh, Humberton?"

"These devil-worship cults have a trick of getting people," the necrologist agreed. "I've known of such cases—at least, I have read of them. If there is a devil, I admire him immensely. He always knows enough to attack a man's strength rather than his weakness."

Clyde shook his head. "I don't get that, Ho."

"Bensen's strength was his versatility. He could do a number of things supremely well." The necrologist held up a long hand, and ticked his points off on his fingers. "First, he was an authority on archaeology. He knew these medieval cults inside and out. He even knew that the Beltonus priests throttled their sacrifices with these tongs—which was something I had never realized, though Servetus hints at it. He was a master goldsmith and jeweler. He was a sculptor—I never even guessed that, but it is very apparent, now. And he must have been a good deal of an electrical expert. He made that marvelous figure of the giant angel, with its lighting effects. That was his masterpiece, I think—the masterpiece of his strength. And that was where the devil started with him."

Sollerby grunted acquiescence, from his place on the couch. "When a man builds an idol, the next step is to worship it," he suggested.

"Precisely. Look up the incident of the Golden Calf, Clyde. I think we can say that he made the angel, and lighted it. Then, as his mind became twisted, all the rest followed: the pine incense, to produce the atmosphere of the woods in which Beltonus was worshipped, the lever motion for tilting the figure downward to kill—that was an idea from a Babylonish temple, I fancy—and finally the theft of valuable articles from the museum. He used these as offerings to his idol, and made imitations to take their places. The last was the imitation angel, itself."

"That's one thing I wanted to ask you," Clyde put in, excitedly. "Where do you suppose the real angel is?"

"Oh, yes!" The necrologist smiled, rather mischievously. "I am near-sighted, yet not entirely lacking in observation." He slid his hand into a trousers pocket. "While you and Sollerby were trying to resuscitate poor Bensen, I found the angel. It stood squarely in front of the giant image—a final offering! Take charge of it, Clyde. To your eyes, no doubt, it looks exactly like the spurious angel, but Isaacs could tell the difference, I assure you!"

The detective accepted the tiny, glistening figure, looked at it with interest for a moment, and callously dropped it into a coat pocket.

"O. K.," he said. "We'll hold it with the other one, for evidence. Probably the poor devils he killed borrowed or stole the fake image to try out some Beltonus stuff with at the house. That's how it happened to be there. My guess is they were on to some of Bensen's stealing, too, and were dumb enough to tell him. That cooked their goose. Think so, Ho?"

Humberton nodded. "No doubt he offered to initiate them into the Beltonus mysteries. When two of them were tied, the rest was easy. He made the marks on their necks with this tongs—for my benefit, I imagine—returned the tongs to this house, and came to my study with his story. It was partly cunning and partly transparent."

"I follow you there, all right. Think he tumbled to the fact that the watchman had left the door open for us?"

"I fear he suspected something, and forced the watchman to confess. He very evidently was waiting for us."

"That's what comes of dealing with a bughouse guy," the detective declared, emphatically. "Those batty bozos know too much. Take the way this guy killed himself. Would anyone with his brains ticking right have figured out how to get his neck beneath that darned Angel's feet, so it would choke him to death when it started forward? Not only that, but he counted on getting us, too—and, believe me, he'd have done it, but, for those wings sticking out a little in front. Why did he ever overlook that, Ho?"

"Because he was insane," the necrologist replied.

Clyde shook his head, doubtfully. "That's too much for me." He glanced toward the recumbent coroner, who now slept peacefully, with even rise and fall of breath. "Let's go. I've sent for a man to guard this place, till your fellows can stop around with the dead wagon. Shall I wake Sollerby? He's likely to be so stiff we'll have to carry him."

"Clyde—" Horatio Humberton smiled —a whimsical, reminiscent smile. "Were you ever a Desert Hoot Owl?"

In the act of stooping to tickle the coroner's nose, the big detective stopped, and straightened up. The look in his face was compounded chiefly of incredulity.

"A *what?*" he demanded.

"Ah, youth! Youth!" The necrologist spoke with a note of gentle sadness. "It was all of twenty-five years ago. I was a Hoot Owl, Clyde. In fact, I rose to be Thrice Opprobrious Screecher of the Order. I had charge of the initiations. Time passes, one's memory grows dim, but it came back to me—even to the opening in the wall, that led to the final passage. Some of the mechanical and electrical arrangements are new—the room where Bensen and his angel, for instance, was where our neophytes crossed the Burning Sands—but—"

"This house—" the detective shouted.

Humberton nodded. "The Order went into bankruptcy; its club house had to be sold. Bensen bought it. I have often wondered what he did with the secret passages. No doubt in his wife's time they were kept blocked off. She was a sane, sensible woman. Well—Sollerby is sleeping very soundly. I fear ordinary measures would not awaken him. Suppose we try this."

The tongs were still in his hand. He extended them, and, with infinite care, used their fingerlike claws to grasp the coroner's uplifted throat. Instantly, he withdrew them again; which was as well, for Sollerby, with a hoarse cry, reached the floor in a bound.

Dead Man's Lottery

by

T. T. Flynn

Author of "The Fourteenth Mummy," etc.

"The numbers are drawn." That dread phrase meant flashing knives and death in the dives of San Francisco's Chinatown. But danger was meat and drink to Denny Eagan. His gambling blood only coursed faster when the game was a Dead Man's Lottery—murder the prize.

CHAPTER ONE

Fog Street

THE gears of the taxi whined in rising crescendo as it rolled swiftly away from the curb. "Pudge" Paget watched the bright red tail-light dwindle to a speck in the fog, vanish. Pudge peered about in the silent opaque night.

A human arm, severed just below the elbow.

"Gosh, what a neighborhood!" he commented disgustedly. "It gives me the creeps Phew! Get a schnozzle full of that smell! Must be a glue factory around here. Sure we didn't unload on the wrong corner?"

Denny Eagan chuckled as he turned his coat collar up about his ears.

"Nope. We're right," he said. "It's a little atmospheric, but then what do you expect from Chinatown, my boy?"

"Chop suey," Pudge said promptly. "Show me bright lights and a table, an' I'll show you an appetite."

"Work before you eat," Denny advised, starting along the sidewalk.

Pudge walked fast to keep up with Denny's long strides. Denny bumped six feet—and Pudge lacked eight inches of that. Denny was slender—and Pudge matched his name, short, stocky, pudgy-looking and slow. Innocent and harmless and good-natured in the bargain. But that was on the surface. Behind the round placid face and constant grumblings Pudge had a brain that worked fast. And more than one man had found out to his sorrow that when Pudge went into action he was destruction.

On the other hand, Denny Eagan was tall and wiry. Beneath the low-pulled brim of his hat his face was lean, keen, humorous. And under all that was a cool intelligence. Which was why Denny Eagan was in Chinatown tonight.

Pudge sighed as they walked. "I'd think better if I ate," he suggested delicately. "It's after seven now."

"Sad," sympathized Denny. "Tighten your belt, Pudge. A little dieting won't hurt you anyway. We don't eat until we see Sam Kong. I'll get twenty from him."

"If it don't go south like that bankroll did this afternoon," Pudge sighed. "Honest, I never thought a dip'd get to your kick like that."

"I'm still feeling foolish," Denny admitted. "But it'll be all right. Sam Kong will take care of us. I'm sure of that."

"Wonder why he sent for you?" Pudge speculated.

"I am too," Denny confessed. "Something's up. Sam wouldn't have called long distance that way if he wasn't disturbed. He always was a secretive old fellow, but he sounded worried this time."

The fog swirled damply around them. Now and then a light pushed feeble, sickly rays through the slow swirling opaque curtains of moisture. But there weren't many lights. The narrow street seemed deserted, dead.

Faintly the shrill muted wail of a Chinese fiddle drifted down from overhead. There were three and four-story warrens to right and left of them. Ramshackle old buildings with faded, peeling fronts, sagging cornices, dirty windows, fetid hallways. Old tenement buildings that seethed and bubbled with hidden life by day and night. And yet tonight none of that life was visible. The fog had driven it inside, blotted it out, much as the fog was blotting out the fronts of the buildings themselves.

A silent padding figure slipped past them. A head turned. Sharp eyes peered at them. And as silently as it had appeared, the figure vanished on in the fog.

Pudge grunted his distaste.

"I'm no hero," he said. "I don't like this neighborhood. Why didn't you have that hack take us where we wanted to go? You had coin enough for that."

"Taxis from uptown stand out like carbuncles around here," Denny said. "Sam insisted this was secret business. We'll walk to his place, and no one else will be wiser."

"You're the boss," Pudge grumbled. "You know this town and I don't. But I'm beginning to understand why you left. It smells like murder and looks like sin."

Denny chuckled. "Some nice people here. Old Sam Kong is all wool and a yard wide. Got a heart of gold."

"I'll tell you more about that after you tell him we're broke," said Pudge cynically.

THEY turned to the right, reached the next street corner and swung to the left. And in the fog Pudge bumped square into a waiting figure that stepped out of a dark doorway.

"Watch your step!" Pudge said indignantly. "They oughta hang tail-lights on guys like you."

The bright beam of a flashlight stabbed into Pudge's face. "And who are you, fresh guy?" a gruff voice demanded.

"What's it to you?" Pudge snarled. "Get that light out of my eyes. One side, mister, one side."

The stranger was still invisible to them, but Denny Eagan went alert as he heard the voice. His hand fell on Pudge's arm. "Come on," he advised Pudge. "If that's the fellow I think it is, he's only a flat-footed tramp, who's not responsible for what he does."

"Oh, yeah?" the gruff voice exploded. The light shifted to Denny's face. "I thought it was you who made that crack, Eagan! So you're back? What's the big idea?"

Denny smiled, crinkling his eyes as he looked into the light. "I was right, then. It's Sergeant 'Bat' Miller himself, in the flesh. The old hero of Chinatown still flattening his feet on the pavement."

Sergeant Miller shifted the light and its reflected rays limned him, and a second figure in the doorway behind him, dimly in the fog. He was a big hulking, broad-shouldered fellow with a bull neck and a flat beefy face, a rock-square chin, a steel trap of a mouth under a bristling mustache and glowering, suspicious eyes.

"Oh, so he's a dick," said Pudge, mollified. "I hope the traffic cops ain't as clumsy as he is. Trucks bump harder than I do."

Sergeant Bat Miller began to lose his temper. "Two smart guys, aren't you?" he snapped. "We'll just see how smart you are. Stand right there, both of you, until I frisk you."

"Now, Sergeant," Denny protested, "my friend and I are peaceful citizens—er—walking for our health. You're making a mistake."

"Rats!" Sergeant Miller snorted. "I don't know your little pal, but I know you, Eagan. I thought you had left town for good. You ain't back here for your health."

"That's it—health," said Denny amiably, raising his arms for the sergeant to pat under them. "My doctor advised me that fog was the thing I needed. So I came back here looking for it. Nice fog, isn't it?"

The sergeant disdained reply. With skill born of long practice he frisked Denny swiftly and thoroughly. Then transferred his attentions to Pudge. Pudge submitted gracefully, too. And when the sergeant had finished with him he suggested: "Down my neck."

"Huh? What's that?"

"I might have a knife hanging down the back of my neck," Pudge suggested. "They carry 'em there sometimes, you know."

A heavy hand smacked between Pudge's shoulder blades ungently. "Smart egg, aren't you?" Sergeant Miller said angrily.

"Well, there might have been a knife there," Pudge comforted meekly.

An angry snort answered that. "What are you two doin' here?"

"Health," said Denny again.

"When did you get in town?"

"Several hours ago."

"Where are you staying?"

"At the Milton."

"I've got a notion to run you both in."

"You might try it," Denny suggested. "No telling what publicity you'll get out of it, Sergeant, old friend, old friend."

"You threatening me, Eagan?"

"Wouldn't think of it," Denny chuckled. "You're a bad man to threaten, Sergeant; aren't you?"

But something had changed the situation entirely. The sergeant lost none of his truculence, but he spoke no more of running them in. "Get along with you," he growled. "But watch your step. The first slip you make I'll pick you up so fast it'll shake your eye teeth loose. Get me?"

"Plainly," said Denny. "Come on, Pudge. Oh, by the way, Sarge, how about loaning me ten dollars?"

"I'll run you in yet!" Sergeant Miller choked. "Get outa here!"

DENNY chuckled again as they walked on, but that mood quickly passed and he became sober, thoughtful. "I'm sorry we ran into Bat Miller there," he said to Pudge. "He's a bad egg and he'd like to pin something on me."

"How so?"

"We tangled once. I bumped into one or two crooked deals Miller was in, and stepped on his toes a few times. It made him wild. He'd give his right arm to get me. Matter of fact, he was the reason I left. He made it his business in life to frame me. Missed fire on a couple of attempts, but I saw the light. It was too hard on the nerves to watch for his dirty tricks all the time. He'd have gotten me sooner or later."

"The dirty rat!" Pudge exploded.

"All in the game," Denny said without rancor. "But I'm sorry about this tonight. I don't know what Sam Kong's got up his sleeve. No telling what he'll want me to do. And Bat Miller will be right on the job where I'm concerned. I wouldn't be surprised if he wasn't tailing us back there in the fog right now. We'll see."

At the next corner Denny turned sharply to the right, flattened himself against the sheer brick wall. Pudge melted beside him.

Not more than two minutes elapsed before quiet furtive steps came out of the fog. The big figure of Sergeant Miller padded softly by, crossed the street in the direction they had been going.

Denny said under his breath: "The son of a gun! I had a hunch he'd be doing that. Well, I've got a trick or two up my sleeve he can't top. He's been around here a long time, but he's got a few things to learn yet. This way, Pudge."

They continued along the cross street, at right angles to the direction in which Sergeant Bat Miller had vanished. For a full ten minutes Denny walked swiftly, pursuing a twisted, tortuous course through the maze of narrow smelly streets. Finally he ducked abruptly out of the fog into a little, dimly lighted store on a corner.

"Phew!" Pudge gasped, as the atmosphere inside the store struck them like a physical blow. "This is awful! You could cut it with a knife!"

Denny grinned. "A little close," he admitted. "But it's all good food."

Pudge, a stranger to places like this, looked around with narrowed eyes. The floor about them was jammed with wooden boxes full of small dried minnows, dried cuttle fish, sharks' fins, sea slugs, pressed dried duck, and numerous other strange and odoriferous foods so dear to the palates of Orientals.

A short scrawny Chinese lost in an oversized brown coat and full black trousers moved forward to meet them. A beaming smile of welcome spread over his saffron face as Denny turned down the collar of his coat and shoved his hat back on his head.

"*Ho la*—velly glad see you! Wheah you been long time?"

"Traveling for my health," Denny grinned, shaking the clawlike hand that was thrust out to him. "Pudge, this is

Mock Yum, the worst old sinner this side of Shanghai. He can do more with a poker hand than you can with dice. The name is Pagget, Mock."

"How do?" Mock Yum beamed.

"Terrific," said Pudge faintly as he expelled the breath he had been holding and clasped Mock Yum's withered hand limply. Pudge cast an appealing glance at Denny. "I guess we better be running along," he suggested.

"Going," said Denny; and to Mock Yum: "Get us through to Sam Kong's place, will you, Mock?" Denny laid a finger alongside his nose gravely. "Can do?"

Mock Yum blinked gravely. "Can do," he assented. "Come along flom dis way."

MOCK YUM trotted to the back of the store, opened a door there, and led them into a narrow, dark, airless hallway. From a nail in the wall he took a small flashlight. Its bobbing ray lighted the way before them.

They went through another door and down a flight of steps into a musty cellar filled with cobwebs and piles of boxes. Mock Yum stopped before the bare wall at the end of the room, pulled a box over on the floor and stepped nimbly on it. He reached up to the ceiling over his head. He didn't use the light so they did not see what his hand did there. But a moment later, with a rusty grating sound, a section of the solid wall turned on a pivot. Mock Yum motioned them in, followed them, and pushed on the section with a grunt. It swung slowly back into place.

They were in a narrow, low-ceilinged tunnel. Mock Yum squeezed by them, led the way with his light again, padding softly in felt-soled slippers. The tunnel turned at right angles, dipped down to a lower level via a flight of damp wooden steps. Now and then another passage led off, but Mock Yum kept straight ahead.

"Some layout," Pudge said admiringly.

"How much of this is there anyhow?"

"Haven't the slightest idea," Denny confessed over his shoulder. "I'd say no man knows all of it. Most of these passages date from the old days. They're not much used now. Sam Kong told me once if I ever wanted to get to his place secretly to go to Mock Yum, and Mock would take care of it. He hinted there was a connection between his place and Mock's store, which is over in the next block. I know Bat Miller never was through here."

Mock Yum heard them talking, asked over his shoulder: "You like?"

"Pretty nice," Denny said.

Mock cackled under his breath. "When young I help dig. No tloble foah me walkee this in dalk." Mock ducked into a side passage, confided as they followed: "This one go Sam Kong place. I show you, an' lun back foah flesh customah. Business plenty pooah now."

The passage ended abruptly. Mock's light flashed against a blank wall of concrete. But when he pushed against it hard, the concrete pivoted harshly as the other door had when they entered. Mock Yum started to slip through.

Denny, who was directly behind him, never did see exactly what happened. But Mock stopped suddenly. A shrill, choking gasp came from his throat. He swayed there in the narrow opening, beating his arms in front of him, so that the flashlight beam danced crazily in the dark space beyond.

Looking past Mock Yum's head, Denny fancied that he saw a flitting shadow outlined for an instant in the light. But he wasn't sure, and the swinging beam was in another spot the next instant. Then the flashlight crashed to the floor and went out.

Pudge swore in startled excitement, behind Denny. "What's the matter?" he demanded.

"Don't know!" Denny threw back at

him. "Mock Yum—what is it? Mock—"

But Mock Yum did not answer. A sobbing, inarticulate groan came from his lips. And a moment later the dull thud of his body striking the floor was audible.

CHAPTER TWO

The Yellow Arm

THE flashlight had gone out as it fell. Inky blackness shrouded them. Mock Yum made no sound or movement after he dropped.

"I knew there was something screwy about this place!" Pudge uttered blankly.

Denny did not answer. He was groping in his pocket for matches. He found the box, struck one hastily. The thin yellow flare showed Mock Yum lying prone before him in the narrow opening. The scrawny little Oriental was still, silent.

"Mock!" Denny said sharply.

Mock Yum did not reply.

The match went out. Denny struck two more, squeezed through the opening as soon as they flared, putting his feet down carefully to avoid stepping on Mock Yum. He saw the flashlight lying on the floor beyond Mock Yum's outstretched hand. He picked it up, pressed the button. The bulb had been smashed by the hard fall; the light was useless. Denny slipped it in his pocket, struck more matches, dropped to a knee beside the still form.

Mock Yum was lying face down on the bare concrete floor of a yawning black cellar. Denny turned him over with an effort. A soft oath slipped through his lips at what he saw.

The carved bone handle of a long dagger was protruding from Mock Yum's chest! He had been stabbed through the heart!

Pudge squeezed through the door, looked down and saw it also as the matches burned low in Denny's fingers and went out.

"Holy cow!" Pudge gasped. "Am I seeing right? Has he got a knife stuck in his chest?"

Denny fumbled for more matches. "He has," he agreed blankly. "He was stabbed in the heart as he started to come through."

"Who did it?"

"I don't know," Denny confessed. "I thought I saw something moving in the cellar here before he dropped the light. Someone must have been standing just on this side of the door, waiting for him."

"Maybe the guy who did it is over there in the dark now!" Pudge rapped out warningly. "Better watch them matches, Denny!"

That was the way Pudge worked. Give him real trouble and he was all business instantly. It was good advice. Denny delayed striking the matches, listened intently. The musty blackness was as still as the inside of an isolated tomb. Still, damp, chill. For the first time in his life Denny felt the short hairs crawl at the back of his neck. Was death waiting over there in the blackness, ready to strike again?

He scratched the matches abruptly on the side of the box, peered about as their flare rolled the inky curtain back. They were in an empty cellar. No packing boxes, crates, odd objects behind which someone might be crouching. Just damp, empty space, dusty, cobwebby—and unoccupied. Pudge looked too. "No one here!" he uttered.

"Doesn't seem to be," Denny agreed, standing up. "But there was! I saw something move in the light—and there had to be someone to use that knife. I'll have a better look."

"Watch your step!" Pudge warned.

"Have to risk it."

USING his shrinking supply of matches sparingly, Denny searched the cellar, peering into the corners, looking for a spot where someone might be hiding. It took only a minute. At the end of that time he was certain they were the only occupants of the cellar. There was a steep stairway over in the opposite corner.

"Whoever did it escaped up that stairway," Denny said, stepping back to the body.

"Didja hear any steps?" Pudge demanded.

"No. But then I wasn't listening for any. I was too startled at Mock Yum's actions. Besides, the noise he made would have drowned out anything like that."

"You sure he's dead?" Pudge asked, regarding the body.

"Not a chance for anything else, with a wound like that," Denny said. But to make sure he knelt again and felt for Mock Yum's pulse. There was not a sign of a heart beat. The sickly match light showed the old man lying there as if he had fallen into a deep sleep. Fright and terror, if any, had smoothed away on his yellow face. The wound was bleeding externally only slightly.

"Why should anyone stick him like that?" Pudge asked, puzzled.

And Denny had to confess that he did not know. "No one could have been expecting him," he pointed out. "We didn't even know ourselves until a quarter of an hour ago that we were going to see him."

"But somebody was waiting here," Pudge insisted.

"He just happened to be here."

"Then why kill the old fellow? He wasn't making trouble."

"Search me," Denny had to confess again. "It's a mystery. Funny things happen here in Chinatown. I'll make a guess though. Whoever did it, didn't even know who they were stabbing. They weren't showing a light. I doubt if Mock Yum's face was visible."

"It coulda been," Pudge declared thoughtfully. "When he pushed that door open I saw the light shine up past his face for a second. Anyone standing on the other side could have got a good look at his mug."

"Might have at that," Denny agreed.

Pudge lighted a cigarette. His round face was serious as he cupped the match before it. "I'm glad your cop friend ain't here right now," he commented. "This looks like the little thing he'd like to pin on you."

"He would," Denny assented. "Say, what's that?"

Pudge had pitched his lighted match aside. It had fallen in a little arc of flame, winked out as it struck the floor. But there had been enough light to show a scrap of color against the wall several feet away. Denny had not noticed it before. He stepped to it now and lighted another match, bent and picked up a small silk scarf that lay there. A woman's scarf. Denny's voice came sharp as he looked at it.

"This has blood on it!"

"Now we're gettin' warm," said Pudge.

"Fresh blood too," said Denny, looking closer at it. "And it's a woman's scarf! Must have been dropped by the person who stabbed Mock Yum!"

"Women are hell with knives," Pudge commented darkly. "I knew a little Mexican girl once who made a pass at me when I told her I wasn't a marrying man. But this bird was too old to be tangled up with a woman."

Pudge's cigarette glowed deeply as he puffed hard on it. "Maybe he wasn't at that," he reversed himself a moment later. "Some old men can make the fur fly."

"You're up the wrong alley," Denny said curtly. "Mock Yum didn't know himself he was coming this way. So how could anyone else? Don't forget that?"

"You got a woman's scarf there, ain't you?" Pudge insisted.

"Yes."

"With fresh blood on it?"

"Yes. But Mock Yum's wound didn't

bleed. This blood couldn't have come from him!"

"I never thought of that," Pudge admitted with chagrin. And then he demanded irritably: "But if it didn't come from him, where did it come from? Fresh blood don't spatter out of the air!"

THEY were both silent for a moment before the flood of questions and contradictions that arose.

"I had a hunch we were gonna find trouble tonight," Pudge said under his breath.

"And we did," Denny agreed. "And it's plenty of trouble. I don't like this. Sam Kong's place is upstairs, according to Mock Yum. Let's go up there."

"And leave him here?"

"Can't take him along. I want to talk to Sam before it's reported to the police. This is no ordinary killing. There's a lot more behind it than we can see, Pudge."

"How so?"

"Evidence. Sam Kong was expecting trouble of some kind when he talked to me over long distance. I could get it in his voice, and the few hints he dropped. I'll bet my last dollar this is hooked up with it."

"Your last dollar was stolen," Pudge reminded. "But you're right. Put it up to him and see if he's got the answer. I've got a hunch we're going to need an answer if we report this, an' your flat-foot friend horns in on it. It's just my luck I had to mention knives to him."

Denny stooped over, caught Mock Yum's shoulder and pulled the body into the cellar, several feet away from the door. Then he stepped back, shoved hard and closed the door.

"What's the idea?" Pudge questioned.

"Just as well no outsiders know about that tunnel unless they have to. Sam Kong would feel that way about it. I'm going to leave this thing up to him, anyway. He can do what he pleases about it.

Let's get out of here while the getting's good. The more I think about Bat Miller the less I like this."

They made their way to the steps, went up them slowly. And as they mounted them faint, quick running steps sounded overhead. A woman's steps. The door at the top opened to Denny's touch, let them into a dimly lighted hallway. They had emerged at the back of another flight of stairs leading up to the second floor. And the hallway was empty. Denny ran to the front door, stepped out, returned in a moment.

"She's gone," he said. "Can't follow her in that fog."

"Wonder if she was the dame dropped that scarf," said Pudge.

"So do I."

"Where are we?" Pudge asked.

"This is Sam Kong's hallway," Denny said, looking around. "I've been in it. You're pale, Pudge. Not afraid, are you?"

Pudge snorted, hunched his shoulders as he looked around too. "I always get that way over the first murder of the night," he said. "Your friend Kong must be small potatoes by the kind of dump he lives in."

Denny smiled at that. "Wait until you see how he lives," he said, walking around and starting up the stairs.

The worn, unpainted treads creaked loudly under their feet. The dimly lighted hall and stair-well were squalid and miserable. Stained dirty paper was peeling from the walls, patches of white plaster were showing.

"I can see how he lives," Pudge grunted. "An' it don't look so hot to me."

A door flush with the top steps blocked their way. In contrast to the flimsy stairs it was strong and massive, bound with strips of metal. Denny pushed a bell button at the side.

"This door is backed with steel," he said casually. "It would take an army to break through and make any time here."

"Why the fort?" Pudge demanded.

"There used to be times when it wasn't safe to be at home to the world. Sam's been around here fifty years at least. He can tell tales that will raise the hair on top of your head."

"He'll have to go some to beat what we ran into tonight."

THERE was no answer to the ring. Denny pushed the button again; and suddenly he looked closely at the door, and pushed against it. The massive door swung in silently on oiled hinges.

"Funny," Denny muttered. "I never knew Sam Kong's door to be unlocked like this before."

He pressed the bell button again. They could hear the faint *buzzzz* inside, but no answering movement.

"I don't like it," Denny said dubiously, fingering the gay silken scarf he still carried in his hand. "I think I'll go in and look around. There's something funny about all this."

Pudge Pagget whistled softly as he followed Denny in. For they stepped out of squalor into a world of richness and magnificence that by contrast was stunning. The entrance hall into which they came had an intricately laid parquet floor of rare woods, waxed, shining. Six ebony chairs, set three to a side along the wall, were one mass of deep carving and gleaming inlaid mother-of-pearl. And on the wall at the end of the short hall hung a large black-and-gold tapestry of five-legged sea dragon bursting out of stormy sea waves. The walls were paneled waist high in ebony. A massive chandelier of hundreds of cut prisms shed light.

The adjoining room, into which Denny went, drew another sharp intake of breath from Pudge. For here was even greater richness and magnificence.

The waxed floor was strewn with hand-woven rugs, carved screens stood in the corners, gold-and-silver-threaded tapestries hung on the walls. A great decorative porcelain vase stood by a far doorway of the big room. An alabaster fretwork panel opened through the wall into another room. And on a teak table a tiny exquisite vase of translucent green jade held a single golden orchid.

"Gosh!" Pudge breathed. "Some class!"

Denny smiled. "I told you to wait. As a matter of fact Sam Kong is a very rich man. The store downstairs is only one of many things that he's connected with."

"Well, at least he'll never be bothered by panhandlers," Pudge said philosophically. "One look at that hallway is enough."

Denny nodded absently, inspecting the big room in which they were standing. The apartment of Sam Kong was as still as—death. The vague uneasy feeling which had gripped him when he found the door unlocked deepened. He raised his voice, called. "Sam Kong! Lee! Anybody in here?"

And there was no answer.

A Chinese newspaper lay on the big teak table beside the little jade vase. Pudge strolled over to it, picked up the newspaper. "It beats me how they can get any sense out of these cat marks," he said, looking at the printing.

And the next instant Pudge's eyes riveted over the edge of the paper in a horrified gaze. His face blanched, his voice trembled as he spoke.

"For God's sake, look at this! Do you see what I see?"

Denny wheeled around, followed Pudge's rigid pointing finger. When Pudge had picked up the newspaper he had uncovered an object lying beneath it. And it was all Denny could do himself to choke back an exclamation.

For on the smooth polished top of the dark teak table there lay a grim and grisly sight. A human arm, severed just below the elbow! A ghastly inanimate member with yellow fingers clenched tight about a strip of red tissue paper.

"Your friend certainly believes in takin' away a fellow's appetite," Pudge gulped, stepping close to the table and staring down at the severed forearm with pallid fascination.

Denny had reached the table in a stride. Now, standing beside Pudge, he reached out and touched the thing. He had hoped for a moment that tricky eyesight had deceived them, hoped that the forearm and those saffron fingers clenched tightly about the strip of red rice paper were artificial. But even as he touched it Denny knew that it was a false hope. This ghastly grisly object on the table had some connection with Mock Yum's death. His finger touched stiff clammy flesh.

"It's real?" asked Pudge.

Denny nodded. "It came off a human body all right. A Chinaman by the looks of the skin."

Pudge drew a shaken breath, smiled a sickly smile. "You came lookin' for trouble an' you certainly found it," he breathed. "What's the answer to this? What's that strip of red tissue paper it's holding?"

Denny tried to pull the paper from those close-clenched fingers, found it impossible. So tight in death were those bony digits stiffened that the tissue would tear unless he pried the fingers apart. He didn't do that. They could see Chinese characters brushed the whole length of the strip. Black characters against a blood-red background.

"Might be a lottery ticket," said Denny. "Only lottery tickets are white, and this is red." Denny looked around. "I'm going to have a look through the apartment," he said abruptly. "There's no blood on this arm. It still doesn't explain the scarf."

CHAPTER THREE

Dead Man's Lottery

SAM KONG'S apartment covered the entire floor of the large building. Room after room, all furnished in the same lavish style they had already encountered. One of them was a woman's bedroom, gay, bright, Occidental in every detail. Denny stopped short in the doorway.

"I didn't know Sam Kong had any woman in his household," he stated wonderingly.

"This ties with that silk scarf, I guess," said Pudge.

"Looks like it. We'll see."

Denny went to a dainty dressing table against the side wall, opened drawers until he found what he sought, a handkerchief that had been used. He sniffed it, then the scarf. "Same perfume," he said briefly.

He picked a small frosted-glass vial out of the row of bottles on the dressing table, uncorked it, breathed deep. "This is the perfume."

"Where's the girl?"

"We haven't searched the whole apartment yet," said Denny.

It was some three minutes later in a tiny bedroom off the kitchen, at the rear of the apartment, that the search came to an end. Denny stopped short as he came abreast of it. Stopped, looking at the bottom of the door.

"I think we've found what we're looking for," he said sharply, and pointed down.

A damp crimson trickle thrust out from under the door, mute, dreadful in its implication of what was on the other side.

Denny grasped the knob, shoved the door in. It only went halfway. Beyond the bottom edge of the door a shock of black hair could be seen on the floor. A man was lying there, sprawled on his back, hands outstretched, eyes wide in a vacant stare.

"It's Lee, Sam Kong's man!" Denny burst out. "Poor old Lee! He was a swell fellow, always smiling and laughing."

He stooped over the body. Like Mock Yum, Lee was an elderly man, his face wrinkled and sharpened by long life. He was quite dead; had been stabbed in the back, Denny found when he turned Lee's body half over. The long thin slit where the knife had gone in was plain. Lee's flesh was still warm. He had not been dead long.

And loosely held in one of Lee's withered hands was a strip of white paper, with a black border. It had a series of small dots made by a tiny brush with India ink. And the same brush had written characters down the side of the slip. Denny pulled it from the loosely clasping fingers and straightened up.

"Chinese lottery ticket," said Denny. "Bought a few in my time, but never won anything."

"What's it doing in his hand?"

Denny looked long and thoughtfully at that flimsy rice-paper lottery ticket; and from it to Lee's body on the floor. Abruptly he folded the ticket, thrust it in his pocket.

"Let's look through the rest of this place," he said hurriedly. "I'm afraid Sam Kong may be dead too."

But they found no trace of Sam Kong, and their search of the spacious apartment was suddenly terminated by the tramp of heavy feet, the rasp of loud voices at the front. Denny went there quickly, was met as he entered the big front room by a loud voice exploding: "What the devil are you doing in here?"

It was Detective Sergeant Miller, in company with another plainclothes officer. And in the room with them was a short, elderly Chinese with a round moon-like face, and a slender willowy girl. Ser-

geant Miller was glaring as his stubby finger pointed at Denny.

A relieved look appeared on the round face of the old Chinese. The girl stared at Denny curiously.

Denny smiled thinly. "I was looking through the apartment," he said, but his eyes as he spoke were on the girl.

SHE could not have been more than twenty-one or two. And she was, without doubt, one of the prettiest girls Denny had ever seen. Her skin was as white as his, her features delicate, clean-cut. She was dressed in modern Occidental clothes. At first glance she might have been a beautiful white girl. A closer look revealed the merest slant of her eyes, the ebony sheen of her black hair. Oriental blood ran in her veins, Denny decided, and the mixture of white and yellow had produced something stunning and unexpected. Sam Kong had never mentioned any woman belonging to his household.

"Looking around the apartment, were you?" Sergeant Miller said sarcastically. "Well, who told you to look; an' what were you lookin' for? And before you start your little story, what do you know about this?" The sergeant pointed to the cold clenched fist on the table.

"Nothing," Denny said coolly as he walked to the table. "I saw that when I came in, and thought I'd better look around. It's a queer decoration, isn't it?"

Miller choked. "Decoration? Are you trying to kid me? What are you doing in here anyway?"

The little rotund Chinese, whose face despite his advanced age, was virtually free from wrinkles, save for little nests of lines around his eyes, said mildly: "Mr. Eagan exceedingly lustrous friend of mine, Sergeant. Tonight telephone call from him inform me graciously he will pay long-deferred visit to old friend Sam Kong. And over telephone I bid him accept my house for his pleasure."

Sam Kong beamed at the sergeant and Denny, like an innocent old Buddha to whom falsehood was impossible. But it only drew a snort from Miller.

"He called, did he? Then why wasn't you here waitin' for him?"

"Forgotten errand drew my attention outside for brief time," Sam murmured gently.

"And while you was gone, this thing was brought in, eh?"

Sam bobbed his head. "Evidence cannot be denied. Sight so upset my granddaughter, Fan Sing, that she run out for help. And good fortune direct me here to meet you."

Miller scowled at the thing on the table, snarled at Denny suddenly: "So this was here when you came in?"

"Hidden under that newspaper," Denny agreed. "It, and the fact I couldn't find anyone in, made me think I'd better look around the apartment."

"It was covered up when you come in?"

"I threw the paper over it before I went out," Fan Sing said in a low voice. "It was too horrible to look at."

She spoke without a trace of accent. And again Denny was puzzled by the feeling that she did not belong in Sam Kong's household. She seemed an outlander, an alien by Sam Kong's standards. He was conscious too that when the others were talking Fan Sing was watching him covertly.

Miller opened the cold clenched fingers roughly and pulled out the slip of red rice paper. "What's this chicken writing say?" he demanded, holding the paper up before Sam Kong.

Sam squinted at it. "It say, 'Peace to your house!'"

"Yeah? Read it again! You know that ain't what it says!" Miller grated.

Sam's bland smile did not change by a muscle. "It say, 'The numbers are drawn,'" he translated.

"That's better. Does it mean anythi to you?"

Sam shrugged, shook his head.

"An' you don't know who left this an here, or why?"

Sam sighed. "Meaning is profoun mystery," he said. "Perhaps mischievor friend play joke."

Denny spoke then, because the matte of Lee would be discovered quickly. "N much of a joke, Sam. I found Lee bac in his bedroom. He's been stabbed death."

The smile left Sam's face. Denn heard the swift intake of breath that Fa Sing drew.

"What?" Miller roared at him. "Some one back there stabbed to death?"

"Yes."

"You fool! Why didn't you speak up Where is he?"

DENNY led the way back to Lee room. Miller took charge of mat ters with a rush, sent his man to th telephone to call the homicide squat fired questions at Denny. Got no satis factory answers, and called Fan Sin into the hallway outside the door.

"You mean to tell me you didn't kno this fellow was lying in here dead whe you went out?" he demanded harshly.

Fan Sing looked at him calmly fror big black eyes. "My room is some di tance from here," she explained. "I calle Lee, and when he did not answer thought he was out."

"When did you see him last?"

"At dinner. I went to my room afte that to read. I slept a little, and then go up and went into the front room. I sa that—that thing on the table. I calle Lee, and then ran out."

"Huh!" Miller snorted, and shot a Sam: "Know who might have done this?

Real grief was visible on Sam Kong' face. Lee had worked for him half a life time. But his voice was calm also as h answered. "I cannot help you. I know nothing. Lee most happily in kitchen when I depart."

The homicide squad arrived with surprising quickness. For an hour the apartment was a scene of heavy activity. Photographs were taken, fingerprints registered, barrages of questions fired.

And in the midst of that one of the homicide men, searching the building, discovered the dead body of Mock Yum in the basement. And the excitement reached a new climax. Miller recognized Mock Yum.

"This guy owns a store over in the next block!" he said loudly. "What's he doing down in this cellar?"

Electric lights had been turned on. Sam Kong was down there, and Denny and Pudge. And a Lieutenant Parker, who had charge of the squad. Sam Kong faced them all like an expressionless old Buddha.

"Mock Yum old friend," he declared. "His presence here is great mystery. I am bowed with grief. I put reward of five hundred dollars for man who killed him."

Not by the flicker of an eyelid did Sam betray the fact that he knew there was a tunnel connecting the damp cellar with Mock Yum's store. And the detectives prowling about the cellar with their flashlights did not suspect it.

Denny said nothing. The scarf and the lottery ticket he had taken from Lee's hand were in his pocket. He knew Sam Kong would wish it. this way, or the old fellow would have mentioned the tunnel himself. Sam must know that Mock Yum had come here through the tunnel. Once or twice Denny caught Sam's eyes on him without expression.

Denny's mind returned often to Fan Sing. The blood-spotted scarf in his pocket had come from her room. If she had been in there until she found the arm,

how had the scarf gotten out? What did she know about it? But all of those questions would have to wait until he could talk alone with Sam Kong.

He had another hour's wait while the medical examiner came, more questions were asked, the bodies taken away. And then finally the last detective left and the apartment was closed against the packed, murmuring crowd of curious Chinese that had gathered outside

They were alone.

FROM a carved wall cabinet Sam Kong brought a small stone bottle, three little glasses. He poured dark liquid into the glasses, handed one to Denny and one to Pudge. Fan Sing had disappeared.

"Poppy wine," said Sam Kong. "Made for me near Canton, by my brother. You will find it refreshing." Sam sighed, showed emotion for the first time as he sipped his wine. "Lee was my friend," he said simply, looking at Denny over the glass.

"Mock Yum brought us through the tunnel, Sam," Denny said.

"Thought steal into my mind," Sam admitted.

Denny told the old man what had happened, pulled the scarf from his pocket and tossed it on the teak table.

"I found this down there. It had fresh blood on it, which couldn't have come from Mock Yum. The same person who got him killed Lee. Must have wiped the knife on it."

Bright and gay in the light the scarf lay, and the blood smears were plain and ugly on it. They looked as if they might have come from a hastily wiped knife blade.

Denny laid the lottery ticket beside it. "This was in Lee's hand."

Sam Kong snatched it up. The troubled look on his face deepened. "In Lee's hand?" he echoed.

"Yes."

Sam sighed. "Death speed through Chinatown, my friend. Lee and Mock Yum are not the first. I suggest trouble over telephone to you, and trouble fly to meet you. Little god of luck save you from walking into cellar first and collecting knife."

"I thought about that," Denny admitted. "What's the answer, Sam?"

Sam spread his hands. "Gentle task delivered to you. Police give many words and find nothing. My friends assure me any sum of money paid delightfully if matter stopped and our people made safe again."

"Who are your friends?" Denny questioned shrewdly.

"The To Fang lottery," said Sam Kong slowly.

Denny did not try to hide his surprise. He knew all about the To Fang lottery, that immensely wealthy syndicate of unknown Chinese who catered to the unquenchable gambling spirit of their countrymen. In three cities and a score of smaller towns the To Fang lottery had numerous agencies where the tickets were sold. Drawings were held every day. The amount of money the organization collected and disbursed in the course of a year was stupendous.

"I didn't know you were connected with the To Fang lottery, Sam."

"Secret not known to many," Sam told him.

"Where does the lottery come in on this?"

Sam Kong's wise, shrewd eyes rested on them. "To Fang lottery has become lottery of ghastly death," he said slowly, and the more impressively because of his deliberation. "It is dying faster than lucky winners die. Chinese afraid to buy tickets now. For lucky winner meets disaster quickly. Sometimes loses all money—each time loses life. Already in ev-

ery Chinatown where To Fang opera[te] fearful word is whispered that To Fa[ng] is unlucky. To Fang lottery tickets a[re] chances for death. And lottery is shun[ned] like plague of evil. Great money loss o[c]curs to lottery owners. And in sha[me] they confront loss of face, having to co[n]fess they are helpless to protect trust[ing] buyers of tickets."

"That doesn't explain Lee," Den[ny] pointed out.

SAM KONG filled the glasses with w[ine] again. His hand did not tremble a[nd] his voice was steady. "Lee flirt with f[or]tune's smile for fifty years, unknow[ing] that his master was behind lottery. Ye[s]terday fortune smile on Lee most sweet[ly] tossing into delirious lap of humble co[ok] sixty thousand gold dollars. Lee promp[t]ly burn soup and spend leisure hours [in] room counting vast sum of money u[n]ceasingly, despite apprehensive maste[r's] advice to deposit money in safe bank. T[o]night false telephone call lure me awa[y.] And now—Lee rejoice with honored a[n]cestors and sixty thousand dollars depa[rt] into unknown."

"Are you sure of that?" Denny aske[d.] "I didn't hear anything said about mo[n]ey."

"I examine place where Lee keep mo[n]ey, finding it sadly vacant," Sam assure[d] him. Sam pointed to the white lotter[y] ticket. "To Fang lottery ticket clutch[ed] in Lee's dead hand. And writing on si[de] of ticket, instead of seller's name, s[ay] most mockingly, 'The prize is Death.'"

"Why didn't you tell some of that [to] the police?"

Sam sighed helplessly. "Police r[un] around in circles and deliver nothing. B[e]sides—lottery ticket highly illegal. M[ore] embarrassing to inform police of secr[et] details. Hence telephone call to you, [my] friend. Chinatown business and wa[ys] well known to you from years spent [in]

Chinatown newspaper beat. To Fang lottery happy to bestow great reward on trusted man who save face and business for them."

"I see the light," Denny murmured. "How about a little money in advance, Sam? I'm broke."

Sam Kong drew a fat wallet from his pocket, leafed out two hundred dollars in twenties and pressed them in Denny's hand, while Pudge stared incredulously. As Denny pocketed them he asked casually: "By the way, what was the real message on that red slip?"

"It say, 'The numbers are drawn,'" said Sam unhappily. "Gentle little hint to To Fang owners that hand of death guide their lottery now."

"Very delicately put," said Denny thoughtfully, picking up his hat. "I'll let you know how things are going."

Sam Kong asked anxiously: "Do thought occur to you how to proceed?"

"Several thoughts occur," Denny grinned. "And I'm going to proceed. Burn a joss stick for luck, Sam. I may need it."

They went out.

CHAPTER FOUR

The Dragon's Blood Club

IN ONE spot in Chinatown there was light, life, gaiety. That was Poppy Street, where ran the street cars and through traffic; where the curio stores, the Chinese theater, the fake joss house, the movies and ornate eating and dancing places were located. Poppy Street— whose history was as old as Chinatown, whose lurid past was as crimson as the neon dragon blazing over the wide, brightly lighted stairway leading up to the Dragon's Blood Club.

Club in name only, the Dragon's Blood catered to anyone who desired the type of entertainment it offered.

"Food!" Pudge uttered ecstatically as he and Denny Eagan mounted the brass-studded steps and entered the Dragon's Blood. "Smell it—look at it!" Pudge gestured around the huge room that opened before them.

Shrewd Chinese business sense had transformed the big room into a mighty arched cavern, over whose walls fantastic dragons writhed and flew, down from whose arched ceiling fierce *papier-mâché* dragons' heads glared. Curtained booths beneath a balcony lined the walls, rows of tables were placed outside them, and there was still room for a large dance floor.

The balcony had more private booths. And the whole place was a kaleidoscope of lights, of music, of dancers and diners, drifting swirls of cigarette smoke, talk, laughter. For Chinatown superstitions and Chinatown fog did not keep the Americans at home, or a certain portion of younger Chinatown itself.

Both kinds were present tonight, and one would never know from a glance over the room that grim tragedy and threat had occurred nearby.

A head waiter hurried to meet them. He was waved back and his place taken by another Chinese who had been standing near the cashier's desk at the right of the entrance.

This man would have stood out in any group of his fellow countrymen. For he was all of six feet tall, broad-shouldered, powerful. Thirty might have been his age. His black hair was cut in a stubby pompadour, and lowering black eyes stared from beneath bushy black brows. A great scar starting in his stubby black hair swept in a vermilion slash down over his cheek to the under side of his chin.

He was smiling as he came to meet them, and that scar-twisted smile managed to be forbidding, malevolent, unpleasant. "Good evening, Mr. Eagan," he greeted in faultless English. "Welcome to our club. We have not seen you for some time. A table for two?"

"A booth up on the balcony," said Denny amiably. "A place where we can look down over the floor while we eat, Blood."

Black eyes flickered for an instant. "You remember my old name which you coined, I see," said the other smoothly. "Certainly. This way."

And with a bow and a wider smile he led them to the balcony stairs and personally conducted them up to a booth. Women turned their heads and looked at him as he moved with catlike grace.

Seated, they ordered steaks, and the big fellow took their order with a deference that was almost mocking. The twisted smile seemed fixed on his face. "You have come back to live?" he asked smoothly.

Denny grinned at him. "Just a little visit, Blood, old boy. I got homesick for the fog. Great stuff, fog, don't you think?"

"It has its uses," said the other, and with a final mocking bow he withdrew.

"Phew!" said Pudge under his breath. "What an ape! So his name's Blood, is it?"

Denny chuckled as he lit a cigarette and looked down over the big floor below. Their booth opened that way, with curtains at the back.

"I nicknamed him Blood," Denny said. "And it stuck with a lot of people. His real name is Gee Foo. Half-breed fellow. Smart as a whip. Came in here about ten years ago without a dime, and now he's getting to be one of the big guns among his countrymen. It was one of his deals that got me in bad with Miller. Blood does a little dope selling and so on. Gets by with it too. Costs him hush money, but he can afford it."

"And Miller lets his palm run his eyes?" Pudge asked shrewdly.

"They're good friends," Denny said casually. "Blood was with Miller tonight. They had been talking in that doorway. Blood stayed back in the shadows and kept quiet, but I saw the light reflected on his scar. He's too big to mistake, anyway."

"I smell a rat," said Pudge quickly. "Two old friends gabbing in a dark doorway don't sound so hot—when they've got a dump like this to chin in."

"Might have met there accidentally," Denny said absently.

THEIR food came. As they ate, Pudge asked: "What are you going to do about old Kong's trouble?"

Denny shook his head. "Don't know. He's in deep. The Chinese lottery is a big thing. It takes someone with a lot on the ball to buck it. And it needed damn smart brains and nerve to enter Sam's house and stab his own cook. We're up against clever killers. They've got something big up their sleeves. They'd never buck the lottery if it wasn't big."

"Looks to me like Mock Yum happened to be in the wrong place at the right time," said Pudge. "The guy who left that prize package on the table, and used his knife on the cook, was trying to scram out through the tunnel. Just as he got there, the door opened and old Mock Yum paraded through. So the fellow planted his knife in him and lammed up the stairs and out on the street."

"That's about the way it happened," Denny agreed.

"That granddaughter's a knockout, ain't she?"

"She'll pass."

"Pass my eye! She'll run away out ahead!" Pudge leaned over the table. "You know, I've been wondering about her and that scarf. She musta been the one who came running down the stairs while we came up from below."

"I didn't say anything about it," Denny said, "but it must have been her."

"All right—then she was in her room all the time someone was moving around the apartment, and sticking his knife in the cook. Funny she didn't hear something. But whether she did or not, that scarf must have been in her room all the time. I looked. Everything is kept strictly in order around that house. Wasn't a sign of any other personal belonging out. So where did the scarf come from?"

"I thought of all that," said Denny. "She didn't drop it, because she came down the stairs after Mock Yum was killed. If she'd been down there in the cellar, she would not have gone upstairs, and then hurried down again."

"Unless," said Pudge triumphantly, "she thought he was alone, and went upstairs to get something—or hide something. And then went out to call help."

"She's Sam's granddaughter. She wouldn't be working against him."

"That's where I stumble," Pudge nodded gloomily. "The facts don't check."

Denny's fork paused halfway to his mouth as Pudge finished; he laid it down and leaned over the balcony railing, staring at a point across the floor.

"There's something that checks!" he said sharply to Pudge. "Sam Kong's granddaughter just went into one of the booths over there."

"Who's with her?"

"She's alone."

"What the devil is she doing here alone?"

Denny put his napkin on the table and stood up. "I'll go and ask her," he said. "I want to talk to her anyway." But before he could get away from the table Denny stopped, a queer look coming over his face. "Guess I won't at that. She's not alone now. Did you see that young fellow who just went in the booth with her?"

"Uh-huh," replied Pudge. "Regular chink Romeo, wasn't he? The movies ought to grab him."

"Jerry Chin's his name. This is serious."

"Nothing wrong with the gal seeing her sweetie here," said Pudge complacently.

"No," said Denny curtly. "But Jerry Chin's not the kind of a fellow to sweetie any granddaughter of Sam Kong's. He's a cheap gambler, race-track tout and woman chaser."

Pudge paused, fork upraised. "Gambler?"

"Exactly! Hit me right off too. I'm going down and pass the time of night with them. Fan Sing has no business in here this late anyway. I'll bet her grandfather doesn't know it. He's strict old-school Chinese. The whole business is beginning to look more and more sour to me."

"Want me along?"

"No. Stay here until I come back."

Denny looked toward the front as he skirted the rear of the dancing floor. Blood was still up at the front, near the cashier's desk; was looking the other way and did not see him. Denny pulled aside the curtains in front of the booth, smiling amiably.

And his smile turned to incredulous amazement. With his own eyes Denny had seen two people go through the curtains. They had not come out. The booth was empty.

DENNY stood there staring foolishly. The music stopped and the dancers streamed toward their tables as he slowly stepped behind the curtains. He couldn't be wrong. This was the right booth. There was a half-smoked cigarette in the glass ash tray on the table, smoke still curling from its end. And Fan Sing and her young man seemed to have vanished into thin air. Denny stood there amazed.

But only for a moment was Denny at a loss. He had not spent years in Chinatown for nothing. The two had not come out the front—ergo, they must have gone some other way.

The sides of the booth were solid wooden panels. Not a chance that way. It had to be back. That settled, Denny inspected the back of the booth. It didn't take him long to locate the cleverly concealed panel at one corner. Took him but little longer to find how to push it open, prying with a table knife. The panel slid back in smoothly greased slots, revealing a narrow passage in the wall beyond.

Denny whirled around suddenly as the curtains were pushed back and a white-coated waiter stepped in. He stopped short at sight of the open panel, his jaw dropped; swift suspicion leaped into his lean yellow face.

"What you do?" he questioned angrily.

"Going through," Denny said airily. "Want to tell Jerry Chin something. He's waiting in there."

Beady black eyes showed mounting suspicion. "Who tell you go back theah?"

"It's all right," Denny said casually. He was edging slowly around the table as he spoke.

"No. I call Gee Foo. This place plivate."

The waiter whirled for the doorway with a startled grunt as Denny lunged at him. Denny's hand caught the waiter's shoulder. His other arm locked around the saffron neck in a strangle clamp. One heave brought the struggling waiter around to the back of the booth.

The other struggled wildly. His hand slipped down inside his coat, flashed out with a knife. Denny saw the motion, guessed what was coming. His arm hooked a swift chop around to the front of the head he held clamped. His clenched fist caught the side of the yel-

low jaw squarely. It was a perfect knockout blow. With a faint sigh of exhaled breath the body went limp against him.

Denny grabbed the knife from the lax fingers, slipped it in his pocket. Due to his quickness there had been no sound audible against the restless cacophony that filled the big room. Denny stepped quickly to the opening, dragged his victim through, slid the panel back.

In the pitch blackness which surrounded them as soon as the panel closed, Denny hesitated. The waiter was out for some time. But to leave him here was inviting discovery by the first person who entered this passage. And Denny was no stranger to the ways of Chinatown. Back here in these passages he was on his own, beyond the reach of the law. He struck a match, saw that the passage, barely wide enough for one person to walk in, ran on the level of the second floor for some thirty feet, with a stairway going up at one end, and stairs going down at the other.

He solved the matter as best he could by dragging the body over toward the descending stairs. No use tying or gagging him. The wall was thin here; he could hear voices on the other side, from some party in a booth. Even a bound man could kick enough to attract attention. He'd have to chance it that he had struck hard enough to keep the fellow quiet for some time.

DENNY went on up, on a hunch. There were gambling rooms on the third floor. It wasn't likely Sam Kong's granddaughter would go down underground. Halfway up the stairs he knew he was right. The faint perfume of her passage still lingered in the still, dead air.

He came to a landing. That would be the third floor. The steps still went up, into the attic possibly. This was a three-story building. A lighted match showed a sliding panel with a handle on the back, opening into the third floor. Silence lay beyond. Denny moved the panel and looked through.

A small short hall with several doors opening off it lay beyond. Many voices were not far off, but the hall itself was empty. Denny stepped out, closed the panel behind him. And as he stood there warily, one of the doors opened suddenly. Sam Kong's granddaughter looked out.

Astonishment, chagrin, apprehension swept over her face at sight of Denny standing there. She moved back in quickly, and closed the door without speaking to him. Denny reached the door an instant later, shoved it open just as Fan Sing was trying to slip a bolt inside. Denny entered without asking permission.

Fan Sing stepped back from him, her face pale. "Good—good evening," she said uncertainly.

It was a small carpeted room holding only a rug, round table and a dozen chairs against the walls. A room used for card games, Denny decided. And they were alone in it.

"Where's Jerry Chin?" Denny asked, as he closed the door and put his back to it.

Fan Sing looked at him silently from her slightly slant eyes. She was very beautiful, very appealing as she stood there. It was hard to think of her in connection with Chinatown. She did not look like it, did not talk like it. And yet —there was the matter of Jerry Chin, and of her presence here.

She puzzled Denny. She was like a beautiful, mysterious flower, that might be harmless—and might be deadly. Her actions at Sam Kong's house were suspicious. Her meeting Jerry Chin when she should be home in bed was suspicious. Her slipping through the panel and up here with him was even more suspicious.

For she had come of her own free will. That much was plain.

"What are you doing here?" Denny asked.

Fan Sing drew herself up, flashed him a look of dislike. "That is my business," she replied haughtily. "How dare you walk in here this way? I—I shall ring for someone to put you out."

Denny ignored her threat. "Are you really Sam Kong's granddaughter?" he asked curiously.

"Certainly I am."

"You don't look like it. Where have you been all this time?"

"I am Chinese," she said with a proud lift to her chin.

"No disgrace. But you're not acting like a granddaughter of Sam Kong."

"Why?" she flashed.

"You wouldn't be here like this. Does Sam Kong know you're here?"

"Yes."

And by her slight hesitation and the way her black eyes shifted, Denny knew she was lying.

"You're not married?"

"No," she denied.

"What do you know about Jerry Chin?"

"He—he is a friend of mine."

"So you admit slipping up here with him? Where is he?"

"I don't admit anything," Fan Sing denied. Her cheeks were flushing now; her eyes were stormy with anger.

"That scarf of yours—how did it get out of your room this evening?" Denny demanded.

"That was not my scarf," Fan Sing denied quickly.

AND she was lying again, standing before him flushed and defiant. Denny experienced an overpowering wish to shake the truth out of her. What kind of a mess was she mixed up with that she should have to lie? She had seen that he had her grandfather's confidence.

"I think," said Denny shrewdly, "that I'd better go down and telephone Sam Kong, and ask him if he knows you are here."

That startled her, frightened her, took a lot of the defiance out of her. "Please don't do that," Fan Sing begged quickly.

"Why not?"

"I—I don't want to worry him. He thinks I'm at home in bed."

"And instead of that you're in one of the dives of the quarter, with a rotten, lying rat who would never dare walk with you before your grandfather."

"Who are you speaking of?"

"Jerry Chin."

Her change from uneasiness to blazing anger was instantaneous. "You lie! You don't know a thing about Jerry! Who asked you to come snooping around this way?"

"How long have you lived with your grandfather?" Denny asked curiously.

Fan Sing was a creature of furious moods. She smiled abruptly. "I have lived in the east all my life until the last three months," she said softly.

"Some people can learn a lot in three months, and some can't," Denny sighed. "Now you're pretty, Fan Sing, and you'd turn almost any man's head. But you're not turning mine with that smile. Suppose you tell me the truth about tonight? You know who killed old Lee, and who knifed Mock Yum. And you know how your scarf got down in the basement."

"I do not!" Fan Sing denied flatly.

"Did you help?" Denny shot out suddenly, taking a step toward her.

Fan Sing backed away with a startled step. There was horror in her wild, "No!"

"You were in your room while all that happened?"

"Y-yes," said Fan Sing.

"And you didn't hear a thing?"

"No."

"Then how did your scarf get out of your room?"

"I—I must have left it in the front room," Fan Sing said hurriedly, and then bit her red under-lip as she saw what she had done.

"That settles the ownership of it anyway," Denny said grimly. "You're lying faster than I can talk, Fan Sing. You're hiding something."

"I'm not," she replied tremulously.

"Do you realize that your grandfather is in a lot of trouble?"

"Yes," faintly.

"Then tell me what you know."

"I don't know anything," she made her monotonous denial again.

Denny sighed in exasperation. "I see I'll have to get your grandfather over here after all." He turned toward the door.

"Don't" Fan Sing pleaded. "I'll go home now. See? I'll go out with you." She snatched her little hat off the table, tucked it down on her head and stepped to the door as Denny waited for her.

He opened the door and Fan Sing preceded him into the hallway. Following her, Denny wondered why she stopped outside the door and then went on quickly. He found out as he stepped out. A figure flattened against the wall there leaped at him. Denny's guarding arm went up too late. A swinging blackjack crashed against the side of his head.

And as everything went black, Denny's last bitter thought was that Sam Kong's granddaughter had seen Jerry Chin outside the door as she stepped through and had deliberately walked on as if there was no one there.

She had double-crossed him neatly.

CHAPTER FIVE

Mr. Jerry Chin

PUDGE PAGGET finished the last of his food lighted a cigarette and glanced uneasily at his watch. It had been a good fifteen minutes since Denny Eagan had entered that curtained booth on the other side of the dance floor. A few minutes after he entered Pudge had seen a white-coated waiter go through the curtains. Since then the waiter had not emerged, and there had been no sign of life about the booth.

Funny, Pudge thought. Waiters didn't belong in a booth that long. Then occurred something that brought Pudge out of his chair. The first girl of a party of four, walking along the line of booths, trailed her hands against the curtains and jerked one back. And Pudge saw that the booth was empty.

Pudge got down there as fast as he could. His eyes had been on the booth all the time. None of the four who should have been in there could have emerged without his seeing them. Pudge's round innocent face was surprisingly hard as he arrived at the booth. And he got another shock as the waiter almost bumped into him coming out. Pudge saw that there was no one else in the booth. He caught the waiter's arm.

"Where's the others who were in here?" he demanded forcefully.

The waiter pulled his arm away impatiently. His hair was tousled. His thin yellow face looked excited.

"Don' no Englis'," the waiter mumbled, and started on.

Pudge grabbed his arm again. "Never mind that 'no savvy' gag!" Pudge said roughly. "I seen three others go in there a while ago, an' they ain't there now."

Pudge reached back and pulled a corner of the curtain out to make sure. Yes, the booth was empty. They had gone in, hadn't come out—and weren't in there now. Pudge noticed now that the waiter's white coat was dirty at the sides and back. It had been clean when he went in.

"Kick through!" said Pudge roughly.

"Who's back of this Houdini act? Where'd they go?"

"Mus' go," the waiter gasped excitedly, and with a mighty effort he jerked away again and cut across the dance floor, making for the cashier's desk. Pudge followed at his heels, swearing under his breath. Something was wrong. He intended to find the answer.

Gee Foo, his face impassive behind the great scar was just coming out of a further door, marked OFFICE. Two men were with him, thin weedy young Chinese. The waiter hurried to Gee Foo, was spilling a torrent of singsong Chinese when Pudge joined them.

"Never mind that stuff!" Pudge said sourly to Gee Foo. "My buddy went in a booth over there. This guy followed him in. He just came back out, and now Eagan ain't there. Where is he?"

AND then without waiting for an answer, Pudge left them standing there and cut across the room. For Pudge had just seen Sam Kong's granddaughter come through a door on the other side of the room and make for the front entrance hurriedly. Pudge planted himself in front of her. "Where did Denny Eagan go?" he snapped.

Fan Sing stopped, a look of dismay on her face. She shook her head. "Is Mr. Eagan here?" she asked blankly.

"You know he is!" Pudge rapped at her. "He went in that booth where you were."

"I think you are mistaken," said Fan Sing nervously.

A soft voice at Pudge's shoulder said with a trace of mocking amusement: "Are you asking about Mr. Eagan? You will find him in my office. He has been talking over the effects of foggy weather."

"Yeah?" said Pudge suspiciously. "Fog, eh?"

Gee Foo bowed slightly. His scarred grin grew broader if anything. "I confess there were other things also. You will find him sitting right inside the door there."

Things were moving a little too fast for Pudge. Here was Sam Kong's granddaughter telling him that he was mistaken about Denny and the booth, and the big fellow assuring him clamly that Denny was over there in the office. Sam Kong's girl ought to know what she was talking about.

"All right, he can tell me what happened!" Pudge snapped, and stalked toward the office.

Gee Foo raised an eyebrow the merest bit. The two yellow men who had come out of the office with him drifted back toward it.

Fan Sing started toward the door again. Gee Foo reached her side with a stride. "If you will come into my office, we will talk this matter over," he smiled.

"No," said Fan Sing. "I am going home."

Gee Foo laid a hand on her arm. "Mr. Eagan has something to say to you. A minute only. Jerry is coming too."

Fan Sing twitched her arm away with a quick jerk. "I am going home," she repeated tonelessly. "That can wait." Her eye met the staring orbs under Gee Foo's bushy black brows. "I will see Mr. Eagan later" said Fan Sing, and hurried to the door.

Blood took a half step after her, and then stopped. There were too many people nearby to allow any noticeable action. And his men had entered the office. He wheeled and strode there with his catlike tread.

The smile was gone from his face now.

DENNY EAGAN rolled over and opened his eyes. He groaned as a club seemed to rise up behind and smack him on the head. But it was only an echo of another blow that had struck him previously. Denny groaned again.

An amused voice said "Bad dreams?"

Denny turned his head. Jerry Chin was sitting close to the cot on which he lay.

Denny threw his legs over the side of the cot and raised himself to a sitting posture with a grunt. "You!" he said.

"Me," Jerry Chin agreed blandly, standing up. He was all that Pudge's first opinion of him had suggested. A dapper, tall and handsome young Chinese. His skin was almost white. His clothes were faultless. His bearing was easy and assured. And if his slant eyes were set a little too close together, if his mouth was thin and calculating, and there was a general lack of sincerity about his face, it would take more than a casual observer to note the defects.

"You almost caved my head in," Denny said, gingerly feeling the back of his skull. There was a big lump there, and he winced as he pressed it.

Jerry Chin was of the younger generation, educated in American schools, speaking English faultlessly, knowing how to dress and act. He grinned maliciously as Denny winced. "That would have been a pleasure," he stated.

"You don't say?" Denny replied.

His eyes wandered about the room. It was small and squalid. The ceiling was low. The walls were varnished wood. The bare floor was wood. But it was the door behind Chin that caught his eye. It was formed of wide planks that looked as if they might be inches thick. There were no windows in the room. Jerry Chin had been smoking, and the blue fog he had made hung thick around the single small light bulb that hung from the wooden ceiling.

"Yes," said Jerry Chin, "it would have saved us some trouble."

"Who is 'us'? And what trouble would it have saved?"

"My—er—friends," replied Jerry Chin, mincing his words with mock carefulness. "You're too curious, Eagan. They decided that you'd better take a little visit out of town."

"You don't say?" Denny said again mildly. "Out of town, eh?"

"That's it."

"And who's going to send me out of town?"

"I'll see that you're started on the road," said Jerry Chin.

"And who'll see that I don't come back?"

Jerry Chin showed gleaming white teeth as he laughed. "You won't be back."

"No," said Denny unpleasantly. "And why not?"

Jerry Chin inspected the carefully manicured fingernails of his left hand, chewed the corner of one for a moment. "You don't come back from the river" he said casually.

"I see," said Denny after a moment. "The river, eh? I might have known you had some dirty trick like that up your lousy sleeve. Smooth snake, aren't you?"

Denny felt in his pockets. The knife he had slipped there was gone, his cigarettes, keys and money also. "Stole my money, eh?" he charged.

"You won't need it," Jerry Chin said indifferently.

"Give me a cigarette."

The sleek young man tossed him a smoke and a clip of matches—one of Denny's own cigarettes by the brand. Denny lighted up inhaled.

"I won't argue with you," he said abruptly. "I know your kind. But tell me this—is Sam Kong's granddaughter working with you?"

"We're going to be married" said Jerry Chin softly.

"I see" said Denny, equally softly.

THAT explained a lot of things that had been puzzling him. Explained why Fan Sing could turn against her grandfather, could betray her grandfather's friend. In love with this sleek young gambler, she walked his road. And it made Denny feel pretty bad to think of the shock Sam Kong was due to get when he found out. It would be doubly bad if Fan Sing had helped with the killing of old Lee, had been implicated in it in any way.

"When does this little murder party come off?" Denny questioned pleasantly.

"In a little while," Jerry Chin assured him, quite as if they were discussing the weather.

"You're a cold-blooded rat, aren't you?"

Jerry Chin yawned, in nowise affected by the slander. "Practical," he said. "Notice my hand stays near my pocket?"

"I see."

"Gun," said Jerry Chin briefly.

Denny yawned too. "Well, if I have to wait for my murder, I might as well lie down and be comfortable. My head aches and my feet hurt. I'll take off my shoes." Denny bent, unlaced his right shoe, pulled it off; and yawned again.

Jerry Chin admired him. "You're a cool one."

"Yes," Denny agreed. "I'm cool all right."

The hand that held the shoe made a sudden hard flirt. The shoe flew from the fingers, heel first. It struck Jerry Chin square between the eyes before he knew what was happening.

As the slim dapper Chinese staggered back, cursing and slapping his hand to his coat pocket, Denny left the cot like an uncoiling steel spring.

The impact of his shoulder drove Jerry Chin clear back against the door. And by that time Denny had clamped his hand on the wrist that was grabbing for a gun. Denny brought his head up under Jerry's chin, driving Jerry's head back against the thick planks of the door. And drove his right fist to the wrist in the unprotected stomach before him.

A gasp of pain burst from Jerry Chin's

lips. He bowed helplessly forward—to meet Denny's fist again; that smashed into his mouth, catapulting his head back against the door with a dull thump. Jerry Chin's knees buckled. He started to sag to the floor. A trickle of blood welled from the corner of his mouth.

Denny held him up long enough to pull the gun out of his pocket, and then pushed him down and backed to the cot.

"I'm practical too," Denny confided as Jerry Chin groaned, gasped for breath, swiped at his bleeding mouth with the back of his hand.

CHAPTER SIX

Murder Money

DENNY fastened his shoe on again, keeping a wary eye cocked toward Jerry Chin, who staggered weakly to his feet.

"Now then," said Denny, getting up with the revolver in his hand, "we're going places and do things. Open up the door and lead out. And the first one of your friends who makes a pass at me buttons trouble for you. Savvy?"

Chin pushed open the door, stumbled out without replying. He was a badly battered and sadly chastened young man; he went without argument, almost slinking. They came out into a narrow passage—a tunnel.

"Underground, eh?" said Denny, looking around. "Which way is the river?"

Chin pointed to the left.

"We go to the right then. And God help you if we go wrong."

Just beyond them a fist hammered on the inside of a door set in the opposite side of the tunnel. A muffled voice shouted: "Hey, Denny! That you out there?"

A prod with the gun brought a key out of Jerry Chin's pocket, unlocked the padlock which secured the door. A disheveled

and wild-eyed Pudge popped out. H[i] face was scratched and one eye was b[e] coming discolored.

"Where've you been?" Pudge d[e] manded in an aggrieved voice.

"On ice," said Denny.

He explained what had happened t[o] him. Pudge matched it.

"I went in the office looking for you, he said, "and two Chinks followed me i[n] an' jumped me. We'd have wrecked th[e] office if one of them hadn't clipped m[e] behind the ear with a pair of brass knuck[s] I woke up in that stinking room. What'[s] the idea?"

"We're too inquisitive," Denny in formed him. "They don't like it aroun[d] here. It seems they picked the river fo[r] us."

"Huh? Going to drown us?"

"Something like that."

Pudge groaned. "I told you I didn'[t] like the looks of this neighborhood. W[e] come to pay a call an' wind up headed for the river. What do we do now?"

Denny considered their sullen captive. "Where there's smoke, there's fire," he said. "If being inquisitive is worth a couple of murders, it's worth a little trouble to be inquisitive. If you get what I mean."

"It sounds like a riddle," said Pudge.

"It's really a lucky break, I think," Denny grinned. He reached out and grabbed Jerry Chin by his well-groomed neck. "Jerry," said Denny coldly, "I ought to kill you. I may yet, and plead self-defense. The more I think about Fan Sing the madder I get. Sam Kong would back me up. But I may let you off if you loosen up and tell me who killed Sam Kong's cook. Think fast. You're walking a tight rope."

Jerry Chin cringed away from him. "I don't know anything about that," he denied sullenly. "I can prove it by witnesses."

"Where were you when it happened?"

"Out riding with Fan Sing," said Jerry promptly. "We stopped in a drug store for a malted milk."

Denny grinned unpleasantly. "So you know all about it? When it happened and everything? Got an alibi too. And so that's where Fan Sing was instead of sleeping in her room?"

Jerry Chin said nothing. His smoothly barbered face suddenly looked haggard and anxious. Denny slammed him against the wall, shoved the pistol muzzle deep in his stomach.

"Who killed Lee?" he rasped. "Last chance, damn you!"

And Jerry Chin abruptly wilted. He was soft underneath, lacked the nerve to brazen it out. "Gee Foo," he stammered. "Why?"

"He wants to start a new lottery."

"Got it!" Denny exclaimed with satisfaction. "That's what's been puzzling me. Get on ahead of us, punk! Take us to Blood's office. We'll have a little family gathering, with mourners' bench and prayers. And I'll be hoping you try to cross me or make a run for it."

DENNY shoved the young gambler along the low tunnel, followed close at his heels. It was lighted for a short distance, then turned abruptly and ended at a flight of steps. The lights stopped there. They mounted the steps into increasing blackness. Reached a landing, went up another flight, in pitch blackness now.

And Jerry Chin stopped and fumbled at the wall. A panel slid back. Light came in. "Go out first, Pudge, and see he doesn't try any tricks," Denny ordered.

He heard Pudge give a gasp. Heard an exclamation as Jerry Chin stepped in. Followed them, and stopped short inside the opening. They were in an office. Desk and safe and file case, table and chairs. And facing them were Gee Foo and Sergeant Bat Miller.

The steel door of the safe was open. The two men had been counting money. A stack of it rested on the desk. A fat sheaf of bills was clutched in Bat Miller's thick fingers.

"What the hell!" Bat Miller exploded.

"We find the law," said Denny.

Miller laid the sheaf of bills on the desk hastily, as if they were suddenly burning his fingers.

"Prisoner for you," Denny said, narrow-eyed. "Charge him with kidnaping, assault with intent to kill, accessory to murder and robbery. That'll hold him. And you can thank me for making the arrest, Sergeant. He ties up with those two killings at Sam Kong's."

"He does, does he?" Miller asked thickly. "How d'you know?"

"Good evidence. You'll probably find a couple of hundred dollars of my money in his pocket, for one thing. That's enough to hold him on."

Miller had been doing all the talking. Gee Foo had stood by the desk, his unwinking eyes fixed on them.

It was Sergeant Miller who made the first move. He reached under his coat and drew out his service revolver.

"I'll handle him," Miller said hurriedly. He stepped to Jerry Chin, grabbed him by the shoulder, pushed him around. "You're under arrest," he said harshly— and with a violent shove he drove the young man against Denny. Followed, using him as a shield, shoved his gun in Denny's face.

"Drop that gat!" Miller said in an ugly tone.

There was a swift movement at the desk. Gee Foo gave a catlike leap to the door, a black-metalled automatic in his hand. He was grinning now. Denny slowly lowered his gun. Jerry Chin snatched it from him.

Pudge, caught by surprise, stood gaping.

Denny shook his head, ignored the

young gambler. "So you're in this thing deep," he said to Miller.

"Shut up!" Miller snarled. "Get back down where you came from."

"You know what that means. Murder," Denny answered.

"Go on!" Miller grated.

"I knew you were rotten, but I didn't think you were this bad," Denny said contemptuously. "If you go through with this and it gets out, you'll burn."

"It won't get out," Miller sneered. "You fool! D'you think I'm going to let you boggle things now—when we're muscling in on a fortune? You know too much!"

"And murder done already!"

"Don't let that worry you," Gee Foo said silkily from the door. "We're handling that all right. A few fools who happened to win the lottery prizes won't be missed." Gee Foo's scarred face was like a mask of evil as he smiled broadly. "And their prize money from the To Fang lottery is swelling my capital for the new lottery. In another month To Fang will be the lottery of dead men, shunned by every man. The new lottery will be welcomed."

"I suppose that's Lee's money you were counting?" said Denny. He was stalling for time, wondering desperately if there was a way out of this.

"Lee's money," Gee Foo grinned. "He squealed like a stuck pig when he fell. And then when I started out through the cellar I had to stop another. I understand you were back of him."

"Fan Sing told you!"

"Yes."

"Stop gabbing!" Miller growled. "Get these two down below and out of the way!"

GEE FOO moved away from the door. Just like a cat stalking its kill, Denny noted. And as he went the door suddenly opened behind him. Catlike, Gee Foo whirled.

Fan Sing stood in the doorway, staring at them.

Gee Foo put his gun behind his back. "Come in," he purred pleasantly.

"What—what is the matter?" Fan Sing stammered.

"Just a little fun. J—"

Jerry Chin moved quickly toward the door, forcing a smile. "It's all right. Come in, dear," he urged.

Fan Sing backed out a step. Jerry Chin leaped after her, the strain showing in his voice as he asked her to come in. But as he reached the doorway, Fan Sing whisked aside.

"Quick!" she gasped to someone there. And a stalwart, blue-coated figure took her place. Four others crowded in behind him.

Jerry Chin tried to slam the door. A burly shoulder drove it in. "What's going on in here?" the officer demanded grimly. He reached for a gun.

Gee Foo shot him. And with the roar of the shot deafening their ears and the officer falling with a queer startled look on his face, Gee Foo leaped for the open panel in the wall.

Pudge made one flying leap, tackled him, brought him crashing to the floor, his head smashing hard against the wall. Pudge swarmed over him, grabbing for the gun.

Sergeant Miller swore and dove for the panel too, swinging his gun at Pudge. Denny knocked it up, drove his fist into Miller's face, and tripped the big detective.

Jerry Chin hastily dropped his gun as bluecoats swarmed into the office with drawn pistols. It was all over in seconds. Gee Foo sitting up groggily; Miller handcuffed and cursing and Jerry Chin held by an arm.

Pandemonium had broken out in the great room beyond. The people there came crowding toward the office door. One of the bluecoats stepped out and drove them back. And Sam Kong edged into the office with Fan Sing following him.

Then questions were fired at Denny. He sketched briefly what had happened.

"Gee Foo decided to muscle in on the lottery racket," he said. "He didn't have much chance as long as the To Fang lottery was running. So he set out to wreck it by killing and robbing the winners. A little of that went a long way. When everyone was afraid to buy To Fang tickets, the new lottery would open up, and get the business. He was playing for a fortune. And Miller was playing with him, furnishing all the protection and inside information he could. Gee Foo killed Sam Kong's cook tonight, stole the old fellow's sixty thousand dollars prize money, and left that dead arm as a warning. Killed Mock Yum too, in the basement. But," Denny finished, "what brought you officers here?"

"The old gent called us out. Said there was trouble here," the leader told him.

A smile broke across Sam Kong's round face. "My granddaughter arrive from guilty absence, overflowing with fears," he said to Denny. "Confess to indignant grandpapa that she have been pursuing clandestine love affair with handsome young man she meet. Tonight when grandpapa summoned out by telephone call, she receive telephone call also, requesting her sweet presence for ride with loved one.

"Foolishly she go. And on arriving back discover trouble and summon help. Then she see her scarf produced with blood on it—and suddenly realize that same scarf was left in loved one's car day before. Most unhappy and confused, she slip out to see loved one and ask explanation. And he cleverly soothe her fears and draw whole story of events of evening from her. Hastily excusing himself he depart. To warn friends undoubtedly. And my friend Eagan, questioning Fan Sing, find

nothing because she still believe in loved one. But loved one make fatal mistake of attacking Eagan when he start to take her home.

"Fan Sing realize then that false steps have bungled things, and hastily return to Grandpapa to confess and ask advice.

"And grandpapa, scenting trouble, summon police and come quickly to pry in trouble. Arriving," said Sam Kong blandly, "at opportune moment."

"Very opportune," agreed Denny drily. "I knew Miller was mixed up in this. That's what brought me here tonight. But I didn't think he'd try what he did. It would have been murder mighty quick."

"How in hell did you know anything about me?" Miller snarled.

"You knew too much," Denny answered gently. "Tonight when Sam Kong read the red slip wrong, you knew it was wrong. And you can't read Chinese, Miller. So someone must have told you what was to be on it. You had been talking to Gee Foo earlier in the evening, where no one would see you. I knew you were crooked and Gee Foo was more so. So I came here to see what I could scratch up."

"That scarf is still puzzling me," Pudge confessed.

Denny swung on Jerry Chin. "What about it?"

Jerry Chin said unhappily: "Gee Foo used it to get the cook to open the door. He said it had been left in his place, and he wanted to return it. The cook had to open the door to take it, and Gee Foo got in."

"And wiped his knife on it and then dropped it," Denny said. "Simple. But it helped a lot."

"Simple things always help," Sam Kong declared. "See what simple scratching uncover. And now I take simple granddaughter home and make not so simple. Fan Sing, come!"

And Fan Sing went—meekly.

The Crippled Corpse

by

Erle Stanley Gardner

Author of "Make It Snappy," etc.

Free-lance bodyguard, crime breaker de luxe—that was Dick Bentley. No case was too tough for him to break, no trap too tight for him to spring. Even when the smoothest gang of all had set it—baited it with a crippled corpse.

He tried to say something, failed — then pitched forward.

CHAPTER ONE

Blind Baggage

THE house was strange and dark and silent. It set back from the road, surrounded by an iron fence, with clumps of shrubbery casting dark patches of mysterious shadow.

Dick Bentley was accustomed to strange silent houses. In his capacity as free-lance bodyguard he had had dealings with many persons who lived in houses that presented an outward atmosphere of mystery.

He rang the bell for the third time without hearing any sound of answering steps from the dark interior of the house. Nor did this disturb him. Many times he had dealt with persons who were reluctant to answer doorbells until after they

63

had assured themselves that the caller was one who meant no harm.

Bentley rather expected, in fact, that there would be the click of lights, a secret survey from some point of vantage, and then a questioning, conducted through some sliding portal in the door. Ever since chance had placed Bentley in his position of acting as a very successful bodyguard for a very prominent millionaire whose life had been threatened by racketeers, Bentley had gone into strange places, met strange people, and seen strange sights.

So certain was he that he would be bathed in a bright light and subjected to a searching inquiry, that it came as rather a shock to him when, without so much as the faintest suggestion of footsteps, or rattling chains, the huge door swung inward, and a man said: "Come in, Mr. Bentley."

Bentley's hand moved swiftly. The fingers were within a matter of inches of the gun butt which hung under his left armpit.

"Good evening," he said, trying to get some glimpse of the man who was standing to one side, waiting for him to come in.

He could see that this man was rather powerfully built, that he was standing with his shoulders hunched forward, a position which might have indicated either the first touch of years, or the position of one who rather expects an attack.

"It was a young lady who telephoned me," said Bentley.

"Yes," said the man, "my daughter."

"I see," said Bentley, and walked past him, into the warm darkness of the hallway.

There was a light somewhere in the rear, and a door that was partially open. Some light seeped through this half opening, and gave sufficient illumination to show the outlines of the man who had invited him to enter.

Dick Bentley walked straight down the hallway, toward the door through which the light came. He wanted to show this man that he was not in the least frightened at darkened hallways or mysterious houses.

"I presume you're George Oliver," he called over his shoulder.

"Yes," said the man in a strangely muffled tone.

Dick Bentley hesitated at the doorway. "Do I go in here?"

"Yes."

"Will you ask your daughter to come in?"

The man's bulk was vague and indefinite in the darkness. "You can talk with me," he said.

Dick Bentley was politely obstinate. "Doubtless I can," he said, "but I was engaged by a young woman, a Miss Aileen Oliver, and I wish to take my instructions from her, personally."

The man's voice seemed choking with some suppressed emotion. "Go in, then, and sit down," he said.

DICK BENTLEY walked into the lighted room. It was a huge library with massive tables, shaded reading lamps, bookcases that tiered up to the dimness of the darkened ceiling.

He dropped into a chair and waited.

Some two or three minutes passed. The spell of the strange house began to impress itself upon Dick Bentley. He had a feeling that eyes that were unfriendly were surveying him through secret apertures in the walls of the room.

Twice he looked around him swiftly—and saw nothing. The shaded reading lamps sent the rays from the light straight downward and made of the ceiling and sides of the room dark pools of shadow.

Then a door opened.

A man in livery came forward and bowed. "You wished to see Miss Oliver?"

"Yes," rasped Bentley.

"And you're Mr. Bentley?"

"Yes."

"Very well. Wait just a moment."

The figure turned, vanished upon smoothly silent feet through the doorway.

Dick Bentley got to his feet, shook his shoulders, as though he had been a dog, shaking off water. The weight of dark mystery which permeated the house seemed like something tangible which was striving to engulf him in a black fog.

He heard low voices engaged in surreptitious conversation, then swift feet upon an upper corridor, then silence again.

Dick Bentley was accustomed to the playing of hunches. Playing hunches had saved his life upon more than one occasion. He played one now. He moved out of the light, into the shadows. And, as he moved, something drew his steps toward a door which showed as a vague outline of ribboned light against the darkness of the walls of the library.

Dick Bentley knew perfectly well that he had no business padding around the house upon a tour of exploration, opening doors, peering into rooms. Yet he followed some strange hunch. Perhaps it was some unconscious recognition that all was not right. Perhaps it was merely a certain nervousness, engendered by the air of mystery with which the place was surrounded.

Be that as it may, Dick opened the door and found himself looking into a dining room, handsomely appointed, stiffly conventional, after the manner of wealthy respectability. From the huge sideboard with its polished silver, to the great table with silver candlesticks and the chairs that were set at regular intervals, the room was just what one would expect to find in a residence of wealth and refinement.

There was one incongruous note, and only one.

A wardrobe trunk was standing within a few feet of the door through which Bentley had entered the room. It was a massive affair, and it seemed strangely out of place.

Bentley's eyes snapped to sharp focus upon that trunk. He tried to determine just what it was, beyond the inherent incongruity of the trunk being there at all, that made him feel that the trunk was connected in some sinister way with the air of mystery and menace which seemed to permeate the house.

Then his eyes caught a bit of cloth, and Bentley knew.

The cloth which protruded from between the edges of the two halves of the trunk was a plaid of rather a coarse figure. It was not an unusual pattern, yet was a striking pattern. And the portion which protruded was undoubtedly a part of the creased trousers of a man. It was only a triangle of cloth, yet the manner in which it emerged from the trunk did not indicate that here was a portion of a garment which had been carelessly hung in the container—

Bentley crossed to the trunk in three swift strides. The lock was not quite in place, the two halves not entirely closed.

He pushed with his powerful shoulders, a hand on either side of the trunk. The halves opened.

The drawers had been ripped out from one side of the trunk, making it all one big cavity on the inside, big enough to hold that which it did hold.

Dick Bentley's eyes widened as he took in the spectacle.

A MAN had been doubled into the interior of that trunk, and the man was quite dead. It needed but one glance at the puttylike color of the skin, at the glassy stare of the filmed eyes to tell Bentley that there was no need of feeling the pulse at the cold wrist.

The man had been well past middle age. Gray side whiskers protruded from either side of a long, thin mouth. The hair was gray and bushy, the eyebrows thick. A pair of glasses dangled from a wide black ribbon.

And the man had been crippled. One leg was decidedly withered, and a thick-soled boot made it the same length as the other leg. Apparently the boots had been carefully made, but the physical defect had been so great that the man must have a cane in order to walk.

And, as though it had been included through some subtle touch of irony, the man's cane had been placed by his side. It was a polished piece of black wood with a silver butt and initials engraved upon the silver.

Bentley noticed that the cause of death had probably been a series of blows upon the back of the head. The white hair was flecked with red stains, and the top of the head had a peculiar shape about it.

Bentley closed the trunk, turned, and walked back into the library. His lips were pressed into a grim line.

He walked toward the light, and a door opened. A young woman, rather beautiful in a striking fashion, with skirts that showed her silk-encased limbs to advantage, was coming toward him, smiling.

"Mr. Bentley?"

He bowed.

She regarded him steadily for a few moments, then said, simply: "I'm Aileen Oliver, and I telephoned you an hour or so ago."

Dick Bentley nodded, said nothing. His eyes were searching her face. Did she know what was in that wardrobe trunk in the next room? Did she surmise that he had been in that room, making an investigation?

If so, she showed it by neither expression nor tone.

She waved a gracious hand toward a chair. "Won't you be seated?" she asked.

Bentley sat down, lit a cigarette, and was interested to note that the hand which held the match was steady as a rock. He glanced up and saw that the girl was also staring at that match flame. He wondered if she had rather expected that the flame might have trembled as the hand which held the match reacted to the after effect of a nervous shock.

The girl started the conversation, settling herself upon the edge of one of the huge chairs, crossing her knees, smoothing down her skirt over the shapely contours.

"I was worried about father," she said. Bentley nodded.

"There have been some people worrying him in a business deal. I think they're racketeers, or blackmailers, or something of the sort. I telephoned you from the hangar as soon as my plane got in. I'd been away at college. He telegraphed for me to come home. I knew he was worried.

"And I'd heard about you. You're a detective. You specialize in protecting people from harm. Anyway, that's what I heard about you. You've gunned it out with a couple of gangs of crooks, and come out on top of the heap. Now I want you to protect this house."

Dick Bentley nodded. "Your father or yourself?" he asked.

"Father, principally."

"Maybe he doesn't want to be protected. He didn't seem very cordial when he let me in."

"No. He didn't like the idea."

"O. K.," said Bentley, "what do I do, and where do I begin?"

"I think," she said, slowly, weighing the words with deliberation, "you'd better begin by watching the grounds."

Bentley frowned. "I'm not a watchman, you know, Miss Oliver. I have taken over the protection of certain clients from certain specific dangers, and I've had a fair degree of success. But I have to handle things in my own way, and I direct what others are going to do by way of cooperation."

SHE gave him a smile that was meant to be dazzling, but which served only to disclose a double row of very white teeth, and to make it quite apparent that she was older than she had seemed at first, for the skin at the corners of her mouth crinkled like dry parchment as the corners of the mouth lifted upward.

"I know how you must feel, and I didn't want to make you seem to be just an employee. But there's really a great deal to worry me. Father won't allow you to remain in the house. The servants are all to be trusted, and any danger must, therefore, come from the outside. We haven't any dog to warn us—and I'm afraid. If you'd consent to spend the night, just walking around the grounds and making certain that no one came in— Well, the pay would be very generous."

She opened a little purse which she carried in her hand, and took out three bills. Each of them amounted to one hundred dollars.

"These," she said, "would be in the way of a retainer."

Bentley hesitated, regarded the extended hand with the hundred-dollar bills twisted about the tapering fingers, and then reached out and took them.

"I'd like to ask a couple of questions."

"Go ahead."

"Have you any idea of the exact danger which you think menaces your father?"

She shook her head.

"Do you know any of the people who might be menacing him? In other words, whether or not there might be a certain physical peculiarity about their appearance, something in the line of a distinguishing mark?"

He finished and watched her face, fascinated.

For the eyes were widening. The color was leaving the skin. She seemed on the verge of fainting. Her hands gripped the arm of the chair. Then she shook her head, vehemently.

"No, no! That's not true! That is, I don't know. I don't know what they look like, or who they are. I can't tell you anything about it. I only know that father has been worried. I know that there have been a couple of mysterious telephone calls. I think that there has been some other trouble—a threatening letter, perhaps. I can't tell. Father won't discuss it."

Bentley got to his feet. "I see," he said. "How did you know about the telephone calls, if you were away at college?"

"Riggs," she said, "the butler. He told me all about it after I got home tonight."

Bentley puffed on his cigarette. "Perhaps," he suggested, "it would be well to talk with this butler."

She shook her head again, vehemently. "No. That would never do. He told me, in confidence. He would never confide in a stranger, never in the world."

Bently grinned. "O. K.," he said. "I'll watch the house. I can't promise that my methods will be orthodox. But—" He broke off, listening.

It seemed that there were sounds coming from the dining room, sounds that came from the general location of the trunk that he had seen within that room.

The girl spoke rapidly, filling up the silence with a barrage of words.

"I don't care about your methods. I want protection. I want protection for father. He's worried to death. I'm afraid of what he might do. He might get violent. You know. If someone tried to blackmail him, I mean. He might kill them."

"I see," said Dick Bentley.

There were no further sounds from the dining room. The girl ushered him to the door. He stepped out onto the porch. The thick door banged shut behind him. There was the sound of a clicking bolt and then silence. The spell of the great house gripped Bentley with a cold and clammy hand, like marsh mists arising from the ground in the chill of the morning.

He sensed that eyes were watching him from the darkened windows as he made his survey of the grounds, walking about, peering behind bushes, looking into patches of shadow; making a routine survey, yet always conscious of the fact that the forbidding house itself dominated the grounds as a corpse dominates a grave.

Nor could he forget the reactions which had been on the girl's face when he had asked her concerning possible physical peculiarities of her father's enemies.

CHAPTER TWO

Trunk of Terror

DICK completed a first patrol of the grounds, then slid in behind a bit of hedge, keeping to the shadows, watching and listening. There was no sound from the great pile of the dark mansion. Here and there a slight ribbon of light showed at a window, coming around the sides of a shade. But, for the most part the house was dark, silent and sombre.

Bentley waited. He wanted to find out more before he notified the police about that corpse. It was his duty to protect his clients. He wouldn't countenance crime, nor cover a murder merely in order to protect those who had employed him; but he was going to make pretty certain that he knew where the cards lay before he started to lead.

Half an hour passed during which there was nothing to be seen at the house, nothing to disturb the quiet of the grounds. Then an automobile swept into the driveway. A man opened the car door.

Dick Bentley moved so that he could command a view of the driveway, and the maneuver did him no good. For the driver of the car switched out his headlights. A man jumped to the ground, ran up the stairs.

Dick could see that he carried a suitcase, that he was of medium height and very active. Beyond that, he could see nothing. For the figure jumped up the steps to the porch with lithe step, the big door swung silently open, and the figure vanished into the dark interior of that unlighted hallway with a purposeful rapidity which somehow suggested a doctor, summoned upon a hurried emergency, rushing ino a house without formality or greeting, his mind absorbed in the problem which is to confront him.

Bentley could make out the shape of a man, sitting behind the wheel of the automobile. A faint pin prick of red light in the darkness, glowing and paling alternately, indicated the presence of a cigarette.

Dick moved toward the machine.

He heard the motor throb to life. Then the wheels churned the gravel. The car lurched into motion, swept around the circle of driveway, and hit the street with sufficient speed to cause the tires to screech a protest on the pavement. The sound of the motor died away to a distant snarl as the car sped down the paved road.

Bentley had his own car parked across the street, and debated with himself whether or not he should follow that speeding car, overtake it, crowd it to the curb and question the driver. But he decided against it. The luminous hands of his strap watch showed that it was not yet eleven o'clock by some forty minutes. The night was still young.

Fifteen or twenty minutes passed, and then the sound of a truck rumbling along the highway brought Dick once more to a position near the front of the house. This was what he had been expecting, what he had been waiting for.

The truck lumbered along into view,

hesitated as though the driver was making certain of house numbers, and then turned into the driveway. The truck stopped. It was a light moving truck, and two very husky men sat on the front seat. These men alighted. The headlights were left on, the motor left running.

The pair walked up to the steps, and, as though their presence had been anticipated for some little time, the door opened once more and a dark figure stood just over the threshold.

But the men from the truck did not go in. Instead, the man on the threshold stood aside, after a brief, low-voiced conference. The pair picked up the huge wardrobe trunk, which had evidently been moved in the meantime to a position in the hallway where it would just clear the opening door.

As the men carried the trunk to the truck, Bentley slipped across the street to his automobile. As the truck lumbered out of the driveway, Dick's foot pressed the starter. He had the motor warmed up before the truck had gone half a block, and was in pursuit as soon as he dared to turn on his headlights.

BENTLEY sped alongside the truck when it had gone some ten blocks, and waved his hand, signifying that he wished the men to stop. As he climbed out of his car and walked over to the truck, his right hand was ready to grab for the automatic which nestled in the shoulder holster.

But the men in the truck seemed merely mildly curious.

"Sorry to bother you, but I got a change in the delivery address on that trunk," said Dick.

"Yeah?" asked one of the men in a tone that showed no emotion of any sort. It was a purely casual, mechanical tone of voice.

"Yes," said Bentley, "Mr. Oliver decided he'd have it sent to another address

for tonight, and then move on later."

"O. K.," said the truck driver impatiently, "what's the address?"

Bentley gave the address of his own apartment. The truck driver repeated it mechanically, said: "O. K., buddy," and pushed the gears into mesh.

It was done that simply.

Dick trailed along behind the truck. Evidently the men were merely moving men who had called for a trunk in response to a telephone call. They considered it all in the day's work. If the man who had sent the trunk wanted to give a change of address, that was all in the game so far as the truckmen were concerned.

Bently parked his car in front of the entrance to his apartment, showed the men where the freight elevator was, rode up with them, and superintended the placing of the trunk in his apartment. He noticed that the men handled the trunk carefully, overheard one of them commenting on the fact that their instructions had been to keep it right side up and to refrain from giving it any hard bumps.

Dick paid them, gave them a tip, saw them to the elevator, walked back to his apartment, locked the door, got a hammer and chisel and set to work on the lock. It took but a matter of seconds to get it open.

"Now then," said Dick, grimly, "we'll start identifying this corpse, and then we'll know what we've got ahead of us."

He pushed back the halves of the trunk, glanced inside, and then abruptly recoiled.

He had expected to see the gruesome figure of the murdered man, probably strapped into position so that he would not slump around inside the trunk when it was lifted. But he was totally unprepared for the sight which actually met his eyes.

A beautiful young woman, hardly more

than twenty, clad in the filmiest of underthings, was sitting on a little three-legged stool which had been wired into position. A sheet had been torn into strips and used to keep the young woman from shifting about, the strips passing around her shoulders, waist and arms, and being tied to cleats which had been nailed to the interior of the trunk on the back.

At first glance Bently thought that the young woman was dead. Her head was lolling on one side, her knees were doubled up under her chin, and her eyes were closed upon pallid cheeks.

But, as soon as he touched her, he realized that she was alive but unconscious. She had evidently been drugged with some very powerful opiate.

He untied the sheets from the cleats, lifted her from the stool. She was well formed, athletic, and heavy. There was no fat on her graceful body, but she was well muscled.

Dick carried her into the bedroom, placed her on a bed, covered her over with a sheet, went to the bathroom, wet a towel with cold water, came back, and sopped the face and throat.

"Wake up! Wake up!" he called.

The eyelids fluttered faintly, but there was no other response.

Dick paused to consider her.

She was beautiful, fresh, young, girlish. The filmy undergarments had evidently been tailored to order from the most expensive materials. Everything about her spoke of wealth and breeding. And Dick knew that it would never do to allow the police to come in on the case, giving the resulting publicity to the press. Whoever this young woman might be, she was one who must be protected.

DICK BENTLEY snapped his jaw shut, his lips clamped into a firm line; he went to the telephone and called a physician in whose discretion he had confidence.

"Get a nurse," he instructed the doctor, "come to my apartment. I'll leave the door open. You'll find your patient in bed, unconscious. See that everything is done that can be done, and get her to talk as soon as you can restore her to consciousness. Be sure that there isn't any one in the room when she does talk, except yourself. I don't want even the nurse to hear what she has to say. Tell her Mr. Bentley took her to his apartment because he thought it was the safest place for her.

"Answer the telephone whenever it rings. If it's anyone you don't know, say you're the valet. If it's my voice, tell me about the patient, but don't tell anyone else. You got that straight?"

And he was reassured to hear the close-clipped voice of the physician over the wire.

"I'll be there with the nurse in fifteen minutes."

Dick hung up the telephone, ran to the elevator, got into his car and speeded back to the mysterious residence where he had been summoned. He shut off his motor when he was two blocks away, switched out headlights and kicked out the clutch. He coasted noiselessly to the curb, parked the car, and went once more into the dark mystery of the well-kept grounds.

He was wondering what had happened to that crippled corpse, and he proposed to find out. Things had gone quite far enough within that dark, sinister house.

He circled the place, cautiously, seeking to make certain that there was no one lurking in the shadows, ready to take him at a disadvantage.

When he had reached the back of the house, he heard voices, voices that seemed to be raised in anger.

Dick moved cautiously forward, found a lighted window where the shade had been pulled. He slipped a gun from its holster, opened a blade of his knife that was equipped with a diamond glass cutter, and cut a circle of glass from the pane. When he had about completed the circle, he chewed up a couple of sticks of gum, pressed them against the glass, completed the circle, and lifted the glass from the window.

The gum held only long enough to enable him to get the glass outside of the pane. Then the circle slipped to the ground. But it struck in soft loam and there was no noise.

Voices were coming from the interior of the room, and they sounded much louder now that Dick had removed a section of the glass. He could hear words now.

". . . do as I say," a man was saying in a harsh, angry voice, "or go to the chair for murder."

"I tell you," rasped a deeper voice, a voice whose owner seemed more given to emotion and less to thought, "that Vera says he had an opportunity to look in the dining room. S'pose he looked in the trunk?"

The first voice answered that question in calm menace. "If he looked in that trunk, he's got to be removed. I don't think he did."

"How you going to remove him?"

"Easy. Same way we did the girl."

"The girl wasn't so dangerous."

"That's true. You do as I say. When Bob comes home we'll stage this thing, and stage it right. I tell you we don't need to worry so much about the others. It's Blaire that'll make us the trouble."

Bentley took the blade of his knife, sharpened until it had an edge like a razor, and gave a quick thrust at the curtain. He paused for a moment, wondering if the protruding knife blade had been discovered, then jerked sharply down and withdrew the blade.

He had a little slit in the curtain now, through which he could peer, and the occupants of the room had not noticed that knife point. They were talking again.

". . . Stella telephoned that she'd done her end of the job, and you can look for them out here at any time."

Dick inserted his finger tip to the slit he had cut in the curtain shade, and gently pulled the gap open so that he could see into the room. He was staring directly at the man who was doing the talking.

His eye widened with utter incredulity. Despite himself, veteran of hundreds of crimes that he was, he felt the breath coming into his lungs in a quick, gasping intake.

For the man who was doing the talking, using a cane to gesticulate with, was an elderly man with gray side whiskers, a long, thin mouth, white hair, eyeglasses that were attached to his coat with a wide black ribbon, a suit of clothes that was a distinctive plaid, and a leg that was evidently shorter than its mate.

It was, in short, if Dick's startled senses were any criterion whatever, the same man he had seen seated in the wardrobe trunk, the top of his head caved in, the gray pallor of death about his skin, the glassy stare in his filmed eyes.

The crippled corpse had come to life!

CHAPTER THREE

The Crippled Corpse

AS BENTLEY was staring in incredulous amazement, he heard the sound of a motor from the front of the house, the noise of a machine turning into the graveled driveway.

The man with the cane was speaking now. "All right, Sam. This is your chance to make a perfect play. Get on the job and do exactly as I have instructed you. Exactly, mind you! This is no time for halfway measures!"

And, with a muttered, "Yes, sir," the liveried form of the butler crossed Dick Bentley's line of vision and made for the doorway which apparently opened into the lower corridor.

Dick Bentley dropped the slit back into place by simply removing his finger. He turned away from the window, and ran to the front of the house. He wanted very much to see this new arrival who had evidently complicated the situation by bringing it to a definite crisis.

He gained the front of the house in time to see a taxicab roll away, while two figures were walking toward the steps of the front stoop. This time the light switch clicked on, and the porch light sharply outlined the two figures against the background of the dark night.

There was a young woman, clad in an evening gown, beautiful, form-revealing. Her wrap had slipped down her bare shoulders and was trailing, unnoticed along the gravel behind her, the cloth making little rasping noises as it rubbed the rounded pebbles together.

She was half supporting a young man in evening clothes, a man who had evidently had one or two drinks too many, yet carried himself proudly, despite the fact that it was necessary for him to lean rather heavily upon the arm of the girl.

He staggered as he started up the steps, and she flung an arm around him for support. Her shoulders gleamed whitely in the light of the incandescent in the top of the porch. She was beautiful of figure and of feature. There was, however, a certain hardness about her, a diamond-like efficiency which made of her beauty something of blued steel.

Dick Bentley caught a glimpse of her profile, and it was like a cameo, not in outline, but in hardness. She was a young and beautiful woman who should have been filled with enthusiasm and with idealistic illusions concerning life; yet she seemed, somehow, to have learned all that life had to teach, to have tasted the dregs of the cup of bitterness. She had retained her beauty, but had lost her soul.

Together, the man and woman wove their uncertain way up the steps. Then they crossed the porch, moving more sedately. The young man was evidently accustomed to carry his liquor, given anything like a reasonable amount of it.

At the doorway, the girl said something to him.

He turned to her, gazed down at her steady eyes, flung an arm around the bare shoulders, drew her to him, and kissed her full upon the half-parted lips.

During the embrace she did not close her eyes, but stared straight into his face with eyes that were wide open, hard and calculating.

Then the door opened, and the liveried form of the butler appeared framed in the oblong. He said something which Dick could not hear, stretched forth a hand, gripped the young man in evening clothes under the left arm, and ushered him into the hallway. The girl crowded along on the other side, supporting the figure in evening clothes.

The cab drove away. The door slammed.

Bentley left his place of concealment, and walked back to the place where he had cut the circle of glass from the window. Somehow, he felt as though the final act of a drama was about to be enacted before his eyes.

HE reached his spot of vantage just as the three came into the room. He could see them in the doorway, the young man in evening clothes, staring somewhat stupidly, the butler, solicitous, the young woman, diamond-hard, steady-eyed.

The man with the cane hobbled forward. "So you're Bob Oliver!" he said, and his words contained a measure of contempt that cut through the consciousness of the young man, befuddled as it was by alcohol.

"Who're you?" he demanded.

The crippled man brandished the cane.

"You've heard of me, young fellow. I'm Frank Blaire, your father's lawyer. And I came here tonight because your father was in serious difficulty. And what do I find? I find you, sir, disgracing this roof, dragging the name of your sister into the mud, by bringing home a woman of the streets, a pick-up, probably, who attached herself to you in some night club.

"For shame! For very shame! That you should bring this disgrace upon the head of your father!"

The words had a very different effect upon the three in the doorway. The butler bowed his head, as though forced to agree with what the crippled man had said. The girl held her head the higher, chin thrust out, eyes blazing. Bob Oliver, the young man in evening clothes, flushed, seemed to lose much of his alcoholic daze, to stand that much straighter.

"You lie!" said the girl, her eyes defiant, her face very pale, and very, very hard.

The crippled lawyer hobbled over to her, thrust his head to a position within a few inches of her face. "No," he said "I can see it in your eyes, street-walker, scum of the gutter, betrayer of innocence! What have you done to this young man?"

The girl snapped out crisp words. "Slap him, Bob!"

And Bob Oliver's right hand swung around in a stinging slap.

"Curb your tongue, damn you!" he stormed. "The girl's as decent as you are, more so—"

He didn't finish.

The crippled lawyer seemed to wilt under the sting of that slap. He staggered backward, raised his cane, lost his balance, toppled down, just out of range of Dick Bentley's vision. Dick heard a jarring thud, heard the young woman scream, heard the butler give a sudden exclamation.

"He's hit his head!" said the butler, and sprang forward.

Bob Oliver was standing very erect now, his arm around the girl's waist. "Let him hit it and be damned to him!" he said. "It will teach him not to lay his slanderous tongue on a young woman about whom he knows nothing. The old fool!"

The voice of the butler came drifting up from beyond Dick Bentley's range of vision. "Quick, this is serious!"

Then the young woman pulled herself free from Bob Oliver's arm, and moved forward. Last to go was Oliver himself. But he had made no more than a couple of steps before the butler was back at his side.

"Quick, you've got to get out of here. This is serious. I'm afraid he's in a bad way."

"Get a doctor," said Bob Oliver.

"I'm afraid it's too late for a doctor. Quick. Let's get out of here and see what's to be done. This is horrible!" The butler grabbed Bob Oliver's arm.

"Where's sis?" asked the young man. "She'll know what to do. You can always bank on good old sis."

The butler pushed him back from the door. "Maybe we can find her, but I think she went out. You've got to get away, sir. Maybe we can hush it up. I'll swear it was an accident, that his cane slipped on a rug and that he fell. The young lady will back me up. You can go back uptown, and we'll say you weren't here at all."

And he pushed young Oliver from the room, raised a hand to the light switch and clicked off the lights.

But, just before the lights were clicked off, Dick Bentley had a chance to move and pull the curtain a little, so that he could see the form of the crippled lawyer. It was lying, sprawled out in a grotesque posture, the head flush against a brass andiron which protruded slightly from the fireplace. The form was lying very still.

Then darkness engulfed the room.

DICK BENTLEY could hear the sound of voices raised in an argument. He could hear the butler's tone of voice whiningly insistent, the girl's cold voice, as sharply outlined as her personality. Then he could hear the dazedly incredulous voice of the young man.

Bentley made a circle of the house. Then he walked up the front steps and rang the bell. The light clicked on, then the door opened. The butler stood on the threshold, looking very uncomfortable.

"What's going on?" asked Bentley.

"Nothing, sir. Master Bob came home. He had been dining, sir, and he made something of a commotion."

"I thought, perhaps, my services would be required," said Bentley.

"No, sir. Miss Oliver wasn't awakened, sir. She's retired. That is, I thought she'd retired, but it seems that she must have gone out somewhere. Master Robert is looking for her, and—" The butler paused to listen to some sound which came from the interior of the gloomy house. His face twitched. He muttered a sharp: "Excuse me, sir," and slammed the door.

Dick Bentley nodded, crossed over to the far side of the driveway, sat down and waited. He had to wait only a few minutes. A taxicab's lights danced down the roadway. The cab swung into the graveled driveway, came to a stop in front of the door, and young Oliver, a suitcase in his hand, overcoat over his arm, attired in a gray business suit and soft hat, came running across the porch.

He ran down to the taxicab, and there was only a slight trace of unsteadiness in his gait. He said something to the taxi driver. The door of the house slammed; the door of the cab slammed. The wheels spurned the gravel, and the cab hit the pavement. After it had gone three or four blocks, Dick Bentley stepped on the starter and followed.

The cab went to a downtown hotel.

Young Oliver entered the hotel and registered. Then he went to the room elevators and vanished.

Dick strolled into the hotel and noticed the name under which Oliver had registered—George Underwood.

Dick got in his car, drove back to his apartment. The nurse greeted him at the door, summoned the doctor. The doctor put his finger to his lips.

"No noise right now. She's going to be all right. Inside of half an hour you can talk with her."

Bentley shook his head doggedly. "Half an hour will be too late. I've got to talk with her now."

"She's been doped, and she's groggy," said the physician.

"Only one question," said Bentley.

"Very well," said the doctor, "only one." He led the way into the bedroom.

The girl was propped up on pillows, hair streaming down around her neck, her eyes showing as lead-heavy circles of utter disinterest.

Bentley walked into the room, and she made no move to follow him with her eyes. He crossed her line of vision, and it was as though she did not know he was in the room.

"Miss Oliver," said Bentley, "who was with you when you telephoned for Dick Bentley to come and protect you and your father?"

The eyes moved. The lids fluttered, drooped, raised. She seemed struggling to partial consciousness from some great depths of oblivion.

"Did anybody else know you had called me? Remember, I told you to keep my coming entirely secret."

She stared at him with lifeless, dejected eyes. "No," she said, slowly.

The doctor shook his head at Bentley.

"Let her come out of it. I'm afraid there's some terrific nervous shock that she's suffered. She keeps talking about a murder."

"What does she say about it?" demanded Bentley.

"Something about her brother," said the doctor.

The girl's eyes suddenly snapped to a more close focus. She seemed almost awake, aware of her surroundings. "Bob," she said, distinctly, "killed Frank Blaire, father's lawyer. He's got to run!" Then the head rolled around on the pillow and the eyes closed.

Dick Bentley turned, nodded, strode from the room.

"Do you know what she's talking about?" asked the doctor.

Bentley nodded, grimly.

"How did you know who she was? She wouldn't tell us. Yet she must have been unconscious when you found her. Did she come in that trunk?"

Bentley gave an impatient gesture with his head. "Can't answer fool questions now," he said. "Every time she makes that crack about Bob Oliver, her brother, murdering a lawyer, tell her that there's nothing to it. Otherwise she may get everything in a mess. Get her so she can talk as soon as you can. I'm on my way."

CHAPTER FOUR

Manhandler

DICK got in his car, drove back to the Oliver residence, and once more shut off the lights and motor, coasted to a parking place. This time he moved like some stealthy shadow, slipping through the night, going down the line of the hedge as a furtive prowler.

He came to the window from which he had cut the circle of glass. The room was dark. Dick Bentley placed his hand through the opening, and managed to reach the catch on the window. He opened it. Then he raised the roller shade, and crawled into the room.

It was dark and silent here, and there was a grim suggestion of an uncanny presence in the room. Dick moved with swift caution. There was a flashlight in his pocket, and he switched on the beam, directed it toward the fireplace.

The man lay there, just as he had seen him through that cut in the window curtain. The head had struck against the brass andiron. The legs were sprawled out. The glasses had fallen from the nose and were held by the black ribbon. The gray hair was flecked with red stains. The grim, uncompromising line of the mouth was firm and resolute, even obstinate. The gray side whiskers furnished a distinctive appearance to the face.

This time Dick intended to make certain that the crippled corpse would stay a corpse. He knelt by the body and felt of the wrist. It was utterly pulseless and cold. He touched the flesh of the face, even went so far as to explore the top of the head where the full strength of the blow had fallen.

The man was dead, beyond question.

Dick got up, switched off the flashlight, felt his way to the door of the room, opened it. He could hear voices. Those voices were humming in a swift buzz of conversation. Apparently two men were talking, and, at intervals, a woman joined in the conversation.

Bentley moved upon furtively silent feet. He went to the staircase, padded his way to the second story. All was quiet here. He used his flashlight to guide him. He tried door after door, went into the rooms, looked around. The fourth room furnished him with what he wanted. It was a bedroom, and the toilet articles on the dresser indicated that it was a woman's room.

Dick found a light suitcase on the floor, back of the dresser. He opened that suitcase, found a miscellaneous assortment of feminine apparel. He dumped this assortment from the suitcase, started exploring the corners.

His hand encountered some papers that crinkled under his touch, and he gave a little exclamation of satisfaction. He pulled out two letters and a telegram. The letters and telegram were all addressed to Miss Aileen Oliver, and the address was a very exclusive sorority house at a college town some hundred and fifty miles away.

Bentley shamelessly read the letters.

They were in a masculine hand, and were addressed to "Dearest Sunflower." The letters were very penitent in tone, and indicated that the writer would sooner have cut off his right hand than have done that which he had done. He mentioned that a reporter was trying to contact him, but that he had managed to elude the reporter.

DICK BENTLEY became absorbed in the letters. He read them twice, letting each phrase soak into his mind, getting himself, as nearly as possible, in mental tune with the writer.

Then he opened the telegram.

REPORTERS FOR SCANDAL SHEET HAVE DATA INDICATING YOU WERE PRESENT IN CHINESE OPIUM DEN SMOKING AT TIME OF RAID STOP THAT YOU ESCAPED ARREST BY POLICE BUT THAT INFORMATION IS ABOUT TO BE GIVEN TO COLLEGE AUTHORITIES IN CONNECTION WITH INVESTIGATION STOP MAN WHO CLAIMS TO BE DETECTIVE OFFERS SUPPRESS PROOF IN RETURN SUBSTANTIAL CASH SETTLEMENT STOP RETURN AT ONCE AND EXPLAIN AS I DON'T INTEND TO PAY THESE BLACKMAILERS ONE CENT BUT WANT FACTS AVAILABLE BEFORE TAKING FINAL ACTION.

The telegram was signed merely by the initials "G. O."

Dick pocketed the telegram. Then he turned his attention to the letters again, studying the envelopes. Each bore a return address of W. B. H. 452 Maplewood, and a postmark which showed that they had been posted within the last three days at the city post office.

Bentley got to his feet, looked around the room, using the beam of the flashlight to guide him, then went to the stairs, down them, along the corridor and out into the night. His face was grim and savage. His brows were level lines over eyes that were hard as flints.

He sought out his car, drove savagely toward town, stopped at the first drug store that was open to telephone the doctor at his apartment.

"Has she talked yet?"

"No, but she's snapping out of it," said the physician.

"O. K.," rasped Bentley. "Put her back to sleep. Don't let her talk, even to you."

"I thought you wanted her to talk."

"Well, I don't—not now."

And Bentley slammed the receiver back on the hook, strode from the drug store, broke several speed limits in getting to the downtown hotel. He got the number of the room which had been assigned to George Underwood, took the elevator, walked down the corridor and knocked on the door.

"Who is it?" called a voice from the other side of the door.

"Open up," gruffed Bentley.

"But who do you want?"

"You, George Underwood."

"What do you want?"

"I want to talk with you, and I don't propose to wait here all night."

The door opened a crack. Young Oliver stood on the threshold. "I'm certain there's some mistake," he said. "You see, I'm not really George Underwood—that is, my name isn't—"

Bentley gave a grunt and shoved his shoulder against the door. The door pushed inward, and young Oliver, swept backward by the shove of the door, sprawled on the bed.

He had on athletic underwear. His face was lined with worry, and the color had gone from his cheeks. But his lips were firm and the eyes were steady. There was the reek of alcohol on his breath.

Bentley kicked the door shut, walked into the bathroom, turned on the cold water in the shower, returned to the bed. He grabbed the young man by a shoulder, jerked him to the floor. "Get under that shower," he said, "and stay there until you're cold sober. Then come back so I can talk to you."

THE young man wavered, caught a glimpse of Dick Bentley's jutting jaw, and moved toward the shower. He divested himself of his underwear with shaking hands, thrust a tentative arm and shoulder inside the shower curtain, then squealed and drew back as the shock of the cold water hit his skin.

"Go on in," said Bentley.

The young man darted back of the curtain, gave a little squawk, and come out, glistening. Dick Bentley caught him, flung him back inside the curtain. "Stay there until I tell you to come out," he said.

The curtain billowed under the struggles of young Oliver as he tried to break out from the shower. Bentley pushed him back until some two or three minutes had elapsed. Then he opened the curtains, threw the lad a towel. "Now come out here and talk to me," he said.

The young man's teeth were chattering, but his eyes were clear, and he scrubbed himself into a glow with the coarse towel. When he spoke his voice held more assurance.

"Where did you get that young woman who came out to the house with you?" asked Bentley.

"You know who I am?" Oliver countered.

"Yes, and I know what you're running away from."

Oliver shuddered. "She was a pick-up," he said. "But she was a superior sort of a girl, and I wasn't going to sit down and have some old buzzard call her a street walker."

"Naturally," agreed Bentley. "Now here's what I want you to do. I want you to go on back and face the music. I want you to go to this address and pick up your sister. You'll find her there, and she may be a bit groggy. Get her in shape and wait for me. I'm going to take you both back with me.

"There'll be a doctor there. I'll tell him you're coming out to get the girl. Don't talk to her about what you think happened, and don't let her talk to you about it."

The young man shuddered. "But you know what it means! There'll be a scandal. I can't prove self-defense against an old man like him. And he was a cripple—"

Dick Bentley was impatient. "Don't be a fool," he said. "Get busy and do what I tell you to. Can I count on you—for your sister's sake?"

"Who are you?" asked Oliver, cautiously.

"A detective your sister hired as soon as she got off the plane. She thought there was some danger threatening your father."

"Is there?"

Bentley nodded. "There is, and I've got to work fast if I'm going to earn my pay on this case. I've got no time to stand here arguing. You going back the way I asked you to, or shall I start doing something about it?"

Oliver sighed. "I'm going back," he said. "I didn't even want to run away in the first place, but they made me do it."

"O. K.," said Bentley. "I'm depending on you. Fail me, and you're putting your sister in a tough spot."

"I won't fail," promised Oliver.

Bentley nodded, unlocked the door.

"And make it snappy!" he called over his shoulder, as he went into the hall.

HE left the hotel, went to his car and drove to 452 Maplewood. It was a small apartment house, narrow, sandwiched in between a couple of small stores on one side and an office building on the other. There were two apartments on each floor, one in front and one in back, and there were five floors.

Bentley scanned the directory of mail boxes and found only one where the initials were W. B. H. That was an apartment in the name of William B. Harlowe.

Dick noted the number, and then went on up the stairs. He did not seem to be in a hurry, nor did he seem to be wasting any time. He moved with a steady, remorseless inflexity of purpose that made him seem like an executioner going to the condemned row to bring out a victim.

He found the apartment and banged on the door.

A sleepy voice from the inside demanded to know who was there. Dick Bentley wasted no time in words. "Open up," he said, grimly.

"Who is it?"

"Telegram for Mister Harlowe."

There was the sound of bedsprings creaking, bare feet slapping the floor, then a muffled, cautious voice, that said: "How do I know it's a telegram?"

"If you don't want it," retorted Bentley, "it don't make any difference to me."

There was a moment of silence.

"O. K.," said Bentley. "I'm going, brother. I tried to deliver it."

He turned away from the door, made loud steps to the stairs, clumped down the first three stairs, then, as he heard the rattle of a bolt on the other side of the door, made a quick, silent leap. He was running toward the door of the room upon stealthy feet, shoulders down, like a running football player, as he heard the knob turn and saw the door open a crack.

Bentley lowered his left shoulder so that it would take the force of the impact, and hurled himself through the air. He slammed into the door with the force of a hundred and eighty-five pounds of momentum behind him. The door crashed back. The figure of the man in pajamas sprawled on the floor.

Bentley caught his balance, kicked the door shut. The man in pajamas got to his feet. He was big, well-formed, some six feet of him, slender-waisted, broad-shouldered, but there was a sallow look about his features, a pasty pallor of unhealthy hue.

"Say," he snarled, "what the hell do you mean by pulling that sort of a stunt?"

Dick Bentley measured the distance.

"I don't like it!" roared the big man, moving to set himself for a blow.

"Try this, then," said Dick Bentley, and crossed his left to the jaw. It was a swift blow, made without the faintest sign of drawing back the hand, the sort of a blow that is picked from the air and smashed home. Yet there was a shoulder follow-through that made the blow gather force as it travelled. It caught the big man in pajamas on the jaw and staggered him.

"Want some more?" asked Bentley, speaking in a conversational tone.

The man bellowed and rushed.

Dick slammed his left to the face, ducked under a vicious right, jabbed his own right to the pit of the stomach, straightened, and brought the fist up with him as he straightened, giving the force of his body muscles to the uppercut.

The man gasped, swung wildly. Dick stepped cooly in, deliberately slammed his shod heel down upon the other's bare instep, crossed a vicious left and right.

Bill Harlowe wilted under the impact of those blows, under the torture of that grinding upon his instep.

"I ain't wasting time," remarked Dick Bentley, casually, as though he had been discussing the weather, or the tendency of the stock market. "Are you going to kick through now, or do you want some more?"

HARLOWE stood on one foot, his face stung to a dull red from the impact of the blows. His eyes were wavering now. He looked an impressive figure of a man, athletic of build, handsome of feature. He was the sort of a man who would have done well on a stage, the kind that would have made a matinée idol.

Yet, contrasted with the rugged virility of Dick Bentley, there was a subtle softness about him. He was like a dollar that appeared to be freshly minted without flaw, yet that did not ring true.

"Kick through with what?" he asked, but his eyes were averted.

Bentley slammed home a right to the jaw. It was done deliberately, without the slightest change of facial expression upon his part. He might have been an indulgent, but just, parent, correcting a wayward child.

The blow sent Harlowe sprawling back on the bed.

Bentley moved a step forward. "Are you going to kick through now, or do you want some more?" he asked.

At the repetition of the words Harlowe flung himself from the bed, fighting as a rat will fight in a corner. He was several inches taller than Bentley. His shoulders were broader, his reach greater. He had everything that seemed necessary to master the man who was so insistent upon his 'kicking through,' save a touch of spirit. But that touch of spirit was painfully obvious. The outcome of the fight which followed was never in doubt for the least fraction of a second. The rugged manhood of Dick Bentley, his calm certainty in himself, made the other's efforts seem like futile, hysterical motions.

Harlowe launched wild blows. He lunged and jumped seemingly without thought, trusting to luck, spending himself in a wild frenzy. Bentley slammed home his blows with cool deliberation. When he had to take a blow from the other man he took it as a part of the game, braced to receive it, rolling his head slightly to break the force. He didn't waste time putting up a guard, but devoted his energy to throwing his fists into the other man's anatomy.

Harlowe staggered, poised.

Bentley pulled a vicious right swing with all of his force behind it. It smashed full in Harlowe's face. There was the sound of crunching bone, a muffled scream, and Harlowe went back on the bed. His nose was flattened, twisted. Blood was streaming down it, as well as from his cut lips.

Bentley bent over him, calmly. "Are you going to kick through?" he asked, "or do you want some more?"

Harlowe hesitated.

Dick Bentley took his left hand and slapped it across the bridge of the man's broken nose. Harlowe screamed with agony.

"Are you going to kick through," asked Bentley again, casually, calmly, "or do you want some more?"

Harlowe flung his hands up in front of his mutilated face. He was a picture of cowering despair.

"What do you want to know?"

"I don't want to know anything," said Bentley. "I know all I need to know. I want confirmation, that's all. You're one of those lounge-lizard blackmailers that makes a business of luring prominent women into compromising positions. You double-crossed Aileen Oliver.

"She was a college kid, a little wild, perhaps, looking for new experiences.

You led her along until you felt sure she'd trust you anywhere. Then you took her into a Chinese dive and arranged to have it raided while she was there. You probably had her leave a purse with her cards in it, or something of the sort.

"Then your gang of blackmailers set to work on her dad. They wanted a bunch of hush money to keep it out of the papers, and all that sort of stuff. You wrote the kid how sorry you were, and strung her along in the same old way you've strung so many of 'em along. Is that right?"

THE man on the bed took his hands away from his face. The blood had streamed down over his silk pajamas. His split lips quivered.

"What makes you think I was in on it?"

"Nobody beside you," said Bentley, "knew that the girl had telephoned for me to come out. Yet when I came to the house I was expected. They didn't even need to turn on the light to see who I was. They just let me right in the house and called me by name. That means somebody had tipped them off. It had to be you.

"I'm sure of my ground up to that point, But I'm not sure of it from there on. Something happened, and I'm not sure what it was unless the butler was in on the blackmail. Was he?"

The man did not answer.

Dick Bentley doubled his fist, drew it back. "Was he?" he asked.

The man's startled eyes stared in abject terror at the menace of that doubled fist. "Yes," he yelled, "he was."

"I thought so," said Dick.

He crossed to the wall where there was a telephone, called police headquarters. The man on the bed was making futile efforts to stop the bleeding of his broken nose, holding a pillow against his bruised face.

Bentley spoke mechanically. "Send the homicide squad out to 452 Maplewood. There's a man you'll find on the fourth floor in the rear apartment. His name's Harlowe. He's got a confession to make about a murder—yeah, the murder of Frank Blaire, a lawyer."

Harlowe screamed a muffled protest. "I wasn't in on the murder. I don't know anything about it."

Bentley slammed the telephone receiver back on the hook, crossed the room, took handcuffs from his pocket.

"Not the murder! I don't know about the murder!" Harlowe whimpered.

"About the murder," said Bentley. "When the cops come, tell them about the murder. Or I'll give you something that'll make these seem like love pats. Remember that!"

He grabbed one of the man's wrists, locked the handcuffs about it. Then he took the other handcuff, passed it through the brass tubing on the foot of the bed, put the other wrist over the top of the tubing and clicked the handcuff into place.

"I'm leaving the key over here on the dresser," he said. "You can tell the cops where it is when they come."

"I'll bleed to death," babbled the man, the blood coursing down his features as he spoke, bubbling from his lips and his mutilated nostrils as he tried to breathe.

"Go right ahead," said Dick Bentley. "Society won't lose anything. I hope you do, but I'm afraid you won't."

And he walked out of the place, leaving the door closed but unlocked.

CHAPTER FIVE

"That's Service!"

HE walked down the flight of stairs, hit the cold street, crossed to his car, and drove to his apartment. He left the elevator, pressed the buzzer on the door. The nurse was white-faced.

"Her brother here?" he asked.

The nurse nodded. "It's awful," she said.

Dick Bentley pushed past her. He walked into the bedroom. The girl was sitting up in bed, crying. Bob Oliver was on the side of the bed, soothing her. His face was very white, very set, very purposeful. The doctor was staring at them with a look in which professional concern was mingled with sympathetic curiosity.

Bentley noticed the girl's eyes come to him, and focus. She was in full possession of her faculties now, a little groggy, perhaps, but perfectly awake.

"You're Dick Bentley," she said.

Dick bowed, said: "And at your service."

She shook her head. "No. I didn't get you soon enough. But I still don't know what happened, or how it happened. Oh, it's awful! Awful! Tell me, will they . . . Bob, you know . . . the thing is just too horrible to think about. Why did he do it? They won't claim it was first-degree—"

Dick shook his head at her. "Forget it. You were given some powerful drug that was a hypnotic, and then they told you that Bob had done what you thought he did."

"But he did do it," she insisted. "He says he did it himself."

Dick's face was grim. "Can you wear some of my clothes?" he asked. "I want you to come with me, and we're going to clear this thing up. You couldn't have known that Bob did anything because he didn't even come home until after you had gone under. You're suffering from a suggestion that they planted in your mind as you were going under the hypnotic. Tell me, do you know who gave it to you?"

She rolled her head in a negative. "It might have been the butler. I know he was near me, and I felt something jab me. Then after a while I began to feel

funny. And there were a lot of people telling me things. They said Bob— Well, you know what they said. I tried to tell them they lied, I couldn't keep awake long enough. I drifted off to sleep. And then Bob came, and he said—"

"Never mind what he said," Bentley snapped at her. "I told him not to talk with you about that. I'm going to get some clothes on you and take you back there."

"How did I get here?"

"You were carried here."

"But this is where you live."

"Yes, I got you a transfer from your intended destination."

"Where was that?"

"I don't know. That is, I'm not sure. I think I know, but I'm going to find out more about it."

The girl looked at the nurse. "Can you get some clothes on me?"

The nurse glanced at the doctor. The doctor nodded.

"Some of my things," said Bentley. "She can wear them. They'll be frightfully big for her, but she can put on a coat."

The nurse spoke up. "I've got a suitcase with some extra things. She can wear a nurse's uniform."

"Dandy," agreed Dick. "Get her dressed. We'll wait in the other room."

HE escorted Bob Oliver into the outer room. Oliver started to ply him with questions. Dick shook his head impatiently, refused to answer them.

"Wait," he said. "We'll see if the theory doesn't check out when we get there. There's no use building air castles when we don't know any of the facts."

He smoked a cigarette, and then the girl appeared in the doorway, a little shaky in appearance, but looking fresh and neat in a nurse's uniform. Bentley took one arm, her brother the other, and they escorted the girl to his car. The fresh air of the ride did her good. By the time they arrived at the gloomy residence which sat back from the street in its shadow-splotched grounds, the girl was feeling much more like herself.

Bentley pressed his finger on the doorbell.

There was a pause, then the sound of a clicking lock. The porch light blazed on. The butler stared at them with eyes that bulged with startled surprise.

"But you can't—it isn't convenient—you mustn't—"

Dick pushed his way into the door. "Right about face, don't make any sudden moves, and don't get out of my sight," he said.

The butler gasped. "But—"

Dick grabbed a shoulder, whirled him around. "That's right about face," he said, "and this means forward march!"

And he swung his boot in a swiftly vicious arc that landed with a thud and lifted the butler an inch or two from the floor. Then Dick's right hand snaked the automatic from its holster and jabbed it into the spine of the butler.

"On your way," growled Bentley, "and no funny stuff."

The butler started marching, stiffly, mouthing protests.

There were loud voices coming from the library. Dick pushed the butler ahead of him, on into the room.

A dignified man with iron-gray hair and tortoise-shell spectacles sat at the big table, a glass of whiskey and soda in front of him. A thin man stood across the room, his bony forefinger leveled at the man in the chair. A rather heavy-set individual was seated in a corner of the room. There were two girls sprawled on a leather couch, one the girl that had claimed to Bentley she was Aileen Oliver, the other the girl who had come to the house with George Oliver.

"Dad," said Aileen, and ran toward the man who sat at the table.

He kissed her, patted her back, then made a motion of dismissal; said: "Run to your room, Aileen. There's an important business conference going on here. Bob, I want you to stay. They told me you'd run away. That didn't seem like an Oliver, somehow. I'm glad you're back."

Bentley walked to the middle of the floor. The automatic was in his hand. "Wait a minute," he said. "Perhaps I can short-cut things a little bit."

The girl who had claimed to be Aileen Oliver jumped from the couch. The thin man shifted his bony forefinger, pointed it at Dick.

"That man is a trouble maker. Either he goes out and stays out, or you can't make any deal with us at all!"

Dick turned to stare at him, slowly shifted the automatic. "Shut up," he said. "I'm going to talk." He turned to the man at the table. "Let's see how near I can come to solving this thing and getting this bunch of blackmailers on the run. You're Mr. George Oliver?"

THE man at the table nodded. He was watching Bentley with eyes that were accustomed to judge character and reach decisions. "Yes," he said. "Go ahead and talk."

Bentley nodded, said: "O. K. A lounge lizard framed your daughter. Blackmailers fastened on you. You threatened to fight and wired for your daughter to come home and face the music. You got Frank Blaire, an attorney with a crippled leg to come here to meet the blackmailers. You went away somewhere, so you wouldn't be around to make statements that might be used against you. You did that probably at the last minute on the advise of your lawyer.

"Then your daughter telephoned for me. Her lounge lizard got wise and tipped the bunch off. That frightened them. They tried to rush things. The lawyer had them checkmated, probably had some pretty damaging knowledge. There was a fight. The crooks lost their temper and hit Blaire over the head. He died.

"They lost their heads, were going to try and ship the body out of here. Then the girl came home. They were afraid she'd find out what had happened, so they slipped her a shot and put her to sleep. They had the body in a trunk they'd found in the storage room here, and had ripped the insides out of it so it'd contain the body. Then they remembered the old fox here, and they telephoned him.

"But about that time I showed up. They wanted to put me where I'd be out of the game. So the butler received me in the dark, pretended he was George Oliver, and told me he didn't want me hanging around. Then he got me in a lighted room, appeared in his true character, ushered in one of the blackmailers, the girl over there, and told me she was Aileen. That girl gave me some phony instructions, and a song and dance.

"Then 'The Fox' arrived, with his bag of tricks. He's an actor, adept at disguises, and a shrewd thinker. He doped out a new scheme. He was going to let Aileen come to consciousness, or almost regain consciousness, tell her her brother had committed the murder and then drug her again. They did that. Then they took her clothes, and put her in the trunk. She was to be shipped to Harlowe's apartment so that she'd find herself in such a compromising position everyone would have to consent to marriage.

"Then The Fox took the clothes from the dead lawyer, made up to look like him, masqueraded around until the other girl could contact Bob Oliver in a speakeasy, get him drunk and bring him home. Then they staged a little show to make Bob think he'd killed the lawyer, and get him to skip out.

"Then you came back. You found the ring with another club over your head. Your son had committed a murder. There was the body lying right where The Fox had done his falling stunt. They switched out the lights. The Fox had taken off the lawyer's clothes, removed his own disguise, dressed the lawyer's body and put it in by the andiron.

"It almost worked, but it didn't. That's where I come in. I sidetracked the trunk so the girl didn't get to Harlowe's apartment, and I beat Harlowe into making a confession. The cops have got him now.

"Now this gang can either sit tight and all go to the chair, or they can pin the murder on the guy that really did it. Probably the squat individual with the surly look over there.

"Only make up your minds fast, folks, because the cops are going to be here in about three minutes."

Bentley stood in the center of the floor. His feet were braced far apart. His eyes were glaring savagely about him at the band of crooks who were staring at him in consternation.

George Oliver heaved a deep sigh. "That," he said, "is service!" And he met his daughter's eyes and smiled.

From the street came the wail of a siren.

"About thirty seconds left," said Bentley.

THE girl with the cameo profile looked at the bony man who had masqueraded as the crippled attorney. Then they both looked at the squat, surly man. That individual caught their glance. His lip curled.

"Oh, all right!" he said. He got to his feet. His eyes were staring steadily at Bentley. "You," he said slowly, "can go to hell. And here's your ticket."

His right hand moved but a few inches. There was the glint of blued steel. He had had an automatic concealed in the left sleeve of his coat. He had only to make a gesture with that arm and the weapon fell, ready to be used, right into his right hand.

One of the women screamed. The gun spat fire, and Dick Bentley, standing with his legs wide apart, lips grim, eyes scornful, shot from the hip.

The squat man doubled up sharply, tried to straighten, coughed and spat blood. He tried to say something, failed, staggered, then pitched forward.

"Anybody else?" asked Bentley.

The man he had referred to as The Fox shook his head. "That wipes the slate," he said. "There's only a blackmail rap against the rest of us. We'd be foolish to swap lead over that."

Dick Bentley stared at him with sombre, savage eyes. "I'm sorry," he said. "I'd hoped you'd try something."

The bony man shook his head, raised his hands high in the air.

The sound of the siren screamed into a crescendo. It was coming up the driveway.

Dick Bentley caught the eye of Aileen Oliver, and bowed. "Next time," he said, "get me earlier. I could have saved you a lot of trouble. And don't worry about your boy friend. He wasn't worth wasting lead on, but he's lost that fatal beauty that made so many romantic girls fall for him.

"And, if you don't mind, I'll slip out of here before the police detain me as a material witness. I'm a free lance you know, and I have to turn my time into money." He slipped to the door, holstered his automatic.

As the police pounded up on the front steps, Dick Bentley slipped to the room where lay the crippled corpse, raised the window, and dropped out into the night.

In due time the police would find him and question him. But, in the meantime, there was another case which he'd promised to attend to as soon as the Oliver case was out of the way. And, as he had so aptly stated, his time was money.

He hit the soft turf, slipped into the shadows of the shrubbery, and the night swallowed him.

Murder in B Minor

by
James A. Goldthwaite

They were only scraps of scribbled music—crazy minors whistled up, night after night, through the fog-wisps. But they webbed the House of Conover with crimson threads of harmony—mad murder singsong—melody of death.

CHAPTER ONE

The Man With No Face

THE sound came quavering through the fog of midnight that filled the old-fashioned side street. A queer, singsong treble, floating upward through the mist, wandering into open windows, beating itself into silence against the brick walls. A sound to make children shrink closer to their mothers and men folk wonder if they had locked the outer doors before going to bed.

—and then the knife was struck from his hand.

In one of the houses that bordered the narrow, forgotten little way of the great city, a shriek rang out. A girl sat up in bed, her hands crushed over her racing heart. Her mouth was parched. The sweltering moist midsummer night pressed her down like a smothering blanket of melted lead.

The whistling man! The same sound that had brought her up sweating, panting for breath, the night before and the night before that. . . .

There was no sound now, only the far away dull roar of the city. The snoring of a great uneasy beast, moaning with the bad dreams and nightmares of wickedness in his sleep.

Mary Conover felt a cold electric shock start at her scalp and surge down her body, the prickling of millions of tiny needle points of ice.

Closer now. Out on the sidewalk under her window. It was nothing human, this tune. A weird, jangling discord of crazy minors, half a dozen notes over and over, the chattering laughter of a beast.

Out on the floor, with the spinules of the rug tickling her bare feet and her two hands jammed over her throat, Mary Conover sank to her knees before the window sill.

In the sea of mist, she could not see even the pavement four yards below. The whistling had stopped. Halfway along the face of the apartment house, to the left, somebody was rattling the door.

Her teeth were chattering. Mary jumped up and ran across the room to the door that opened into the hall of the apartment.

Further down the hall, another door was opening. An old man with gray hair stepped out into the hall. He stood motionless, listening. In the glary shine of the electric light bulb, his face was the color of raw dough. In one hand he held an ancient pistol more than a foot long.

At the sound of the girl's step, he spun round. A choked cry blurted from his lips. He saw who it was and the gun melted to his side.

"Uncle! What are you going to do?" the girl cried. "Who is out there?"

"Who's out there—nobody." The old man wet his lips. "What are you up for, Mary?"

"I heard somebody whistling. They tried the door."

"Only some drunks. They've gone along now. Better go back to bed."

"Then what are you out here for, with a pistol?" The girl flung her arms around the old man's neck. Her voice was a sob. "Uncle! Promise me you won't do anything foolish?" She shuddered. "Don't go out there—"

The old man patted her shoulder. "No, I won't go out, Mary. Everything's all right now. You're trembling like a leaf. Go back to bed and don't worry, dear."

The girl stood off and looked at him. "You're sure—that everything's all right? Will you go back to bed yourself, and lock your windows?"

Her uncle nodded. "I will, Mary. They won't come again, now. Good night—"

MARY CONOVER waited till she saw her uncle's door shut and heard the key snap in the lock before she went back into her own room. She was shivering with a nervous chill as she crawled into bed.

Outside, the beast of the city lay rumbling and moaning under the fog. The whistling was gone. In her imagination it kept jangling its mocking singsong over and over through her ears. With a sob, she pulled the covers over her head.

An hour, two hours later, she wakened again. She was wringing wet with perspiration as she threw off the covers and sat up in bed.

Out in the fog, the city beast lay doped and stupefied at last in his jungle.

Somewhere in the house, voices, rising and falling in murmuring waves. . . . One voice or two or three, she could not tell.

Mary slipped out of bed, fumbled for a wrap in the closet, ran across to the door, unlocked it, stepped outside and stole down the corridor to her uncle's door.

She tried the knob. The door was still locked. She called.

"Uncle Jerry! Uncle Jerry Conover!"

Up and down the passage her voice clattered eerily through the stillness. The murmuring voices were still. Silence, through all the house, silence, horrible, uncanny, more nerve-racking than any sound. . . .

She rattled the knob and called again.

"Uncle Jerry—"

She whirled. The door into the apartment had opened. On the threshold stood old Peter McNally, the janitor. McNally's room was directly underneath, in the basement. He had pulled on his coat and trousers over his nightshirt. He was shivering as though with cold.

"He doesn't answer. I'm afraid something has happened," the girl whispered. "I've been calling and calling—"

McNally nodded. He wet his lips. "We'll have to get in there—"

"Wait a minute. . I'll get something. Don't go away—"

Mary ran back down the passage to the kitchen and got a flatiron. McNally took it and smashed open a panel of the door.

He bent to peer in through the hole. There was no light in the room. There was no sound of talking, in there. There was another sound. The sound of a leaky soda fountain fizzing and fizzing.

McNally swore and crossed himself. He reached through the hole, turned the key on the inside and opened the door.

The windows were oblong gray eyes staring wide with horror in a flat black face. The shine of the corner arc-lights seeped through them with a seasick yellow glow. The glare of the electric bulb out in the hall behind threw long shadows over the threshold into the room. The table and bed in the corner bulked mysterious as crouching beasts.

The hall-light threw other shadows. Long, twisted shadows of the things that lay on the floor, halfway across the room. Two motionless bodies.

McNally stumbled forward, his teeth chattering, groping for the electric light switch. Behind him, he heard the girl's nightgown swish as she started to follow him. Then he heard her scream. He knew what she had screamed at. It was on his feet, too. But he had slippers on, and she was barefoot.

McNally found the switch. He tried three times before he could grip the swinging little chain and pull it. The light struck him between the eyes. He turned around and looked on the floor.

MARY CONOVER was standing with her little white feet in a river of red. It was trickling out of the head of the man who lay nearest her and spreading out slowly over the floor. McNally did not know whether he had ever seen the man before or not, because he had no face.

The other man was the one who was making the soda-fountain sound. He was Jerry Conover. His face was the color of crushed blueberries. He was blowing creamy soap-bubbles out of his purple lips.

McNally dropped on his knees at his side. He slid his fingers around his neck and whispered a prayer. He stood up, felt in his pants pocket, pulled out his pocket knife and opened it as he dropped to his knees again. He slid the point of the blade between the puffed-up weals of flesh on Conover's neck, and tugged.

A length of rope dropped off. It had been tied around Jerry's neck. Conover gasped and writhed in a convulsion as the air sucked into his lungs.

McNally stooped and picked him up in both arms.

"Bless God, he'll be alive, after all," he whispered. "Do ye get back to your own room, Mary dear, an' I'll be bringin' him there."

The girl walked in front of him down the hall. She swayed from side to side like a sleep-walker. Her feet left sticky red marks on the bare boards.

She stood on the threshold, clutching the doorjambs with both hands while Mc-Nally put her uncle onto her bed.

"Is he—will he—" she breathed.

The little janitor bustled past her.

"Sure, an' he'll be as good as new in five minutes. Don't ye be worryin', darlin'," he muttered.

He was wiping the sweat from his forehead. Mary heard him running water from the tap in the kitchen. He came back with a glassful, sat down on the bed and started to bathe Jerry Conover's face.

Mary looked at her feet. She bit her lips till they bled. She stumbled across to the bathroom. She went in and shut the door and turned the water on in the tub.

She went back to the bedroom. Jerry Conover lay with his eyes shut, breathing hard. His color was better.

McNally looked up at her. "He'll do now," he whispered. "Do ye go an' get dressed Mary, while I phone the cops."

CHAPTER TWO

The Melody of Death

INSPECTOR Daniel Shannon of Central Office peered over the head of Sergeant Meiggs at the young fellow who had just breezed, unsummoned, into the sanctum. With his natty blue suit, slick brown hair and pink cheeks, he looked more like a college freshman escaped from the campus than a graduate of the police academy.

The inspector clamped his jaw around the butt of a Corona-Corona and jerked his head.

"Come in here, Prentice. Get the high-low on this. It's right up your street." He turned back to Meiggs.

"The door was locked on the inside, you say the janitor and the girl told you. Key in the lock. Two men on the floor inside. One dead, with his skull knocked in. The other one—"

"Knocked in is the word," Meiggs said. "A piece of the bone had been cut out and then driven down a couple of inches into the head—"

Prentice had slid up and perched himself on a corner of the inspector's desk, with a late afternoon edition of an afternoon tabloid spread out in front of him.

"It says here that the piece of bone had a funny shape—"

"Like a triangle," Meiggs said. "About an inch on a side. The edges of the hole were what were the prettiest. They weren't smashed out. They were cut out. Cut as clean as if the thing had been driven down with a steel die."

"And the other man—"

"Old Conover. He was in a corner, trussed hands and legs like a picked chicken, McNally said. He was choking to death one breath at a time—"

"Who was doing it?"

"Nobody—not then. Some one had hog-shackled him first and then tied a piece of some funny kind of rope around his neck. Snug, but not tight enough to kill him. And then *wet it*. That made it shrink. It was made of something that shrank fast. As it tightened, a little at a time, it was shutting off the old man's wind. When McNally and the girl got there, he was the color of blueberry crush and blowing bubbles like a baby whale. Another sixty seconds would have finished him. Cute little business, what?"

Shannon chewed his Corona. "This one

that was killed. Who was he? Identified him yet?"

"Identified him—with what?" Meiggs jerked back. "I told you his face was gone, didn't I? Wiped clean off. Another funny thing about that. It wasn't done with the same tool that killed him. It was done with a hammer or a chisel—after he was killed. Quite a while after, because it wasn't bleeding so much."

"Meant a lot to somebody to keep dark who he was," Shannon mused. "How about the windows? There might have been another man, got out that way—"

"Locked on the inside when they went in, McNally and the girl said, every one of them."

"And the door, too. . . . Well, who pulled the job, then?"

"The guy that was croaked tied up Conover, that's a cinch," Meiggs said. He wouldn't—couldn't—have trussed himself up like that."

"Yeah? Then who knocked off the other guy and massaged his face with an axe? The spirits?" Shannon growled. "You say yourself that Conover couldn't wiggle anything but his eyelashes. And what did he do it with? You frisked the place from the key holes to the drain pipe and there wasn't a thing that could have hit a man and left a three-cornered mark like that.

"Another thing. Figure that a man did have a hammer with a trianguar head, or something, how hard would he have to hit to cut out a piece of bone an inch on a side and drive it into the middle of the brain?"

Prentice yawned. "He'd have to have dynamite behind it. It didn't happen, that's all."

"All right, you tell it, then," Meiggs grunted, getting up. He looked at his watch. "I've got to get up to the inquest."

Prentice slid off the desk to the floor and shook out another cigarette from his paper pack. "Guess I'll go too, Dan, if you haven't anything else for me," he said. "I'd like to see that skull with the two-inch hole in it."

Shannon nodded. "It's Tom's job, remember. But go ahead. Maybe you'll read the answer out of a dream book."

Meiggs laughed without mirth as he picked up his hat. "I'll make him a present of it. Come along, Sherlock. Got your gum shoes and telescope?"

Shannon's bleak gray eyes smiled with a queer look as they followed the figures of the grizzled detective sergeant and the brown-haired youngster through the door. Grown gray in the service of the department, Meiggs was a first-class man, steady, fearless, reliable and level-headed.

But he had not and never would have the thing that Prentice had been born with —the restless, oddly working brain, birthplace of incomprehensible hunches, that was camouflaged behind the vapid exterior of a college nitwit.

AT THE door of the Conover house, Prentice left Meiggs to go into the inquest.

As he loafed down the hallway toward the rear of the apartment, he saw that the room on the left where the killing had happened was jammed to the doors. Over the shoulders of a bunch of bluecoats, he made out the big, blond figure of Sven Skrenjold, a new coroner. Already Skrenjold had made a name as a strong-man publicity hound. His rasping shouts to a witness cut like a buzzsaw over the rumbling of voices. Between two figures on the outskirts of the crowd, Prentice caught a glimpse of a girl, her face frightened and tear-stained as she shrank back from the bulldozing official.

Prentice shrugged and went on. He came to the dining room and kitchen. Both were empty. Beyond, at the end of the hall, was a back door. The other side of this, a tiny entry. Out of the entry, a flight of stairs till he came to a cement cellar floor. Around a corner, a smallish, gray-haired and gray-eyed man sat in a dilapidated rocking chair before an open basement door, smoking a clay pipe.

The little man glanced up as Prentice paused in the door, regarding him with shrewdly narrowed eyes from behind the fog of smoke.

Prentice grinned. "Good morning."

The little man nodded noncommittally. "Good morning, sor-r-r."

Prentice lighted a cigarette and lounged up to the door. "I suppose you're the superintendent of this building?" he suggested casually.

The little man took out his pipe and spat into a crack. "Superintendent—av a dozen packages o' kindling wood tied up with rotten wall-paper," he retorted sarcastically. "Superintendent—yes. Name of McNally. Yours?"

Prentice laughed and gave his name. "Superintendent or not, you're comfortable down here. Lot of excitement upstairs, isn't there?"

McNally smoked silently a moment, his bright eyes boring into Prentice. Then: "Aye. Excitement enough. . . You'll be a detective, I suppose? Or wan av thim reporters, like?"

"I've got a friend upstairs, at the inquest," Prentice said. "I was just looking around for someone to talk to while I waited for him. Haven't you been up there yet—haven't they called you to testify?"

McNally took his pipe out with a jerk. "Aye—that I have!" he snapped. "Up to be bullied by that yellow-haired rascal with the brogue. It's little he found out from me, the haythen!"

Prentice nodded. "Skrenjold's rough. He'd get more out of his witnesses if he wasn't. He was grilling a girl just now as I came past. She was crying. Pretty little thing—know who she was?"

The janitor's eyes snapped. "If he har-rms her, the blackguard, I'll break ivery bone in his body!" he barked. " 'Tis Mary Conover, the old man's niece, the sweetest, loveliest lass this side o' County Kerry, mister. What she wouldn't do, and hasn't done, for her uncle, the old fool. . . . And of all the hell's divilment she's had to put up with from him one way and another, the last month—"

THE little janitor knocked the ashes out of his pipe and clattered to his feet, upsetting the chair.

"I vowed I'd not be telling a soul, mister, but I've got to," he exclaimed. "The things that happened in this house last night and the night before and the night before that—sure, they'd drive a body wild with the thought of 'em if he didn't tell it to someone. Listen here, Mr. Prentice sor-r—"

McNally paced the floor an instant, muttering to himself.

"There's no need o' me telling ye what iverybody knows by this time—how I heard Miss Mary screamin' for help an' put me pants on an' come up to her, an' what divil's picnic we found there in that room," he blurted at last. "But have ye heard the rest av it? The music part, an' the whistlin'?"

Prentice shook his head. To all appearances, the little janitor's story bored him. He was peering intently at a sparrow fluttering about in a pool of water.

"Whistling? Music? No. What about it?" he yawned.

"What about it? That's what I'd like to know!" McNally snorted. "Somebody whistlin' outside the house, at midnight. Footsteps tricklin' up and down, up and down, the way it sounded like a wild animal thryin' to find a place to get in—"

"One set of steps, or two?" Prentice interrupted.

"Wan set or two or three, how could I tell, all scufflin' an' mixed up the way they were?" McNally exclaimed. "An' whistlin'. Over and over the same. No kind of a chune that I ever heard before, mister. No chune that any human man iver made up. Some banshee's gibberish that fair dragged the heart o' me into my throat."

"Somebody whistling for Conover to let them in, probably," Prentice said. "Somebody he knew. That dead man up there—you ever see him hanging around here before?"

"Not me, the bloody ape," McNally growled. "Somebody whistlin' for auld Jerry to let 'em in, ye say? All right. And the same thing the night before and the night before that for goin' on a month. Whoiver it was wanted to see him, wanted him bad, I'm thinkin'. . . . Now then, what about these, mister? What are they—love letters?"

Out of his pocket McNally pulled a handful of fragments of paper. He spread them out on the bench beside Prentice.

"Out of Conover's wastebasket I got these," he muttered. "Wan at a time, ivery two or three days, for the last month or so."

Prentice looked down and nodded. "What's wonderful about that? Nothing but pieces of music scribbled in pencil. Looks like some one is studying harmony. What does Mary play—the piano?"

McNally came over to Prentice and stood looking up at him. The little man's cheeks were flushed. He reached out and gripped Prentice's arm in his thorny, work-calloused fingers.

"What does Mary play? Listen, mister," he whispered. "What I've told nivver a soul in the wor-rld yet. And then see what ye make av it. Not wan musical thing in the wor-rld does Mary play— piano nor fiddle nor nothing else. Nor she doesn't write music. I asked her once.

The auld man neither. Not wan thing do they know about it, at all—except that they hate it and they're scared to death av it! Now then?"

Prentice looked at McNally, reached over and picked up the music papers. "That's funny. If you don't want these for a day or two, I'd like to take them home and look them over," he said. "I know a little about music. I might think of something—"

There was a noise behind them. They looked around.

AT THE foot of the stairs stood a slender, timid-looking little man with a thin white face and mild blue eyes behind the lenses of his old-fashioned, gold-rimmed glasses. The eyes were bulged to the whites. The little man was staring at the scraps of paper in Prentice's hand.

"Oh, I beg p-pardon!" he stuttered. "I didn't mean to intrude, I'm s-sure."

"That's all right, Mr. Plum," McNally exclaimed. "Come right along. Meet Mr. Prentice, Mr. Plum. Mr. Prentice is a friend av mine, jist dropped in to talk things over, like."

Plum touched the tips of his clammy white fingers to Prentice's palm and giggled nervously. He had a high falsetto treble like a girl's. He wore cream-colored spats—in August.

"D-dreadful, wasn't it? I just got through with that—that ruffian upstairs. My, how he roared at me! I just w-wanted to s-slap his face!"

Plum giggled again in his queer, girlish way. He peered suddenly at Prentice out of his bird-bright blue eyes.

"I'd have given an orange sundae to see you do it," Prentice said. "He's up there, yet. Why don't you go back and do it now?"

"Eh? I d-don't understand," Plum chattered back. "Are you t-trying to m-make f-fun of me?"

"Mr. Plum has a room in the apartment over Conover's," McNally broke in, wiping off a grin with the back of his hand. "But he slept all through the racket last night. Didn't you, Mr. Plum?"

Plum ashed his cigarette. "All the w-way," he admitted smugly. "And I'm g-glad of it, too—I'm such a t-timid little thing. I'd have b-been scared out of my w-wits if I'd heard any of those n-noises."

"You know the Conovers?" Prentice asked.

"I'll s-say I do. P—particularly M-Mary. I've been d-dropping in there most every day, all s-summer. M-Mary's a real nice girl—maybe you've noticed that, P-Prentice. And the old man's been p-poorly and he l-likes to h-have company."

Prentice nodded. "I wonder if you would do me a favor, Plum?"

"Eh?" The little man's eyes popped behind his thick lenses.

"Don't get frightened. Nothing dangerous. Just take me up and introduce me to the Conovers," Prentice grinned.

Plum's relief was comical. He stared at Prentice a moment and then burst out laughing. "D-do you know what I was th-thinking of for a minute?" he twittered. "I th-thought you might be g-going to ask me to st-step down and s-see the c-captain. That's the w-way they do, isn't it?"

"I'm sure I don't know," Prentice said. "Better ask some cop."

At the foot of the stairs he turned to the little janitor. "Well, so long, McNally. I'll be seeing you—"

McNally waved his hand. "Good-by, Mr. Prentice. Come again—"

THE inquest was over upstairs. The hallway of the apartment was empty except for a pair of the medical examiner's men who were getting ready to take the body away. The kitchen door was shut. A drone of voices came from behind it. Plum knocked.

The door opened. He whispered a moment through the crack, then turned to Prentice.

"M-Mary says that her uncle is too s-sick to talk to anyone, and she is all tired out after last night and everything, and she can't see you."

Prentice nodded. "Some other time."

He walked a dozen feet down the hall and turned into the room where the murder had happened. The dead man lay on the floor. In life he had been a strapping customer, gaunt and big-boned. He had a mat of bristly gray hair. Under the ruin of what had once been a face were the remnants of a mouth and chin like a prize bull dog's. But his hands were white and soft. . .

Prentice stopped to peer at the wound in his head, a little way down the slope from the crown toward the neck, and on one side. As Meiggs had said, a triangle of flesh and bone fully an inch on a side had been cut out as cleanly as if by the impact of a tool-steel die, and driven a finger's length into the brain. And this done with the only other man in the room tied hand and foot, and all the exits locked.

Prentice bent lower. He ran his hands over the man's clothing. Of course he had been frisked already. But you never could tell. Sometimes things had been found on the second trip.

The pockets were empty. Inside the lining of the vest, at the bottom, a round, flat shape. . .

With a blade of his pocket knife, Prentice ripped a slit in the cloth. The medical examiner's men were standing back, waiting for him to get through. He slipped the thing out, covering it with his hand. Over his shoulder he heard Plum's voice twittering like a sparrow.

"Oh, you f-found something! Wh-what

is it, Mr. P-Prentice? Hadn't you ought to g-give it to the c-cops?"

"Just a button," Prentice said. "I'm beginning to think you're a cop yourself, the way you hang around."

He stood still, letting his eyes travel around the room. There were only a few pieces of furniture—rug, bed, table, a couple of chairs. And against the opposite wall, the one substantial-looking article in the place—one of those tall cumbersome combinations of secretary and bookcase of a sort in vogue a hundred years ago, with a cupboard below and glassed-in shelves above the writing desk. Evidently a family heirloom of generations back.

Prentice strolled casually around the room, bringing up at last in front of the thing. He bent to peer at it as he lighted a cigarette.

What he had thought he saw from the door was correct. Around three sides of the margin of the old secretary ran an ornamental scroll of hand-carved wood. The design was grimed and faded with the wear of time. But in and out of the flowing garlands of roses and whirligigs ran a curious thread of symbols—the five horizontal lines and four spaces of a music clef, with the notes of a theme or tune in the key of B scattered up and down over them. From corner to corner of the cabinet the music scroll ran, a matter of six or seven feet of length in all.

Music. Music running through the Conover case like a sinister thread. Whistling, midnight after midnight, a weird diabolical chant that curdled the blood . . . Scraps of scribbled music, crushed, ripped into shreds, torn to ribbons, flung into the wastebaskets . . . Music symbols carved decades ago into the very frame and substance of the old secretary . . . Strange, time-dimmed notes looking down on the very spot where the stranger without a face lay with his skull drilled to the center.

CHAPTER THREE

Mr. Plum Suggests

PRENTICE opened the door. of the inspector's office without knocking. He paused on the threshold. Shannon and Meiggs were sitting on opposite sides of the desk. Across from them were two strangers. Men with faces nicely tooled out of chilled steel, with eyes to match.

Shannon nodded from Prentice to the pair. "Mr. Prentice, gentlemen. Mr. Jones and Mr. Van Vorst, Waldo. Secret Service of the United States of America."

Prentice nodded and went in. He slid up onto the corner of the desk and lit a cigarette. "Glad to know you, gentlemen," he grinned. "I suppose it's all over by now. You fellows always dig out the answer while we're trying to get the example written down. Who killed Cock Robin?"

"I'm afraid you're suffering a little from the heat, Mr.—er, Prentice," the one nearest him said dryly. "What led you to suppose that the Secret Service is available for the purpose of digging the police department out of its holes?"

"As a matter of fact, Waldo, these gentlemen came here for us to help them dig out of their own hole," Shannon broke in, crunching the butt of his smoke. "It seems that they are taking a hell of an interest in every little thing that happened up there at 49 Pin Street last night."

"If your department doesn't see fit to place the information it has at the disposal of the United States, there are ways of extracting it," Van Vorst broke in, curtly.

"Such as?" Prentice yawned. "I'm not speaking for the inspector, of course, but I imagine he would be willing to play ball fifty-fifty with you, if you asked him real nice, like that."

Shannon nodded. "Exactly. See here, gentlemen. A funny job was pulled last night. You're interested a whole lot. So are we. We know some things and so do you. Help us and we'll help you. Who are these birds you are after? What are they trying to put over?"

Van Vorst smiled chillily and shook his head. "We're not trading any, inspector. If you don't see fit to help us, we'll do it ourselves. And when the finish comes, we'll make it our particular pleasure to publish on the front page of every newspaper in the country the fact that the detective bureau of New York refused help when we asked for it. Good morning."

Shannon sat gloomily chewing the butt of his dry smoke as the callers got up and bustled themselves out.

"Blast 'em, I suppose I've done it now," he muttered. "Let the commissioner hear of this and I'll go back to picking potato bugs in County Kerry. But it riled me the way those two came in here, ordering this and that, P.D.Q. and special delivery."

He drifted his gaze from Meiggs to Prentice and back again. "When Washington comes in like this, there's a lot more to the job than we figured," he mused heavily. "Meiggs is stopped for now. You find out anything, Waldo? Who was the dead man?"

Prentice dug two fingers into his vest pocket. He pulled out the little flat article that he had ripped out of the lining of the faceless man's pocket and rolled it across the desk toward the chief.

"I don't know who he is, but I found that in his pocket," he yawned.

SHANNON picked the thing up. It was a small, flat, round object of polished metal, engraved on one side.

"I don't suppose you've got any more idea than a baby what this thing is, have you, Waldo?" he barked. "Nothing but a dog tag of the Secret Service."

Meiggs jumped out of his chair. He went to look over Shannon's shoulder.

"That dead man was what these government birds were looking for, then," he exclaimed. "One of their pals rubbed out of the picture. They didn't know for sure it was him. But they had a damn good hunch."

He picked his hat off the desk. "Which puts the rap plum in old Conover's lap. Those Washington dicks were right on top of him. He was on a hot spot and had to cover. I'm going up there again and ask him to tell me how he explains this and that."

"If he knows his answers like I think he does," Prentice cut in, "he'll ask you to tell him how he could have killed that S.S. man, wiped off his face, gone out and put his hammer away, come back, locked the door on the inside, tied his hands and feet, trussed that wet rope around his neck and commenced choking himself to death so pretty. Suppose McNally and the girl hadn't showed up right when they did? In another minute he'd have passed out."

"How do we know that he would?" Meiggs barked back. "How do we know how tight those ropes were? We didn't see any of them on him, remember. All we've got is McNally's word for it. And he was scared so stiff that he would have taken his own grandmother for a pink-eyed elephant."

"Yeah—perhaps. But then what do you make of this? Prentice stuffed his hand into his pocket and scattered over the desk the dozen fragments of music that McNaly had given him.

Meiggs stared at the pieces. "I give up. Where did you get it and what's it good for?"

"McNally had them. He didn't say saything to Skrenjold about them because Skrenjold yelled at him. He got them out of Conover's waste basket—been picking them out for weeks, he says. And the whistling—he tell you about that?"

Meiggs shook his head. "Shoot."

Prentice repeated McNally's story about hearing the whistling outside the apartment. Then he told about the scroll of carved music running around the edge of the old secretary.

"Music. Music all through the case like an evil omen. The old man hates music—he knows nothing about it—fears it—yet he has someone whistling under his window every night. He throws music into his waste basket, he has a bookcase with music carved all around it like a motto."

"I suppose it was music that bashed that hole in so-and-so's skull and wiped the flesh and blood off his face?" Shannon growled. "Go up and get Conover and bring him down here, and we'll maybe get him to whistle the answer to us."

Meiggs grinned at Prentice. "I'm on my way. Want to come?"

"We'll probably find Jones and Van Vorst taking the house to pieces and numbering the bricks," Prentice grunted back. "Let's go."

PRENTICE and Meiggs left the red police car around the corner in the avenue and walked the last block to Conover's apartment.

"Also we'll go in by McNally's side door and not by the front, if it's all the same to you," Prentice said.

"Figuring they'll lock us out if they see us coming?" Meiggs grunted.

"Figuring that you and I are not the only ones that are spotting down that lay," Prentice grinned back.

"You're still dreaming that somebody else besides old Conover could have pulled that job?" Meiggs said, incredulously.

"No puzzle is ever done till it's put together, my son," Prentice returned sagely. "You've got yours finished. Mine's got a hole in it yet—these." He held out a handful of the music scraps.

"Rats," Meiggs said. "Here we are."

McNally saw them coming and let them in without ringing. Up in the Conover apartment, a drone of voices came from behind a closed door. Meiggs knocked. A girl opened the door. She had a complexion of roses on snow, deep blue eyes, hair like an armful of spun midnight. Lines of worry sagged her cheeks. Her eyes went wide at sight of the officers.

"Police department," Meiggs said. "We want to talk to your uncle, Miss Conover."

Prentice saw the girl's face go white as she stepped back. He grinned at her. "Don't worry," he whispered, jerking his thumb at Meiggs. "He hasn't got anything on him."

Jerry Conover was sitting in an arm-chair, a pillow behind his head. He was a little, wiry man with a red, clean-shaven face and a thick short nose curiously flattened at one side. His hair was snow white. Against the background of this, his little eyes glittered like frozen blue flames. He wore a collar above the opening of his unbuttoned shirt. A collar of purple-yellow, seared around his neck. He had on an old blue coat with big silver buttons on the sleeves. Prentice noticed the buttons especially.

Meiggs pulled up a chair and sat down facing him.

"We've been going over your case down at headquarters, Conover, and we've got all the answers but two or three. I'm not here to tell bed-time stories. I'm here to give you a chance to come clean to me before I take you down and lock you up for murder. Don't say anything yet. Listen.

"Last night McNally and your niece found you in a room with a man that had been chewed by a steam roller or something. The doors and windows were locked on the inside. No one else was there. No one else could have gone in and come out again. Will you tell me why any jury in the country won't burn you for murder on that evidence?"

Conover did not say anything for a moment. Under his baggy clothes he seemed to be swelling up like a balloon, as he listened. His little knowing blue eyes shrank to beady pin-points of hate.

Suddenly he burst out laughing. A torrent of cackling mockery that exploded like firecrackers on his writhing lips. "So I killed him, did I?" he shrilled. "With my hands and feet tied and a rope around my neck? Would anyone but a fool of a cop ever have thought of a thing like that?"

"The ropes were a blind. You killed him, went out and hid your hammer or whatever it was, came back, locked the door, lay down on the floor and tied those ropes on yourself. McNally was too excited to notice how loose they were when he cut them off. You weren't choking to death any more than I am. What did you do it with—an axe?"

Meiggs jumped to his feet, upsetting the chair as he staggered back. A yell screeched from Conover's throat. He surged to his feet. His long white hands with the fingers writhing like talons jabbed at the detective's face.

"You fool! You bloody, driveling idiot!" he howled. "I tied that rope around my own neck? God's life, you let me put it onto you the way he did onto me—"

The girl was at the old man's side. Her arm around him, she coaxed him back into his chair. He was panting for breath. A line of foam edged his snarling lips. He was mumbling wordless curses over and over as he sat glaring up at the officer.

Meiggs stood grinning at him, his hands in his pockets. "All right, then. You didn't do it," he shot. "Somebody else did. Who was it? What did he look like? How did he get in and out again?"

Conover did not answer. Slowly the color ebbed from his face. His tongue travelled around his lips and he swallowed twice. "I—I don't know," he mumbled. "It was dark. I couldn't see—"

Meiggs strode a step forward, grabbed the old man by the arm and jerked him up to his feet.

"It was dark, was it? But not so dark that you didn't know that the man you killed was an operative of the United States Government," he shouted. "The Secret Service is after you and you know it, Conover. You knew it when you killed him. What for? What did he want you for?"

For an instant, the only sound in the room was the wheezy whistling of old Conover's breath as it sucked agonizedly in and out. His face had turned sickly yellow. His jaw sagged. His flabby cheeks sucked in like the sides of a pricked balloon. His legs wilted. He slipped out of Meiggs' grip and caved down in his chair.

The girl bent over him, chafing his blue, bloodless wrists between her hands. Over her shoulder, her eyes blazed at Meiggs.

"You coward! You— Oh, there aren't any words fit to call you!" she cried. "To come torturing a defenseless old man—"

The girl's voice broke in a gasp. Meiggs whirled around. Over his shoulder as he came plunging across the room, Prentice saw Conover's eyes, bulging pools of utter terror in his livid face.

From outside the house, in the street, had come the sound of whistling. A crazy chant of minors and jangling discords, weird, diabolical—

Meiggs was half a stride behind Prentice as he reaced down the hall of the apartment to the outer door and plunged out onto the sidewalk.

The whistling had stopped. Up and down, both ways, only half a dozen straggling figures were in sight—two old women about their errands, a postman, a scattering of pedestrians. The sun shone down warm and peaceful in the little street.

Meiggs was looking oddly at Prentice

as they turned and went back. "Conover knows what that is. He knows all about it," he muttered between his teeth. "I'm going to shake it out of him if I have to break his neck—"

Prentice squeezed his arm. Out of the shadows at the top of the steps, a little natty figure came into sight. It was Mr. Plum. His face was red and twitching with excitement.

"J-just a minute, Mr. P-Prentice," he twittered. He gripped Prentice's arm and pulled him into a corner.

"That w-was it—the wh-whistling. J-just like what I've heard b-before. You know what I think it m-means? They—whoever they are—haven't g-got done in here yet. S-something more is g-going to happen. Instead of arresting Conover, w-why don't you w-wait till tomorrow? C-come here tonight without anyone knowing and s-see w-what happens f-for yourselves?"

Prentice looked at Meiggs. "How about it? He can't get away. You can take him tomorrow as well as today. Only you'd have to admit that the music means something—"

"Says you," Meiggs grunted.

He went back into the sitting room. Conover lay slumped back on the pillows, white to the eyes.

"O. K., Conover, you win—for today," Meiggs said. "I'm giving you twenty-four hours to think it over. I'll be back tomorrow, same time. Get something ready to tell me that I can believe."

Out in the hall again, Prentice beckoned to Plum. "Keep this dark. Not a word to a soul, you know. Or you'll get your fingers burned. There's a big number somewhere behind this."

"D-don't I know it!" the little man twittered back. "I'm s-scared to death. D-don't worry. I won't wh-whisper a syllable!"

CHAPTER FOUR

The Devil Prowls

THE residents of Pin Street went to bed early. Not a soul save a couple of galloping cats was in sight at eleven o'clock that night when Prentice and Meiggs, five minutes apart, crept down in the shadows of the house fronts and stole soundlessly in through McNally's basement door.

Prentice shut the door behind him and stood listening.

"There's nobody here," Meiggs' whisper came out of the dark. "I've been all over the cellar. Funny that door was open, though. Let's go upstairs."

He led the way up to the Conover apartment and down to the room where the killing had happened. A sweep of light from his electric torch around the room showed it was empty.

"I'm going to wait here a while and see if anything happens. You go take a look-see around outside, Waldo," he whispered.

Out in the hall again, Prentice turned toward the rear. That morning he had noticed that Conover had had his bed made up in the little sitting room. He turned the knob, pushed open the door and stood listening.

There is something that, even in a pitch-dark room, tells if it is occupied. Some infinitesimal, sixth-sense aura of life and human presence.

This room was not occupied. There was nobody in it.

Prentice felt his way over to the side of the bed and flashed his torch. The covers were thrown back. He stooped and felt. Warm. Conover had been gone less than a minute.

Back in the hall, he turned to the left, toward the chamber of the girl. From behind the closed door came a funny sound—the sound of a leaky soda fountain fizzing off.

The door was unlocked. He threw it open. In the faint glow coming in from the street lights, he could see the chain dangling from the wall bracket at the head of the bed. He reached up and pulled. The switch clicked, but no light came. Someone had pulled the fuse.

He threw the shine of his torch down onto the long, gently rounded form under the sheet. Mary Conover, tied hand and foot. Mary Conover, her face the hue of raw steak, with a little froth of creamy white around her writhing lips.

His torch under his armpit, Prentice dug for his pocket knife and knelt on the bed at her side. He felt under the weals of puffed-up flesh on her slender neck, found the wet cord knotted around it and cut it through.

A gasp of air whistled into the girl's lungs. In the bathroom, Prentice filled a glass with water, ran back, and started throwing it in her face. She stirred and groaned. Little by little, the heaving of her bosom grew less. Her face paled from terrible congested crimson to pink.

Prentice cut the ropes that bound her ankles and wrists, stooped and shook her by the shoulder.

"Miss Conover!" he whispered.

He bent lower, breathing deep. A smell that he had not noticed before. Chloroform! He lifted the girl's eyelids. Drugged, all right. Asleep for hours to come.

As he straightened, the girl's clutching right hand relaxed from its spasmodic grip. Out of the opening fingers, a shiny thing fell and tinkled merrily on the floor.

Prentice stooped and picked it up. He held it under the beam of the flash an instant and then slipped it into his pocket.

A big silver button, with a tag of blue cloth, where it had been torn from the fabric. One of the silver buttons off Jerry Conover's coat.

OUT in the hall again, with the door locked and the key in his pocket . . . The other rooms of the apartment were empty. Prentice tiptoed down the corridor to the door, opened it and stole out into the main hall of the building.

For a moment, no sound but the faint rushing of the traffic out in the avenue. Then somethng that prompted Prentice to stoop and slip off his shoes. Out of the blackness above, a whisper of movement, vague, shadowy, like ghostly garments trailing against the night.

Two steps at a time, Prentice sprinted up the stair. At the top, he halted to listen again. Still ahead of him, and closer, now, the swish-swish of hurrying feet. They were travelling down the long hallway of the second floor headed away from him, toward the rear of the building.

Prentice ran a dozen feet and then jammed the button of his flashlight. In the frame of the glare a short, wiry, figure in a fluttering bathrobe. He jerked one look back over his shoulder and snarled out an oath. Jerry Conover.

"Stand where you are!"

Prentice's whispered shout echoed through space. With another gritting curse, Conover had jumped into a run. The skirts of his bathrobe trailing behind him, he popped around a corner and out of sight.

When Prentice got to the point where he had vanished, a long vista of naked walls opened under the beam of his flash. From somewhere below, a draught of cold air came rushing up. A door clicked shut and the air current ceased.

In bottomless blackness, his torch extinguished, Prentice crept back to the head of the stairs and then down to the bottom. Through the pitch darkness of the hall he felt his way to the Conover door. Inside, he fumbled along the wall to the door of the murder room. He turned the knob and stepped over the threshold.

"Tom, you better quit this in here, and come out with me. There's things doing," he whispered. "Somebody tried to send Mary across with the wet collar. Conover's out on a rampage—"

Prentice heard his voice break, trail away to a shadow and then blot out. Silence in the room. Cold, sinister stillness that gripped his heart in a throttling clamp. He felt beads of sweat run down his back as he fumbled for the switch to his flash. He tried three times before the dazzling finger of white cut into the darkness.

Meiggs lay face down on the floor. A little river of crimson bubbled up out of the triangular-shaped hole in the back of his head and welled its way toward his feet across the other dark brown stain on the boards.

Prentice stepped around him and went to look at the windows. Locked on the inside. But the door to the hall had been unlocked.

Meiggs had been hit and killed in the pitch darkness. Killed by someone who had been in the room all the time, lying in wait. Hit and killed before he had dreamed that the man was there. Smashed dead in the pitch dark with a diabolic accuracy that drove the triangle home at the exact spot on his skull where the Secret Service man had been hit.

Prentice went out into the hall again. He locked the door and pocketed the key. Two locked doors, now, with their grisly secrets waiting for answers.

He started toward the telephone in the rear hall of the apartment, and paused, thinking. There was nothing that the boys from headquarters could do for Tom Meiggs, now. Mary was all right, for the present. And somewhere in that black, soundless house, a wild beast in human form was a-prowl.

OUT in the main hall of the building once more, with the key of the Conover apartment making a third in his pocket, Prentice crept back up the stairs to a turn halfway to the top. In the angle of the two walls, he squeezed back and stood listening.

Five minutes, ten . . . Now another sound. The scuff-scuff of feet coming toward him, down the stairs. Sinister, uncanny whisperings, in the pitch blackness.

The man was talking to himself. Muttering jerky prayers and curses mixed, under his breath. Nearer yet . . .

Prentice relaxed. His half-drawn gun dropped back into his pocket. Not Conover. The husky, close-clipped brogue of McNally, the janitor.

Not to dazzle the little Irishman, Prentice focused the beam of his flashlight, one brief ray, onto the floor.

"McNally, this is Prentice," he whispered. "What's up?"

McNally jumped and gurgled an oath. "Saints preserve us! Ye gave me a turn, so ye did," he chattered. "What brings ye here at all, Mr. Prentice, sor-r? Sure, there's hell's own monkey business loose in the house this night."

Prentice could feel the little man shivering at his side. He gripped his arm. "Meiggs, my partner, is dead down there in Conover's room," he whispered. "Killed the same way as the man last night. I found Mary tied up and strangling with a wet rope around her neck. Conover is out of his room. I trailed him up here and then lost him. You seen anything?"

"God curse his dirty soul! What I was afraid of, meself," McNally gritted through his clenched teeth. His hand came groping through the dark and closed over Prentice's wrist.

"Listen, Mr. Prentice, sor-r. I don't know who killed your friend. But I do know who tied up Jerry Conover last night and Mary tonight, may God burn him in hell. Listen—"

McNally's breath broke in a curious gasp. Prentice waited an instant, then shook his arm.

"Yes? Who was it? Talk fast—"

Instead of answering, McNally swayed forward, the weight of his body lunging against Prentice. His knees caved in. His arm jerked out of Prentice's grip.

In the white glare of the electric torch that Prentice sent jabbing downward, a fluttering rag doll of flopping arms and legs was tumbling over and over down the stairs. One split-second glimpse Prentice had of his white, upturned face, jaw sagging, eyes glazed. And then the flashlight was struck from his hand.

He felt the numbing pain of a knife blade through his wrist and lunged into the dark with the other fist.

The blow fanned air. He staggered off balance and pitched headlong.

Arms wrapped themselves around him as he fell. One arm that gripped him around the neck while the other worked with the knife.

The crash of Prentice's head on one of the stair treads half stunned him. In a daze he battled with lead-heavy hands against the hungry steel tongue that came jabbing, jabbing through the dark. Dull, far away darts of pain flicked in his brain like shooting stars. The hands he was fighting with—strange numbed hands that would not do as he willed them—were stickily wet.

They lay on the floor at the bottom of the stairs. Somebody was crouching with his knees on Prentice's chest. He was nuzzling steel hooks of fingers around his throat to stifle his yelling.

Outside the house, in the street, a strange, blood-curdling little tune was whistling itself. Little devils with waving black tails were dancing to the music in Prentice's brain.

Somebody was rattling at the street door.

CHAPTER FIVE

The Whistling Man

MEIGGS killed and Prentice gone. Evaporated into thin air like the fog that dissolved out of Pin Street under the morning sun, leaving the mocking nakedness of asphalt and brick walls.

Conover and Mary still living at the apartment, with little McNally laid out in decent black in his tiny basement room and Mr. Plum chattering and stuttering to the plainclothesmen and reporters. A couple of blue-coats out on the sidewalk barring the door to all save those who could prove business with a big B.

And one thing more, seen by two million pairs of eyes that August afternoon—the strange exhibit that flared in the middle of the first page of half a dozen different newspapers. It was nothing but four lines of music, with a melody of skipping black notes written over them. A melody that utterly dismayed the few curious ones who tried to run it over on their pianos. It looked plausible, but there was no harmony, no tune or meaning to it. Nothing but a senseless jumble of notes. Minor chords in B.

The night came on sultry and damp, sticky with the heat wave that had shut down on the city. There was no wind. Ripples of lightning flickered against low banks of leaden clouds in the west.

With sundown, the two patrolmen departed from before the Conover house, thankful to go. An hour later, at nine o'clock, all the lights in the streets for two blocks on either side went out. The storm on the wires, people said. But the lights did not come on again. From end to end, Pin Street lay drowned in the pitch blackness of dreadful heat.

Inside the house, Mary sat in her bedroom, dressed. There was no light in the room. The door into the hall was locked. Before it, inside the room, a plainclothesman from the homicide bureau sat in a rocking chair mopping the sweat from his forehead. A flashlight and automatic balanced across his lap.

In the other room, where Meiggs and the Secret Service man had been killed, the big black walnut bed and the old secretary threw fantastically flickering shadows across the jagged brown stains on the floor, as the lightning rippled blue-white shimmerings around the edges of the shades. The door into the hall yawned wide open.

Midnight. The storm was coming closer. The thunder banged a legion of titanic kettle drums over the house tops. Around the cracks in the curtains, the cold blue flickering of the lightning throbbed like dragons' tongues.

Now a figure was moving across the room. The jagged flashes of the lightning showed him, a big-shouldered, stooped-over form, in baggy clothes.

A match flared, puny will-o'-the-wisp in the hot gloom. It wavered and went out. The man was halfway across the room. In the garbled, split-second alternations of dazzling black-and-white his face jerked in a leer of greed and fear. Teeth glistening saliva between the drawn-back lips.

Overhead, a thunderbolt broke with a long humming drone. A second match flame spurted yellow, puffed out as though blown by a wind. In the glare of the blue ocean that boiled around the window frames, something lay sprawled on the floor, arms outspread. Midway of his forehead, a triangular hole was spurting blood.

Out in the street, the storm swept down with a deluge of rain that wiped out the lightning. Silence now in the room with the motionless thing on the floor.

FIVE minutes might have passed—ten. Now, more sounds in the pitch blackness there. The rustle of feet and clothing. The white beam of a flashlight jumped out and went skipping around the walls. It played over the black walnut bed in the corner, it flitted across the table and chairs and the old secretary, and came to rest at last on the thing on the floor. It held steady, focusing on the face, while the man behind it walked slowly forward.

The man stooped. A hand came stealing into the light ray. Swiftly it ran over the dead man, turning his pockets out, frisking him for a gun.

Suddenly, the hand froze. The light went out. The rustle of clothes again, the click of the loose board in front of the door. Silence.

A quarter of a minute or less, and yet other sounds from the hall. Two men, this time. This pair came softly, albeit confidently, as those who were expected and had a right to be there.

The white fingers of two flashlights, this time, jerked out and focused long converging gushers of light against the wall. They flitted back and forth and then whipped down to the dead man. A voice snarled amazement.

"Moses, by God!"

"So that's where he was when we started," another voice jerked back. "He beat it out in a hurry to get here first. He was going to cross us, the rat. Well, he got it, and got it right."

"He always was a rat," the first voice growled. "And now the trap's got him."

The second voice husked out a laugh. "How Andy would squirm in hell if he knew that it was still knocking 'em off! How many is this in all now, Peter—five?"

The one called Peter did not answer. "Never mind Andy, you mug," he muttered. "What we've got to think of now is ourselves. One little bit of a wrong move, Ed, and you and me will be chawing dirt right there side of Moses. What the hell's keeping Jerry? He said he would be here and let us in. This damned place is too quiet. What's happened to the light all around everywhere?"

"He left the door open, didn't he?" Ed growled. "He'll be along. He damn well knows better than not to. We've rode him till his guts are soup."

The other one—Peter—swore again and moved nervously.

"Maybe. This lay gives me the jim-jams. What did Moses want to go monkeying around for, anyhow? Didn't he know it was poison? God! What's that—"

From outside, down the hall, slippered feet were scuffing over the boards. A halo of yellow light billowed in around the jamb of the door, making the thing on the floor cast long twisted shadows over toward the door of the old cabinet.

Around the corner a bent figure in trailing blue bathrobe hobbled into the room. Jerry Conover. He held the candle in one withered hand. The other was empty.

"Damn you, what do you go crawling around for like that? You give me the shivers," Peter snarled. "What the hell kept you? Hurry up and let's get this over with." He laughed croakingly. "I see Moses figgered he'd get here in plenty of time. He did."

Old Conover did not move. He stood motionless in the middle of the floor, looking up at the other two. The shine of the candle flame illuminated their faces now for the first time. Big, bearded faces of men past middle age. Faces sin-bitten, hard as riven steel. Eyes like crouching beasts, poison beads of greed and hate, under bushy gray brows.

Without a word, Jerry Conover turned toward the old secretary. One on either side of him, the other two trailed a step behind.

In front of the big walnut cabinet, Jerry paused, bending forward. His shrunken, blue-veined old hands reached out, fumbled among the knobs and scrolls around the edge.

A drawer slid open. The things that Jerry took out with both hands were heavy, by the way he held them. In the wavering candle light, they looked like a pair of copper bricks.

JERRY half turned and set the things down on the little table behind him. Not a word had been spoken. Only Peter's breath had sucked in with a hissing sound as he saw the things. A look passed between him and Ed.

Four hands shot out. Jerry gasped a squeak like a rabbit grabbed by a wolf.

The next instant, he was lying on his back on the floor. Working with grim, soundless expertness, the other two gagged him and tied him hand and foot.

Out of his pocket, Peter pulled a length of soft brown rope. He stooped and knotted it around Jerry's neck.

"We won't stop to give you the wet one this time, brother dear," he croaked. "Somebody might come in and find you in the next twenty minutes. We'll do you one favor in return for the stuff, you sniveling rat. We'll give you a quick croak and a merry one."

With a twist of his big hands, Peter jerked the rope tight and knotted it. He turned to stand up, gurgled a strangling cry and pitched forward onto his face.

Standing above him, with his automatic switched end for end in his hand, Ed had waited till Peter had finished with Jerry. He swung the gun in a hooking arc and brought the steel-shod butt crashing on Peter's head.

The blow went through the skull like paper. One long second Ed stood peering down.

"There's for you, damn you! The end of the Colemans—all but one," he snarled. "All of you gone to hell, and me with the stuff—"

The rambling monologue jerked off.

Holding the heavy bricklike objects under his coat with his left hand, Ed flipped his pistol back, with the butt in his fingers. He blurted a gasping cry and staggered back.

No sound had come from beyond the open door into the hall. With the suddenness of a lightning bolt, the white beam of a flashlight glared through the opening and focused on Ed.

The two rays—Ed's and the newcomer's—met and crossed in the middle of the room. They spot-lighted Ed's rage-twisted snarling mug, they photographed in meticulous black and white detail the narrow, vicious face and beady blue eyes of the slender little figure that stood on the threshold.

The little man fired before Ed could get his gun back into position. But his bullet went wild.

From the dark corner behind the black walnut bedstead a battery of white lights had blazed out. A gun spat a streak of flame. The blue-eyed killer's gun-arm dropped limp at his side as the bullet shattered his shoulder.

Ed spun around, amazement gripping his face, to meet a rush of figures that came vaulting over the bed. Shannon was on top of him like a charging bull. A blow from the inspector's hamlike fist drove him backward, gasping. Before he could get his feet under him, the inspector's gun jabbed in his stomach. The cold steel of the handcuffs shivered across his arms.

Lights blazed in the room.

Prentice, one arm in a sling, whipped out his pocket knife with his other hand and cut Jerry Conover loose. Over across, half a dozen burly figures in plain clothes crowded the door. In their midst the rat-faced little man had gone berserk as the squad closed in on him. Foaming at the lips, he was biting, gouging and kicking. A blue-coat rapped him over the head with a night stick and the commotion ceased.

Two of the headquarters detail came forging in and took charge of Ed. The pair that had been behind the bed with Shannon and Prentice picked Jerry up and sat him in a chair, gulping for breath, but otherwise none the worse.

The copper-brick-looking objects still lay on the floor where Ed had dropped them. As Jones and Van Vorst turned back from attending to Conover, Prentice shoved them out of sight under the secretary with his foot.

He looked up at the bearded giant who stood foaming blasphemies between a couple of plainclothesmen.

"Gentlemen, let me introduce Mr. Ed Coleman, the whistling man," he grinned. "As friend Eddie himself remarked, he is—or would have been—the last of the Coleman boys."

CHAPTER SIX

Mr. X

SHANNON jerked his head at the pair of motionless figures on the floor. "Get those rats out of here, some of you, before we commence to talk," he said. "Put 'em in the other room and somebody call the medical examiner."

When the grisly forms had been removed, he turned to Prentice.

"You promised us action, and you sure kept the date," he grunted. "Now if we could trouble you for one more little thing. Tell us what the hell it's all about—"

"It's too long a story for a hot night. I'll just hit the high spots," Prentice said.

"There were five of the Coleman brothers, to start with—Moses, Edward, Jerry, Andrew and Peter. Andrew was a law-abiding citizen, but the other four were the brains of the famous Coleman gang. Twenty years ago they were the world's best in the line of queer-money pushers, plain and fancy swindling, bank robbing and general bad men. After a while, Jerry fell in love with a good woman, gave himself up, confessed and offered to take his medicine. He got off with five years. Soon after this first split, Moses and company got careless, were caught, convicted and sent up for life.

"When Jerry finished his stretch, his sweetheart wasn't waiting for him at the gate. She was married to another man. Jerry stuck to his good resolutions all the same. He changed his name to Conover, hid away with his niece Mary, orphaned daughter of his brother Andrew, and led a decent life.

"Everything was jake till about six months ago when Edward, Moses and Peter broke stir and headed east. It took them exactly half of that time to locate Jerry here.

"Somewhere the Coleman boys had picked up an ingenious music code which they used for their secret communications with one another. The messages could either be whistled or written. As soon as the three stir-bugs had spotted down Jerry's hideaway they began flooding him with demands in the code. They wanted him to return something—they didn't say what—evidently a relic of the old days that chanced to be in his possession. But its recovery meant a fortune to whoever got it.

"Jerry was pretty well scared, but he sat tight and stalled them off, although Eddie here would walk past under his window every night and whistle the old gang call that meant he was on a red hot spot and getting hotter. Twice Jerry let him in. Ed stormed and threatened, but Jerry didn't buckle down worth a cent.

"Moses, Peter and Ed weren't the only crowd that were interested in Jerry. Just about the time they showed up, the Secret Service had tumbled to the fact that he was one of the long-lost Colemans. Also they had a heavy hunch that he was hoarding something that they had been running circles trying to locate for many moons.

"Phelan, one of the government operatives, had been trailing Jerry so long and so close that he had seen Eddie go past the house, heard him whistle his call—and seen him get in twice when he did it. Night before last, he must have decided to try it himself. Jerry heard him and of course thought it was Ed. He didn't intend to open the door at first. But all at once he got so thundering mad at the thought of these gorillas pestering him and Mary half to death that he suddenly decided to have it out with him, once and for all—kill him if necessary. So he went and let him in. Imagine his feelings when the man he saw was a stranger!

"Once inside, Phelan got overambitious —he lost his head. Finding he couldn't make Jerry talk, he pulled a gun on him. He backed him into a corner and went to fooling around with the old secretary, trying to open it. And then, gentlemen, was when he was killed. Not by Jerry Conover, not by any one alive now. He was killed by the hand of a good man, a man dead these fifteen years—Andrew Coleman, Mary's father."

There was a moment's silence.

"If Conover, or Coleman, or whoever he is, could make you believe that I'll sell you the Brooklyn Bridge," Van Vorst grunted.

"O. K. by me," Prentice grinned. "I'll buy it. But first I want you to step up here and do what Phelan did—try to open this." He motioned at the old walnut cabinet.

"You're staging the hokum, I'm not," Van Vorst growled. "Go ahead with your show."

"All right, then. Shut up and keep back."

STANDING four or five feet away from the secretary, Prentice began poking around the front with a cane that stood in a corner. At his third jab, a gritting metallic clang jarred out. A steel arm some four feet long, swinging from a pivot in the vertical back of the cabinet, crashed down with the force of a trip hammer.

There was a whirring sound and the arm started to rise. Prentice grabbed it and held it down.

"This battle axe would smash in the skull of an ox." He pointed at the projecting triangular piece at the top of the lever.

"That looks like wood, but it is really steel—the head of the hammer. And it falls exactly where the head of a man bending over and trying to work the combination would naturally come."

He let go of the arm. It rose slowly and smoothly into place, fitting so accurately into its socket that not a trace of the outline was visible.

"Andrew Coleman was an expert mechanic. He made the cabinet for his brothers to keep their valuable papers in— as they told him. There was one right way to work the knobs that opened the secret drawer, and a hundred and one wrong ones, any one of which would drop the hammer. To guard against any of the brothers forgetting the combination, Andrew built the directions for working it right into the wood, in this music code around the edge. The mechanism inside that runs the show was set once, twenty years ago. And it's still working.

"When Phelan hit the wrong knob, it got him. He dropped where he stood. Jerry was petrified. While he stood there racking his brain to think what to do, the door suddenly opened and another man stood in the room.

"This third man I will call Mr. X for a minute. He had done time in the same prison out west with the Coleman boys,

and he had wormed out of them enough of the story of the thing that Jerry had in the cabinet to figure it was worth going a long way to get hold of. He had been hanging around for weeks, watching Jerry like a hawk, waiting for a good chance to put the screws on him and make him talk. When he saw the dead man on the floor, his first thought was that the fuss this killing would make would ruin his racket for keeps—particularly if Phelan were identified as a government operative. One thing he could do about that would be to spoil his face so he couldn't be recognized.

"So he pulled a gun on Jerry, made him lie down on the floor, tied him up and gagged him. Then he went out, got a hammer and fixed Phelan so his own mother wouldn't know him. While he was in stir, he had picked up from the Coleman boys the story of their old stunt of torturing a man with a wet rope around his neck till he came through and told whatever it was they wanted to know. So he trussed a couple of layers of cord he had found in the cellar around Jerry's neck and commenced telling him how nice it would feel choking to death, and hadn't he better loosen up with the lowdown, how to get into the cabinet?

"It was X's voice that Mary heard in her room and that wakened her. He didn't have time to get out before she came. He was still in here when McNally smashed the door, hiding over there behind the bed. He got out when McNally and Mary took Jerry down to her room.

"So that was that. From then on, Jerry was scared white. He was on a hot spot and he knew it. If he talked he was afraid of what Washington would do to him about the stuff he had in the cabinet. If he didn't talk, X would get him, sooner or later.

"Then that next night, when Tom Meiggs and I came up here alone. Meiggs was rubbed out the same way that Phelan was—he went monkeying around the secretary, without having the ghost of an idea that it was loaded. X was on the rampage that night. I figure that what he was probably trying to do was to put everybody that might possibly suspect him and his racket out of the way, break open the cabinet with an axe and skip. He started Mary on her way with chloroform and the wet rope. To throw a sour trail he left in her hand a button he had pulled off her uncle's coat. He went looking for Jerry, but Jerry was hunting him, too. McNally must have had a hunch of the truth. He was just starting to tell it to me, when he was stabbed through the heart. X had heard us talking there in the dark and stolen down on us, in his stocking feet.

"I was another one that was just spoiling life for Mr. X. We had a grand mix-up all the way down stairs. He would have got me for the big wash-up if Jerry hadn't heard the rumpus and come on the run. X heard him and beat it before he got there.

"That night, with Meiggs lying dead here and Mary fighting for life, Jerry came clean with me. He told me almost all that I've told you just now. I had managed to read the music cipher before that—during the day. It wasn't so hard. So Jerry and I doped out the play that's just been finished. I was to lie low the next day, and fix it with the inspector that it was to be given out that I was killed. An ad in the music cipher was run in the evening papers. It was to Moses and Peter and Ed over Jerry's name. He told them that he was sick of fighting. The house would be empty of cops that night. If they would come, he would give them the stuff.

"So they came—each set to double-cross the others. Moses got here first and when he tried to open the cabinet in the dark he slipped and the hammer got him. He probably wasn't as familiar with the

secret as the others, in the first place and remember—he hadn't seen the secretary for years. Then Ed and Peter appeared and found him—which is about all, except for one thing."

PRENTICE stooped and pulled the objects he had hidden out from under the secretary. He picked them up and turned to Jones and Van Vorst.

"I forget which one of you it was that said how cooperation was our middle name," he grinned. "Just to make it unanimous, let me present you—"

Jones grabbed two of the four objects that he held out and Van Vorst snatched the others. There was a surge of figures from the corners of the room to look over their shoulders.

Under the bright lights, the bricklike things resolved themselves into orange-yellow oblongs of metal, marvelously engraved.

"Gentlemen, the counterfeit plates of the Coleman boys," Prentice said. "Absolutely the finest article in engraved goods ever made. The stuff they turned out wasn't imitation. It was better than the mint's own brand. No wonder the Comptroller of the Currency died of dyspepsia with those things loose. Moses, Peter and Eddie—not to mention Mr. X—were going to rub them up and put them to work again—"

Jones and Van Vorst looked a trifle sheepish as they turned to Prentice.

"No use trying to act peeved," Jones grinned wryly, holding out his hand. "You've certainly clicked all right. You'll maybe get a letter from the President for this. But you're chiseling on us, at that. This Mr. X—who is he? Or did you just ghost him up to make the story exciting?"

Prentice looked over the knot of shoulders around him and nodded to the man at the door. Two blue-coats came in from the hall. Between them they dragged a diminutive little figure, slender and blue-eyed, who lunged at his beefy guardians like a wildcat, the while he spat a torrent of verbal sewage between his jerking lips.

"Gentlemen, meet Mr. Plum—Mr. X—Mr. Nicholas Grey, otherwise known as 'Stuttering Nellie,' wanted for arson, burglary, murder and I don't know what else. He planned this job like a watch. And almost finished it too. Only for Jerry Conover and his hoss pistol . . . Take him away—"

As the foaming of Plum's curses muffled out in the scuffing of his feet on the way to the door, Prentice turned to Jerry Conover. He sat white-faced and motionless in his chair, still breathing hard. Mary had slipped into the room and sat beside him, her arm linked through his. The girl had gasped out a cry and gone white as Plum had appeared, snarling viciously, between the officers.

"You two will never know how lucky you were," Prentice grinned to the old man and the girl. "There were about nine thousand different ways that things could have gone blooey that didn't. About those green-goods plates, you don't have to worry, either. I'll fix things with Jones and Van Vorst. You were just keeping them out of harm's way. You had no intention of using them—"

He reached down and patted Mary's hand.

"Forget him. It'll be easy—now that you've seen him under the grease paint. Your uncle is going to be a heap better and he'll need you."

The girl smiled as she pressed his hand. "I know. I'm going to be happy now—"

The room was emptying. Prentice fell in along side of Shannon as the inspector turned to go.

"Another fancy job, son—done to the king's taste." The veteran's voice was prideful as he gripped the lad's arm. "You and your music hunch—"

"What we can't do, though, none of us, is get the man that killed Tom Meiggs," Prentice said. "That was where I fell down. I ought to have guessed out that killing machine about twenty-four hours before I did."

Out in the street, it had cleared off. It was cool. The stars spattered the sky like blobs of yellow paint.

"No—we can't do nothing for Tom—none of us," Shannon sighed. "But you couldn't help it, son. You doped the thing out as soon as you could—quicker than anybody else in the house . . . Well, let's be going and having a bite to eat before we turn in. Tomorrow's another day."

Pipe Line

of

PERIL

by

Maxwell Hawkins

Author of "Monkey Murder," etc.

It looked like an accident—that flaming holocaust which charred Cullen to a crisp. But Sheriff O'-Neill had his doubts about it. He knew a murder when he saw one —knew blood won't mix with oil.

The well became a seething cauldron of flame.

BEFORE he stepped onto the derrick floor, Sam Cullen paused to glance at the white face of the gauge on the gas line. It registered the pressure of the titanic store of natural gas three thousand feet below, which Cullen's well had tapped only a few days before.

"Nine hundred pounds!" Cullen exclaimed. "That's a lot of rock pressure, Bert."

Bert Buckley, Cullen's lease foreman, rolled his chaw of scrap around in his fat tanned cheeks. Then he squirted a stream of muddy juice on the white pine of the derrick before answering.

"She's a powerful big well. I figure she'd make around fifty million cubic feet a day, if we opened her wide. And that's enough to burn up the state of Oklahoma," he added.

Cullen strolled across the derrick floor, sat down on the "lazy bench," and crossed his legs, which were encased in high field boots, oil-stained and worn. His kindly but shrewd eyes rested on the mammoth gate valve that crowned the casing of the big gas well and diverted the precious vapor into the gathering line of the Oklahoma Natural Gas Company.

"Has old Jackson Blackwing been around here doing any more of his grumbling?" he asked, turning to the foreman.

Buckley, who was tugging at the big wheel which operated the top gate on the valve, shook his head.

"Haven't seen him since day before yesterday," he replied, releasing a thin stream of tobacco juice. "He rode past the lease house and over to his shack about dark. But he didn't stop or say anything. Just gave me a dirty look, when he saw me in the doorway."

The foreman applied a final tug to the wheel. He wanted to be certain the top gate was closed; open, the well would belch its highly inflammable and dangerous gas up through the derrick with tornado violence.

"Is Blackwing living in his shack now?" Cullen asked.

"No. He's moved into Weemulgee."

"He thinks I swindled him on this lease," Cullen said softly, shaking his head. "But I didn't. I gave him a good price, when this was rank wildcat country. There wasn't a well within five miles."

"Don't worry about him. If he tries to start anything, you can have Sheriff O'Neill throw him in the calaboose," Buckley grunted.

Cullen shrugged. "I'm not worrying. But I play this oil game on the level, and I don't want anybody to say I gypped him—even a greasy quarter-breed like Blackwing. Guess he's getting old and doesn't understand things very well," he added.

"He's crazy, if you ask me," Buckley replied. He put his hand on the gate valve. "This gas is wringing wet, Mr. Cullen. There's oil on this lease as sure as you're a foot high."

Cullen nodded. "You bet there is! Remember Gregory?"

Buckley shot a quick searching glance at the lease owner. "Remember him? I ought to. He lived at the lease house

with me for two days, when he was out here working for you."

"That's true!" Cullen laughed. Well, Gregory has figured out the geology on this property. He reported that it's the best-looking piece in the pool."

The foreman pursed his lips. "Then it's probably worth a couple of million," he murmured. He rolled the last word around in his mouth, almost in awe.

"I hope so," Cullen smiled. "We'll know soon. We're going to haul in the rig for the second well tomorrow."

"Where are you going to drill it?"

Cullen lifted his long frame from the lazy bench and stretched. Then he walked to the edge of the derrick floor and looked out over the expanse of broken terrain that comprised his lease.

It was a late November day, chill and drizzly, the air heavy with moisture. From the gas well, which was on a little hill, he could see grayly the lease house and tool shanty in the opposite corner of the quarter section. Between lay two deep gullies, dry most of the year, but now running with streams several feet wide. The hill that separated them was rocky, covered with a tangled growth of blackjack and sage.

"Gregory says to drill that corner," Cullen replied finally. "And as long as I've paid good money for a geologist's advice, I might as well use it." He raised his hand and pointed off to the right.

"You get a stake driven for the location this afternoon. I'll order the rig in Weemulgee on my way to Tulsa."

He stood in thoughtful silence for a moment, then stepped down from the derrick, his field boots making a squashy sound as they sank in the mud.

"And by the way," Cullen continued, as Buckley followed him, "you had better check our gas line out to the Oklahoma Natural's gathering line."

The foreman gave him a questioning look. "What's tha matter?"

"There's a leak somewhere," Cullen said, his nostrils twitching reminiscently. "Smelled it in the deep ravine as I walked over here. This damp atmosphere blankets it down in all the low places."

"Well—" Buckley hesitated, then nodded slowly. "Maybe there's a break in the two-inch line to the lease house," he said, referring to the pipe that carried gas from the well for use in lighting and heating the two buildings on the lease.

"Fix it," Cullen said crisply. "It's bad business having leaky lines weather like this. The gas hugs the ground. We don't want any accidents." He shook his head dubiously. "A roustabout was killed on a lease I once owned up in the Osage, because of a leaky gas line."

They moved away from the big gasser. Behind them a faint hissing was audible. It came from the inflammable vapor that hundreds of pounds of pressure from the belly of the earth was causing to seep around the valve joints.

It sounded like a den of angered snakes. But there was more menace in that hissing of natural gas. It was more deadly, and in a far different way. It stood for quick death; death in an infernal cauldron of flame, if a man was careless.

CULLEN and Buckley walked single file along the rough road that led from the derrick down to the first gully. They waded through the stream and along the foot of the hill. When they came to the spot where the road cut up over the rise to dip again into the second and deeper of the ravines, which it followed for a hundred yards, Buckley halted.

"I think I'll go over and drive that stake for the new well now," he said.

"I've got to figure out a route for a road to haul the rig in, too," he added.

"All right, Bert," Cullen nodded. "I'll be out again tomorrow."

As the two men parted, the lease owner looked at his watch. It was almost noon. When he had picked his way over the slippery rocks to the top of the hill between the gullies, Cullen halted to recover his breath. His eyes swept the landscape.

The heavy downpour of the previous night had ended with the dawn. But the air was thick, saturated with moisture that seemed to be a combination of drizzle from the low-hanging clouds and mist that rose from the soaked ground.

A medley of sounds came to his ears, sounds that were muffled by distance. The chugging of a steam drilling engine and the clank of the tools at a well which was being put down on one of the adjoining leases beyond the road. In the grove over there, someone was hammering on metal. The ring of steel on steel was unmistakable.

"The Goliath Company must be building more tankage," Cullen said to himself. He smiled. He, too, would be erecting tanks in which to store valuable oil before many weeks. The lease was a sure-shot for "black gold."

He began the steep descent into the ravine. The two-inch gas line which Buckley had mentioned crossed the road halfway up the gully. It ran in gentle curves along the top of the ground, visible wherever the soil was too fallow to support vegetation.

As Cullen neared the point where the line crossed the road, he wrinkled his nose, sniffed audibly.

"This draw is full of gas," he muttered. "I'd better stop at the tool house and leave word for the roustabouts to watch out for it."

He suddenly stopped in his tracks and listened, head cocked slightly to one side.

From the far slope of the gully, and a short distance ahead of him, came a low steady hiss. Like a punctured automobile tire.

"By golly, that's where it is!" he told himself. "There's a break right at that bend."

He plunged into the stream. A couple of seconds later, he was on the other side and starting toward the sizzling gas line.

At that instant hell was let loose in the narrow gully!

A dull rumbling boom accompanied a blinding, searing wall of flame that swept from the upper to the lower end in the space of two or three seconds. It painted the low-hanging clouds a ghastly red.

Cullen opened his lips to scream. The sound gagged in his throat. The fiery air rushed into his mouth, down his windpipe, filled his chest. Clothes ablaze, arms threshing with agony, he staggered a short step. He stumbled and pitched forward on his face.

With a superhuman effort he gained his feet. Now he was groping, his eyes blinded by the fire. He reeled forward like a drunken man, then tripped again and fell heavily, his body writhing about on the steaming ground. Abruptly he quivered, stiffened, and lay motionless. Cullen was dead, his lungs burned out by the deadly fire.

BERT BUCKLEY, clouded with signs of grief, sat in Sheriff "Sleepy" O'Neill's office in Weemulgee and related the events that had preceded the brief moment when the gully on the Cullen lease had been turned into a roaring volcano of blazing gas.

"That was the last time I saw Cullen alive," Buckley said, swallowing hard. "He left me and climbed over the hill. I went on toward the location of the new well.

"Then I heard the noise when the gas caught and looked back. I couldn't see into the ravine—couldn't see Cullen—but the flames were twenty or thirty feet high. They ran the length of that draw like a flash."

O'Neill made a low clucking sound with his tongue against his teeth. He tugged at his scraggly mustache with gnarled fingers.

"Cullen dead when you got to him?" he asked, his voice dropping some of its characteristic drawl.

"Yes. His clothes were still smouldering. I smothered the fire out. But it didn't make any difference. He was done for, poor devil."

The sheriff tilted his chair and lifted one foot to the top of his desk. With the back of his hand, he pushed his ten-gallon hat up till his hair, red hair with a sprinkling of gray, was visible. He let his glance wander out the window to the wet street; then back to Buckley's round face.

"Gas's dangerous," he said laconically.

"I've worked with it all my life, almost," the foreman replied. "This is the first accident I've ever had on a lease I was boss of. Gas is all right if you're careful."

"Think it was an accident, huh?"

"Yes, I do." Buckley suddenly became thoughtful. "That is, I can't imagine anyone touching that gas off on purpose."

"What do you suppose set it afire?" O'Neill asked, squinting one of his gray eyes.

Buckley frowned. "It's got me stumped."

"Gas don't light itself," O'Neill said with dry persistence. "See anybody snooping around that part of the lease?"

"The only other men around the lease were the two roustabouts," the foreman replied. "And they were both working at the tool shack. They came running up while I was putting out the fire in Cullen's clothes."

"Damn funny," the sheriff grunted.

"It is," Buckley agreed. "But I can only figure it as an accident of some kind. We brought the body into town, and I knew I'd better give you a report on what happened."

Sheriff O'Neil was silent. His gray eyes almost closed, giving his lean leathery face the look of a man about to doze off. It was a habit that had brought him his nickname of "Sleepy" as long ago as the days when Oklahoma was a territory.

But there were plenty of men who'd crossed Sleepy O'Neill's path in the fifteen years he'd been sheriff that would have told you it was a misleading trick. When the wiry bowlegged law officer looked sleepiest, his mind was most wide awake.

Buckley stood up. "Guess that's all, sheriff. I'll be moving along. I've got to phone the Tulsa office about what's happened."

The sheriff's eyes snapped open. He waved Buckley back into his chair.

"No hurry! This kind of riles my interest," he said softly. "Tell me something about Cullen."

Buckley slowly resumed his seat. "I don't know very much. I've only been working for him since he started that gas well. Three months, about."

"Pretty rich man? Big operator?"

"Not so very big. He'd been an oil producer for twenty odd years. But he told me he'd never made a killing. Up to now, anyway."

"Why up to now?" O'Neill demanded sharply.

Buckley explained. "Well, that lease is certain to prove up for oil—big oil! It'd have made him a millionaire."

"Make somebody else a millionaire now I suppose," the sheriff murmured.

"His family," Buckley nodded. "He's got a wife and a couple of kids in Tulsa."

"Did Cullen have any enemies?" The sheriff put the question casually, but Buckley suddenly seemed to grow tense.

"Why—why, do you think somebody lit that gas?" the foreman asked. "That Cullen was—" He didn't finish the sentence.

Sleepy O'Neill's voice was almost querulous as he answered. "How the hell do I know? The first I'd heard Cullen was burned to death was when you told me a few minutes ago."

Buckley's eyes narrowed. "Sheriff, do you know old Jackson Blackwing, who owns the land Cullen's lease covers?"

O'Neill nodded.

"He thinks Cullen swindled him on that lease," the foreman said slowly.

"Hm!" the sheriff said, screwing up his lips thoughtfully. "Ever make any threats against Cullen?"

"Not exactly. But he's always growling around to anyone who'll listen, that he was cheated out of his rights."

For a long moment O'Neill's eyes assumed that slumbrous look. Then he jerked his five feet four of tough muscle out of the chair, yanked his big hat low on his forehead.

"Come on!" he exclaimed briskly. "I want to take a look at that gully where Cullen was burned up!"

OUTSIDE the courthouse, in which the sheriff's office was situated, Buckley turned to O'Neill.

"I've got to phone Tulsa. Then I'll drive you out in my car. Meet me at the Gusher Garage in ten minutes."

O'Neill nodded, and the foreman cut across the muddy street toward a one-story brick building, which was identified as the telephone company's office by a blue metal sign shaped like a bell.

"Bad fire they had on the Cullen

lease," a voice at the short man's elbow said.

Sleepy O'Neill glanced around and saw that the speaker was George McAllister, the county recorder.

"Yep. But accidents'll happen now and then in the oil fields. Kind of tough on Cullen. To go like that just when he had a million in his fingers.

McAllister nodded gravely. "Guess he only owned a half interest, though. Sold the other half."

"That so?" O'Neill said, with a sudden lift of his chin. "How'd you know that?"

"Young fellow just left an assignment of a half interest in the property to be put on record."

"Well, the other half'll be enough to provide for the widow and kids," O'Neill said. "They'll have a million, anyway, from what I gather the lease is worth."

McAllister laughed. "You and I could use that, Sleepy," he said, moving up the courthouse steps. "But we were born handsome and not lucky."

O'Neill sauntered down the main street of Weemulgee to the Gusher Garage. A few minutes later he was joined by Buckley. In the foreman's flivver, a brand-new job with a tool rack on the rear, they were soon bouncing over the slippery rutted road toward the Cullen lease.

It was midafternoon, but the sun was completely hidden behind the thick clouds. The air was still filled with the fine drizzle that had blanketed down the fatal gas in the gully earlier.

As they turned in the gate and rolled toward the tool house, O'Neill saw a tall man in field clothes standing beside a roadster. He walked toward their car the minute Buckley brought it to a stop.

"I just heard about Cullen!" he exclaimed. "They told me about it in the

recorder's office. It's terrible, Bert, terrible!"

"Certainly is, Mr. Gregory," the foreman replied. "Meet Sheriff O'Neill. He's out here to investigate the accident."

"Glad to meet you sheriff," Gregory said holding out his hand.

O'Neill nodded acknowledgement of the introduction and shook the proferred hand. His gray eyes took in the tall figure in a single quick glance—the rather studious face, with a thin nose and close-set eyes; the hunched shoulders and unusually long arms.

"Mr. Gregory is a geologist," Buckley explained. "He worked out the formations under the lease and decided it was good for oil."

The tall man smiled deprecatingly. "I thought so much of it," he said, "that I bought a half interest."

"Must have cost you a pretty penny," the sheriff remarked shrewdly.

"I got a bargain. Cullen needed money to develop the property, and I happened to have a bit of ready cash."

O'Neill climbed out of the car. "Let's look over the ravine," he said.

Buckley led the way, O'Neill and Gregory following a few steps behind. As the three men entered the ravine, they saw on all sides grim reminders of the horrible wall of fire that had roared through it only a few hours before. The blackjack and grass, even though they had been soaking wet, had been blackened by the intense heat of the holocaust.

A couple of roustabouts were bucking up the two-inch line, when O'Neill and the others reached the middle of the gully. The leaky section was lying at one side.

"That's how the gas escaped, huh?" the sheriff asked, pointing to the discarded joint of pipe.

"Yes. There's a hole in it. Looks as

if it might have been dropped on a sharp rock," Buckley replied.

The sheriff walked to the twenty-foot length of line and examined it. Near the collar end, he found the leak. It was a small indentation, about the size of a quarter and pierced in the center by a slightly smaller hole. O'Neill squatted on his heels and studied the break. Finally, he stood erect.

"No, sir," he said quietly, "that hole wasn't made by a rock. It's perfectly round—like it had been made with a punch, perhaps."

"What do you think made the gas catch fire?" Gregory asked.

The sheriff merely shrugged, but Buckley answered: "We're both trying to figure that out."

'Maybe Cullen didn't notice the gas collected here, and lit a cigar or cigarette," the geologist suggested.

O'Neill turned quickly to Buckley. "Cullen smoke?"

The foreman thought a moment. "No, he didn't," he said hesitantly. "At least, I never saw him."

At that moment, they were interrupted by the arrival of a man on horseback, a dirty-looking saturnine individual, whose swarthy face was scored with fine wrinkles.

SHERIFF O'NEILL'S eyelids flickered as he saw the horseman. "Hello, Blackwing," he said affably. "Taking a little ride in the rain?"

The quarter-breed pulled up his horse and looked down at the sheriff and Buckley for a few moments. His burning, deep-set eyes swung past Gregory and came to rest on the two roustabouts working on the gas line. Then they dropped to the joint of pipe lying at O'Neill's feet. There was something sinister in his deliberation that held them all speechless.

"Cullen dead?" Blackwing asked at last.

A faint grim smile curled the corners of O'Neill's mouth. "Yes. Burned to death right about where you've got your pony."

After a few seconds silence, Blackwing gave a grunt and muttered: "That's what he gets for cheating people." He tapped his horse, and the animal moved off up the ravine at a trot.

"Seemed sorry to hear about it, didn't he," Buckley remarked sarcastically. O'Neill didn't seem to hear him. His glance, now dull and sleepy, followed the man on the horse till he swung out of the ravine and headed toward the gate that opened onto the Weemulgee road.

"He's been over at his shack again," Buckley said.

"Shack?" O'Neill repeated quickly.

The foreman nodded. "He's got a place over by the gas well. Used to live there. Lately he's been living in town, but he comes out here occasionally and hangs around for a couple of hours."

One of the roustabouts broke in. "All finished, Bert! What's next?"

Buckley walked over to the new joint of pipe and gave it a tentative kick. "Turn the gas back into the line and take this old pipe back to the tool shack," he directed.

O'Neill was pulling ruminatively at his mustache.

"Guess I'll take a look at Blackwing's shack," he said finally. "How do I get there?"

"It's about a hundred yards east of the well by the south fence," Buckley replied. "I'll show you."

"Don't bother," the sheriff said brusquely. "I'll find it. I just want to browse around a little. You and Mr. Gregory can go on back to the lease house."

Buckley's forehead wrinkled into a little frown. It was evident that the sheriff was not eager to have his company. He took the hint with good grace.

"Stop at the lease house and I'll drive you back to town," the foreman said. "If you need me, just shout."

Blackwing's shack, in the middle of a patch of scrub oak, was built of rough lumber, the cracks chinked with mud and stones. It was a small place; just one room and a lean-to.

The windows were gaping holes in the walls, devoid of frames or glass, and the door, too, hung crazily open. Through it, O'Neill caught a glimpse of the gloomy, dirty interior, the bare ground forming the floor.

He entered. There was little furnishing; only a pine table, a bench and a rusted stove. On a hook on the wall hung a grimy suit of overalls and an old straw hat. A tipsy shelf held a few cracked dishes, a frying pan and a pot. That was all, but the sheriff guessed that Blackwing followed the custom of so many mixed bloods and slept on a pallet on the floor like a true Indian.

O'Neill examined the various articles with what appeared to be casual interest. Actually, his glance took in every detail. He walked through the doorless oblong into the lean-to. It was without windows; the only light in it seeped through the cracks in the boards, which were unchinked.

At first, he thought it was entirely empty. Gradually his eyes became accustomed to the gloom, however, and he caught sight of something on the floor that sent him across the lean-to in a quick stride. A few moments later, he had transferred his find into the shack proper and placed it on the table.

O'Neill sucked in his breath slowly, then expelled it in a soft whistle, while he studied the objects before him.

They consisted of an old-fashioned automobile spark coil, a half dozen dry batteries and a roll of two-strand elec-

tric wire. The last item was covered with mud, and he could see that the insulation had been burned from a large part of it. Fastened to one end was a blackened spark-plug. Yellow mud clung to the bottom of the coil and batteries, too.

"Murder," he said, his lips barely moving. "It was murder."

The little sheriff's saddle-leather face grew taut and grim. His gnarled hand went from force of habit to his upper lip and stroked his scraggly mustache.

Outside the door, a branch creaked. He spun on his heel. But even then it was too late. Blackwing, a long-barreled old-style Colt in his hand, was covering him from the doorway.

"Don't move!"

The quarter-breed snarled the words in a tone that bristled with insane menace.

FOR a few seconds they faced each other, Blackwing training his gun on the sheriff's heart. He was an erect figure of medium height, but the myriad wrinkles on his ugly face revealed his age. There were more of them than usual now, as he lowered his brows over his burning eyes and drew back his lips, showing the stumps of yellow teeth.

O'Neill looked at him with a slow conciliatory smile. "Put up your shooting-iron," he said. "You know me."

"What you doin' in my house?" The quarter-breed's eyes shot sparks of hate.

"Dropped in hoping to see you. The door was open."

"You're a liar! You saw me down in the ravine! Thought I'd gone to town. But I fooled you! Just rode round the lease and come back!"

He gave a wild laugh that grated on O'Neill's usually steady nerves. And that crazy light in Blackwing's eyes gave the sheriff an uncomfortable feeling that he was dealing with a man who was out of his mind.

"Cullen's dead!" Again that crazy laugh. Then Blackwing suddenly grew serious, sullen, deadly. "I've a notion to send you after him so you can tell him I'm glad he's dead and gone to hell!"

"What'd you have against Cullen?" O'Neill asked soothingly.

He was stalling for time. As long as the man opposite him was talking, he probably wouldn't shoot. Meanwhile, the sheriff's brain was twisting this way and that behind his sleepy expression, clutching for a means to outwit the quarter-breed.

Blackwing spat out a curse. "He robbed me!"

"Paid you for this lease, didn't he?" O'Neill asked.

"Eight hundred dollars for the lease and royalty!" the man in the door screamed. "Eight hundred dollars! It's worth a million! It's worth a billion, by God!"

"When did he buy it from you?" the sheriff murmured. He edged an inch or two toward the door.

Blackwing's grip on the gun tightened. "Stand still!" he snarled. He glared at O'Neill for a few seconds suspiciously. "What'd you want to know when he bought it for?"

The sheriff shrugged. "Don't make any difference. I was just curious."

"He bought it off me four years ago last month! And he cheated me!"

"*Hmm!* That wasn't much money for it," O'Neill said.

But he didn't mean his words. He knew that Cullen had paid a liberal price for the lease at the time. The vagaries of luck, so important in the oil business, had since made the thousand-to-one shot come through, that was all. But O'Neill realized the logic of that couldn't simmer into Blackwing's decaying brain.

"What'd you kill him for?"

"Who says I killed him?" the quarter-breed demanded craftily. "The gas killed him! The gas that was mine by rights! It burned him! Roasted him to a cinder —and he's roasting in hell now!" He uttered that blood-chilling laugh again. "You'll be there, too, in a minute!"

O'Neill had been watching the old man's trigger finger closely. He wondered just how long it would take Blackwing to squeeze that relic of frontier days into spitting its messenger of death. A second, perhaps. Hardly enough time to permit the sheriff to spring across the six feet that separated them. Or to draw and fire his own gun.

Looking squarely into the muzzle, O'Neill studied the ancient weapon. His eyes suddenly grew dreamy, but almost imperceptibly his muscles tightened. He could see the bullets in the chambers. But now he noticed that it wasn't, as he'd thought at first glance, a sixgun. It was an old five-shot forty-five caliber. There were only five chambers in the cylinder.

And the instant the realization came to him, he hurled himself forward!

Blackwing's trigger finger crooked convulsively. But there was no response, no thunderous lethal blast. Before the quarter-breed had recovered from his surprise, the barrel of Sleepy O'Neill's pistol on his skull crashed him into unconsciousness.

BUCKLEY drove O'Neill and his thoroughly cowed prisoner into Weemulgee in the new tool car. Gregory, so the foreman said, had gone on into Tulsa some time before.

The drizzle still saturated the air. But night was beginning to turn the grayness of the day to black when they reached the edge of town. There the car began to balk, the engine hitting on only three cylinders, so Buckley stopped at the Gusher Garage. The sheriff marched Blackwing on foot to the county lock-up a block away.

From the cells in the basement, the

sheriff climbed to the main floor of the courthouse and entered the office of the country recorder. McAllister was just closing up for the night, but when he saw the sheriff, he stopped putting his record books in the vault and dropped into a chair.

"Sit down!" he exclaimed. "You look as if you'd been busy."

Sleepy O'Neill drawled: "Oh, kinda busy, George. Didn't you say you had that assignment of a half interest in the Cullen lease here?"

McAllister nodded. "Put it on the books today. The original instrument's ready to be sent back. I was just going to take the mail to the post office as soon as I locked up."

"Let me take a look at it" O'Neill said.

The recorder reached for a pile of envelopes and flipped through them. Then, selecting one, he tore it open and handed the single sheet it contained to the sheriff.

O'Neill ran his eye down the page rapidly. It was a standard lease assignment form. It transferred a half interest in the oil and gas lease under the one hundred and sixty acres known as the Blackwing allotment to Maurice A. Gregory, of Tulsa.

He glanced at the signature. Samuel S. Cullen. Everything was regular, so far as he could see, and a faint shadow crossed the bronzed face of the sheriff. He folded the document thoughtfully, tucked it in his pocket and turned to leave.

"Thanks, George," he murmured.

"Hey!" McAllister burst out. "Where you going with that? I've got to mail it back to Tulsa!"

Sleepy O'Neill gave him a wink and a little wave of his hand.

"I'll take good care of it, George. But I need it in my business till tomorrow afternoon."

"The county recorder looked dubious.

"Why—why—" he spluttered, "it ain't regular!"

"Neither's murder!" O'Neill snapped.

McAllister's mouth sagged. "M-m-murder?"

"Yep! Sam Cullen was murdered on his lease by someone who filled a gully with gas and touched it off with a spark coil."

Taking pity on the amazed curiosity which was evident in the recorder's face, O'Neill related what he had learned and what he had gone through in the afternoon.

"Blackwing, eh? That crabby old quarter-breed killed Cullen!" the recorder exclaimed, with a wagging of his head.

"Well, he's half crazy. All crazy on the subject of his land," the sheriff said. "But I haven't got enough to pin the killing on him yet. So I've got him locked up temporarily for assaulting a peace officer."

From the courthouse, O'Neill walked hurriedly to the Gusher Garage, hoping to find Buckley. Wilcox, who owned the garage, met him at the door and informed him that the foreman had gone back to the lease as soon as his car had been repaired.

"I fixed up his flivver, and he pulled right out," Wilcox said. "Too bad about Cullen, wasn't it. He was a fine man. Bought that tool car Buckley drives, from me."

"Hell of a car," O'Neill grinned. "First rainy weather we get it goes on the bum."

"It's O. K.," Wilcox protested. "Just a little ignition trouble."

A few minutes later, O'Neill left the Gusher Garage and walked slowly back to his office. He sat for a long time with one foot on his desk, his chair tilted back at a precarious angle. His eyes were almost closed in thought, and not until he had consumed two stogies in meditative silence did he depart for the Eureka Hotel and supper.

THE nine-twenty Frisco train snorted to a halt before the one-story brick station in Tulsa only ten minutes late the next morning. The damp drizzle of the previous day had continued, and the prospect of the city was wet and unpleasant as Sheriff O'Neill swung down the steps of the smoking car.

He strode briskly across the platform and beckoned to a taxi. Presently he was whirling up Boston Avenue toward the Kennedy Building, where he paid off the driver and entered.

In front of a door on the fifth floor, he halted, while he read the black lettering on it: Samuel S. Cullen, Oil Producer. Then he turned the knob, and walked in.

Cullen's office consisted of one room looking out on an inner court of the building. As the sheriff closed the door behind him, a dark-haired girl, who looked as if she might have been crying, glanced up from her typewriter.

"I'm Sheriff O'Neill of Weemulgee County," he explained with a friendly smile. "I want to find someone who can give me a little help in connection with Mr. Cullen's m-ah-death."

"I'm Miss Alloway, Mr. Cullen's secretary and bookkeeper," she replied, her voice tinged with sadness. "I'm the only one employed in the office. Perhaps I can help you."

"Guess you can," O'Neill nodded. "Glad I found you here."

"You wouldn't, if you'd come a little later. I'm closing the office until after Mr. Cullen's funeral tomorrow."

O'Neill was sympathetic. "Too bad about Mr. Cullen," he said. "I'm investigating the circumstances of his death. The usual formality," he added with a little gesture.

From the inside pocket of his coat, he drew the assignment which he had taken from the county recorder's office the previous day. He unfolded it, then handed it to Miss Alloway.

As she read it, her carefully plucked eyebrows lifted in surprise "Oh," she murmured, "so Mr. Cullen sold a half interest in the Blackwing lease to Mr. Gregory. He didn't mention it to me. But then, of course, he didn't always tell me about his deals," she added hastily.

O'Neill was watching her closely. "Do you recognize the signature?" he asked.

Her eyes dropped to the bottom of the sheet. She nodded, then looked at him with a smile. The sheriff's heart sank.

"Oh, yes, indeed," she replied, with a little laugh. "I recognize it perfectly."

O'NEILL caught the noon train south from Tulsa and an hour and a half later reached Weemulgee. In his own rattling roadster, he headed as fast as it would travel for the Cullen lease. As he approached, he heard in the distance a whistling roar, like a vast number of locomotives with their safety valves open at the same time.

"The gas well's blowing wide," the sheriff muttered to himself. "Wonder what's the idea."

The roustabouts working at the tool house gave him the answer. "Bert's at the well," one of them shouted. "The pressure's increasing and he was afraid it might lift the casing out of the hole, if he didn't open it up for a spell."

Cullen strode up the death ravine and across the hill to the second gully. The roar of the gas was growing more deafening with each step he took. It sounded as if the earth were screaming with rage because a hole had been drilled deep into it.

There was no one in sight as O'Neill drew near the rig. But when he rounded the engine house, he saw the foreman standing some distance back from the derrick. And beside him was a tall stoop-shouldered figure, which the sheriff recognized as Gregory, the geologist.

The two men were deep in conversation although they had to cup their hands and shout into each other's ears to make themselves heard.

Buckley was scowling. But suddenly he caught sight of the sheriff, and his scowl changed to an ingratiating smile. O'Neill observed, however, that he gave the man beside him a sharp nudge, almost like a warning signal.

Sleepy O'Neill, an enigmatic twist on one corner of his lips, walked directly to Buckley. The foreman waved a greeting. But the sheriff ignored it. He put one hand on the foreman's elbow; the other slid across his belt. When it came to a stop, an efficient-looking pistol was sticking out from it.

O'Neill raised his voice to its full strength. "You're coming with me— under arrest!"

Buckley's eyes grew black, but his fat face paled beneath the heavy tan. "What the hell!" he exclaimed.

"For Cullen's murder!"

"You're crazy!"

Sleepy O'Neill smiled dangerously. He released Buckley's elbow, but kept his pistol jammed in his side. Then he put his free hand in his pocket and when it came out two spark-plugs were lying in the palm.

The foreman's eyes opened wide, he started to say something, then set his lips. But only for a moment. As he looked at O'Neill's brittle gaze, he seemed suddenly to wilt. "All—all right," he said, although the sheriff got the words more by reading his lips than from the sound.

Buckley squared his shoulders. "I'll have to shut in the well first!" he yelled.

O'Neill nodded, waved him toward the rig with his pistol. He followed a few feet behind the foreman till they were within a dozen yards of the derrick. Then he stopped. While Buckley tugged at the wheel that closed the top gate of the massive valve, O'Neill kept him covered. Out of one corner of his eye, he had watched Gregory. But the geologist was standing motionless. Apparently, he didn't understand what it was all about.

Gradually the roar of the gas diminished as the valve gate closed. The silence that followed was acute; it made O'Neill's ears ring. Buckley gave a final tug at the wheel. Then he suddenly darted behind the valve. His hand went into his pocket and came out with a pistol.

"Now, by God!" he screamed, "try and get me!"

O'Neill brought his gun up. But he didn't squeeze the trigger. There wasn't any use. Buckley was well shielded by the huge valve.

"If you shoot, you'll set that gas off and burn up!" O'Neill warned.

"If you try to come into this derrick, I'll blow us to hell together!" Buckley snarled.

For a few seconds there was a tense silence. O'Neill cursed himself inwardly for having let the foreman outsmart him. Now they were deadlocked.

Buckley was protected from O'Neill's pistol by his metal shield. On the other hand, Buckley didn't dare to shoot. The derrick was reeking with gas from the well; the flash of his gun would turn it into a fiery furnace.

A sudden breath of air fanned O'Neill's cheek. His jaw jutted out desperately. That faint breeze was swinging the balance in Buckley's favor. In a few minutes it would blow the gas from the derrick and then the foreman could risk a shot from behind his barrier.

The foreman shifted his position. For a second, part of his body was exposed. O'Neill's gun roared. The bullet clanged against the metal valve. But the sound was immediately lost in a hideous roar as the derrick filled with fire. The bullet had struck a spark on the valve and ignited the gas!

O'Neill leaped back from the devastating blast of heat. Through the flames, he saw Buckley, arms covering his face, stagger to the edge of the derrick floor. He swayed for a second, then plunged head first into the water and muck of the slush pit on the far side of the rig.

But in that fleeting space of time since O'Neill had fired, the foreman had gone through the same living hell he had designed for Cullen. It was a ghastly, horrifying spectacle, and O'Neill, for all his hard-bitten training, turned away. It was over in a few seconds. The gas was consumed, and only the burning timbers of the rig and a couple of small streaks of flame where the valve leaked slightly, remained as reminders of the gruesome affair.

Gregory had stood rooted to the ground. His head was sticking forward, as if drawn toward the flames by some strange fascination. But suddenly he galvanized into action, whirled on his heels and started down the hill toward the gully.

O'Neill shouted to him to halt. But he plunged recklessly on. The sheriff's gun snapped up, barked once again, and the geologist tumbled the last few steps into the muddy stream that was racing through the draw.

SLEEPY O'NEILL finished telling about the fight at the Cullen lease. McAllister's popping eyes were shiny with admiration.

"So Buckley died," the recorder murmured.

O'Neill nodded.

"Gregory's wound isn't serious. We'll try him for being an accessory to murder—and convict him!" he added with a snap.

"How'd you know Buckley did it?"

McAllister asked the sheriff wonderingly.

"Well, George, I had to pinch old Blackwing because he went loco" the sheriff drawled. "But that old quarterbreed didn't know anything about automobiles. He couldn't have rigged up a death trap like Cullen died in. That was clear as spring water to me."

"Yes, but what put it on Buckley?" the recorder persisted.

"A spark-plug!"

"Huh?"

O'Neill smiled, and took the two spark plugs he had shown Buckley at the gas well from his pocket. One of them was blackened by fire. The other, oil-stained and with the porcelain cracked, was of a different brand. The sheriff pointed to the blackened plug.

"That's from Buckley's new flivver originally," he explained. "It's the kind they put in the cars when they make 'em. The other one's just an old plug Buckley put in the car when he took the good one out. But it didn't work very well. Gave out just as we were getting into town last night."

McAllister was plainly puzzled.

"Buckley wanted to be sure that the spark for his death trap would be a good hot one. He only had some old plugs around the lease, and so he took one out of his car, figuring to replace it later. Meanwhile, he put an old plug in the car. That one there!"

"How'd you find that out?"

"Wilcox, over at the garage, told me about fixing Buckley's car. Said it was funny how that old plug got into a new machine." The sheriff grinned faintly. "That made me doggone suspicious of Buckley. But there was other things that clinched it for me."

"What things?" McAllister demanded eagerly.

"Oh, for one thing, I inquired at the phone office and found out Buckley didn't call Cullen's office. He called

Gregory's office in Tulsa, while I was waiting for him. Guess he didn't know Gregory was already out at the lease. Then there was that assignment."

"The one you got from me?"

"Yep. It looked kind of strange for Cullen to sell a half interest in that lease to an individual. Not many men can dig down in their pocket for the money it would be worth. If the assignment had been to a big oil company, it wouldn't have surprised me."

He suddenly gave a chuckle. "I just took that assignment up to Tulsa on a hunch and Cullen's secretary identified the signature for me."

"Then it was all regular?" McAllister murmured.

"Hell no!" O'Neill laughed. "She identified it—as her own handwriting!"

"What are you talking about?" the recorder said incredulously.

The sheriff nodded. "It was a forgery all right. But you might say Gregory was too smart. He forged a forgery, so to speak. The only copy of Cullen's signature he had was on a letter Cullen had written him. So that's what he copied. But Miss Alloway, Cullen's secretary, had typed that letter, and just signed her boss's name to it.

He squinted at McAllister. "And that tied the two murderers into a double hitch! Buckley planted that coil and other stuff in old Blackwing's shack to throw suspicion on him, in case I couldn't be made to think Cullen's death was an accident."

"Well, I'll be— Yes, sir, I'll be damned," McAllister muttered. "Speaking of Blackwing, Sleepy, how'd you know you'd have time to jump him before he could shoot you out at his shack?"

"I've been around this country a long time George," O'Neill drawled. "And I've learned lots about guns. When I discovered Blackwing was toting a five-shot forty-five Colt, I knew it was a single-action gun. All of 'em always was, see? But I guess Blackwing didn't know that—or he'd forgotten about it, being used to a regular sixgun.

"He hadn't cocked that old Colt. And you know as well as I do you got to cock a single-action gun before you can shoot it. That meant nothing would happen if he squeezed the trigger, when I jumped on him."

Sleepy O'Neill pulled out one of his favorite stogies. When it was nicely burning, he waved it at McAillister.

"How about going to the Lyric Picture Theatre with me tonight, George," he suggested. "There's a big city gangster film on. I'd kind of like to see something exciting for a change."

No Magic Mumbling

DO YOU remember when Dr. Coué came over from Europe a few years ago with his singular formula for well-being: "Every day in every way I'm getting better and better?" And the amazing furor which swept the country in the wake of the good doctor? We were always a bit dubious and skeptical as to just how efficacious his method might be. Possibly it had its worthy points but at the first faint traces of even the most minor sort of indisposition we hustled up to our family physician for some of his old-fashioned, orthodox treatment. And it didn't include any magic mumbling of a catch phrase either.

We believe that the same general rule is applicable to the building of a magazine. We could sit here and reiterate the obvious fact that every month in a dozen different ways DIME DETECTIVE MAGAZINE gets better and better. We know it to be true but merely saying so over and over again wouldn't go very far toward keeping up the good work. It takes more than that. A lot more. Plenty of the good old-fashioned, orthodox treatment, in fact, to supplement the catch phrases.

And the treatment in this case consists in going after the best writers in the market; getting them to outdo even their own previous efforts in furnishing new mystery and thrills for the ever increasing army of loyal DIME DETECTIVE readers; and making each issue one galaxy of exciting detective action from the front cover to the back.

This month we are proud to introduce a new master-mystery author to the readers of DIME DETECTIVE in the person of J. Paul Suter, whose splendid hair-raiser, *The Angel of the Damned*, opens the issue and is illustrated on the cover. He writes from his home in Youngstown, Ohio to tell us something about himself and his unique necrologist-detective, Horatio Humberton.

Since you asked me—my gosh, was it a week ago, and here I am only just replying?—for information as to where that tall, gaunt person with the thick glasses, Mr. Horatio Humberton, came from, I have been casting about in what I optimistically term my mind to find out whether I know, myself.

The result is appalling. For several years I have been writing about Humberton, and suddenly, as the result of your query, I find that I never realized who the man really is. I realize it now. And I am rather alarmed. For it has come to me that, in all essentials, Ho Humberton is a highly respected banker of my acquaintance, who never conducted a funeral nor tracked down a murderer in his life.

To be sure, the banker doesn't wear thick glasses, and he doesn't smoke long, black cigars, and if the embalming of the dead is a hobby with him he certainly keeps that fact a profound secret from his friends; but it is he, nevertheless. If he *were* a

J. PAUL SUTER

necrologist—if he *did* dabble in detective lore—he would be Humberton.

Do most of your writers plot their stories out in advance, so that they know just where they are going, from first word to last? I wish I could. My method is so unscientific that it becomes laughable. The murder mystery comes to me first. I get to wondering about it—what a heck of a thing for someone to do!—why should anybody pull off a killing like that?—who did it, and why, in the name of common sense? I wonder, without arriving at any conclusion; and then, some fateful evening, I sit down to the typewriter, throw Humberton onto the job, and let him do his stuff. As the story progresses, I begin to sense who the murderer is. Sometimes I am right; but more often, I find toward the end of the story that someone I did not suspect is the real criminal, and then, of course, I have to go back and do a lot of rewriting.

That, it seems to me, is about the hardest way to write a detective story. I know a lot of easier ways, but with me they don't seem to click. If I can tell in advance who did the horrid deed, the story is more than likely to be a flop.

As for my personal tastes, if they are of interest to anyone, I play volley ball and pitch horse shoes (doing neither very well), I believe in ghosts and am profoundly interested in all sorts of psychic phenomena. I like to read all manner of books, with a slant toward ancient Egypt. I don't drink or smoke, but I do over-eat—with the result that I have to diet, every once in a while, to keep the old waist line below my chest measurement. Also, I am inclined to "reach for a sweet," and you know what that does.

Married; five children, and about three thousand books. Wife can write much better than I, but she doesn't know it. Consider myself pretty nifty at humorous writing, but the editors don't. Turn out a few ghost stories each year. Do most of my writing at night, all alone, in a down-town office building. Have had the family train the Graflex on me a time or two, so you are likely to see a picture of me shortly. If it doesn't seem good enough for publication, let me know, and I will send a snapshot of my brother-in-law. He has "it."

Thank you, Mr. Suter. We appreciate your letter and hope to hear more from you in the near future.

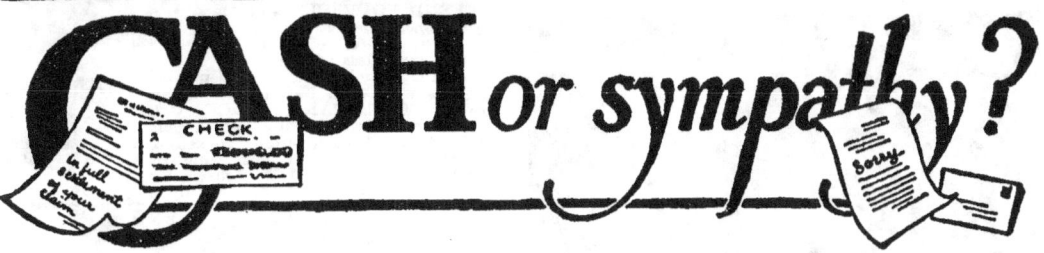

 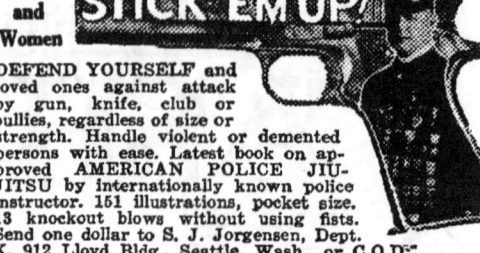
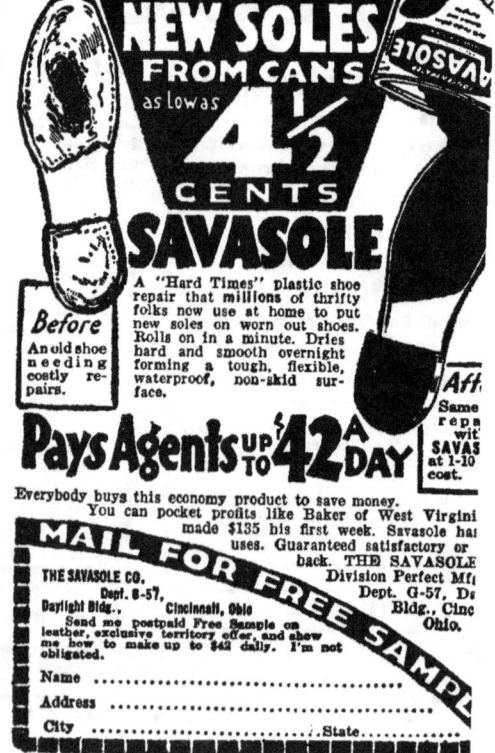

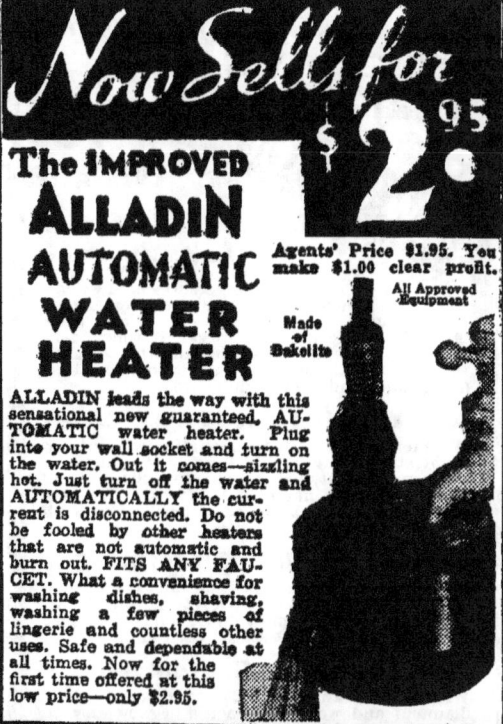

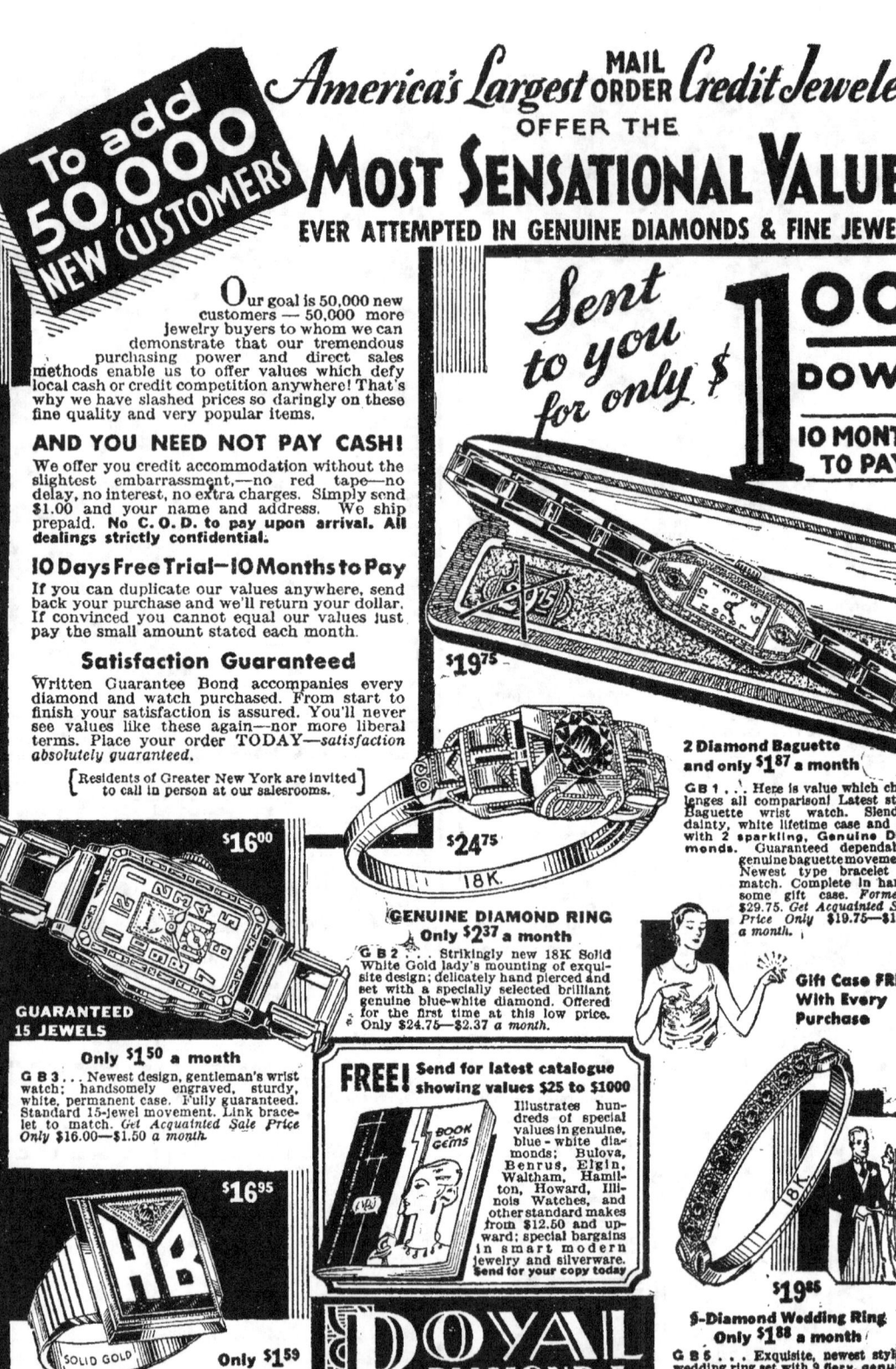